LOVE Bites

A PARANORMAL
ROMANTIC COMEDY

D1522225

USA TODAY BESTSELLING AUTHOR

CYNTHIA ST. AUBiN

COPYRIGHT © Cynthia St. Aubin

Published by Oliver-Heber Books

0 9 8 7 6 5 4 3 2 1

*For Ted, without whose gentle (but insistent) encouragement,
this book might have stayed safely tucked in my desk drawer.
Thank you for doing Life with me and for being my Person.*

ACKNOWLEDGMENTS

My undying gratitude to Kerrigan Byrne, who read this book in its earliest (and ugliest) iterations and said nice things anyway. Thank you for being my Platonic Life Partner, my Emotional Support Human, and most importantly, my friend. GutterBear and TrashPanda 4 Life!
My sincere thanks to Casey Harris-Parks, editor, reader, friend and fellow cheese-lover, for helping me make this book infinitely more readable.

My thanks (and apologies) to Lynne Harter, my beloved WordNerd, this book's first editor and excellent teacher, who made my work better in every way.

Huge thanks to Melissa McArthur, eagle-eyed and quick-witted.

And lastly, but certainly not leastly, thanks to Rebecca Poole, cover designer extraordinaire, talented writer, and lovely friend. You're the bestest.

*A*rt reminds me of everything, and everything reminds me of art.

The corpse downhill was something Goya—the eighteenth century's answer to a death-obsessed emo kid—would have painted.

She lay bent among the skeletons of bare bushes, her hair tangled into the fingers of branches. Even from my station ten yards beyond the ribbon of yellow crime scene tape, I could see the angry red cavern where her throat should be. Rapid brushstrokes of blood spattered her cheeks and creamy silk blouse, pale among the dead leaves. Her slim legs splayed from her skirt at odd angles, her arms thrown over her head like a broken ballerina. Filmy eyes stared up toward the sky, their color seemingly leached away by death.

Stars cartwheeled at the edges of my vision, a mockery of Van Gogh's *Starry Night*. I sat down hard on my heels and took a deep breath.

"You okay, honey?" The uniformed officer leaned down and put a warm hand on my shoulder.

"Yes, I'll be fine. Just got a little dizzy."

"You're with Detective Morrison?" Her spark-plug-shaped body stacked itself into an upright position as she glanced toward the creek.

I followed her eyes to where Morrison crouched, barking orders to the group of forensics technicians flapping around him like startled ducks.

"For the moment," I said.

"Pain in the ass, isn't he?" Her soft, haunted eyes flicked over my face. "It gets easier, you know. After a while, it's like watching a movie. You're here, but you're not here."

In my mind, I was already somewhere else. Leaning back into my memory, sliding into the comfort of my mental catalogue of paintings, I could make this all into a slide show. Something happening to someone else.

"Morrison said you were an expert witness. What do you do?"

I'm the assistant to the guy who might have done this. And Morrison wants me to see his handiwork so badly he'll say anything just to get me into a crime scene.

"Canine forensics." It sounded ridiculous but was the first idea that came to my head.

"Oh wow. You're here because of—" The officer looked toward the body and turned back to me, pressing a hand against her throat.

I nodded.

"Don't you need to get a closer look? I can take you past the crime scene tape."

"No!" I coughed, hoping to cover my hasty refusal, then took a deep breath and began again. "No. I don't need to get any closer than this to tell you that whatever did this wasn't human." That much was true, however I'd meant it.

Her eyes grew wide. "What do you think it was?"

A werewolf. "Could be a feral dog. Especially this close to the canyon."

"Oh, right," she said, perhaps eager to have information not yet available to her plentiful male counterparts. "Can I bring you a blanket or anything?"

I shook my head and pushed myself to my feet. "No, I'll be okay. Thanks though."

Morrison climbed the embankment to where I stood, shivering from the combination of cold and horror.

"Who is she?"

His face was set in dogged pursuit of fresh clues. He took a moment to relish his words.

"The woman *your boss* left the gallery with last night."

A terrible tableau splashed across my mind. Pictures, details, descriptions. The other women. The other murders.

One idea rose quietly above the cacophony of panicked, useless thoughts.

I could be next.

CHAPTER 1

TWO WEEKS EARLIER...

"*G*ilbert, we *need* this job."

If cats were cars, Gilbert would be a 1981 Cadillac Fleetwood—long, wide, and heavy on his wheels. Parked next to where I sat cross-legged on the wood floor, he flicked his tail as if to say, *No shit, lady. You think we like the Dollar Tree swill you've been slopping us with for the past three months?*

During that three months, this small studio apartment had been our entire world. And why leave when this one room offered all the amenities a girl needed during the complete mental breakdown phase of an ugly divorce? A bed—perfect for hours of endless sobbing. A couch—a must-have for those weeks-long TV binges. A coffee table—absolutely essential for those solo frozen food dinners, collecting piles of unpaid bills, and even hiding under when your ex stops by unannounced.

Currently, Gilbert and I occupied the vanity, aka, the full-length mirror I'd propped against the closet door next to my bed. I squinted into the dust-speckled glass and tried to force the nervous twitch out of my hand as I redrew my eyeliner for the third time.

"Don't look at me like that," I said. "It's not like you

could do better. You don't even have opposable thumbs."

I reached for the mini medieval torture device in my makeup bag and began to pinch my lashes into an expression of perpetual shock. They'd calm down to something like mild surprise after I added mascara.

"Anyway, if I get this job, we'll be able to afford rent, and Fancy Feast, and a cell phone, and cheese. Oh God. *Cheese.*"

The wand dropped involuntarily, leaving a fat black smudge on my cheekbone.

I licked my finger and wiped off the errant mascara, and with it, a strip of my liberally applied blush. The patch of pasty skin beneath hadn't seen the sun for the better part of ninety days.

"You know, if I were the heroine in a romance novel, my skin wouldn't be *pasty*. It would be the creamy ivory of the finest porcelain. And my eyes would be the gray-green of the sea under storm clouds. Can you believe they refused to put that on my driver's license? I mean, it was the least they could do for recording my height as *five foot eleven inches* instead of *mutant,* like I requested."

Gilbert spread his paw and commenced addressing the space between the pink-padded toes with his sand-papery tongue. I took that as a sign of his distaste for the dull gray hell of government-run offices that any discussion of driver's licenses brought to mind.

"I know, right?"

He yawned, stretched, and sauntered over to the couch where Stewie and Stella, my other feline life partners, were already sleeping soundly like breathing bookends. The three cats, along with the furniture crowding the front room of my studio apartment and a mountain of debt, had been my lot in the "property division" phase of the divorce. My husband—my *ex*-husband, *thank you very much*—had made off with anything that could be plugged into a wall along with the contents of our savings account.

Ass nugget.

Hauling myself into a standing position, I fluffed the wavy tangle of my auburn hair and pulled my sweater a little lower, as much to reveal an extra half-inch of cleavage as to cover the slacks I'd had to secure with a hair tie, a safety pin, and the will of Jesus.

"Not a total loss, right?" I said to Gilbert, who had curled himself into a cozy heap on the end of the couch nearest the old brass radiator.

My motives for choosing this apartment had been hopeful, though it had since become a crushing post-divorce prison for my soul. During my first visit to the sleepy mountain town of Georgetown, Colorado, while searching for a spot to begin repairing my fractured psyche and equally afflicted credit, I'd seen the For Rent sign propped in the window of the old Victorian house. During my brief tour, the landlord had mentioned this house had been completed in 1890. While this would mean absolutely nothing to most people, I took it as an auspicious sign. It was this same year Vincent Van Gogh—my art historical boyfriend—had completed *Wheatfield with Crows*—my favorite painting.

I'd rented it on the spot, then proceeded to be passed over for every single job I'd applied for in the following months.

And if I didn't cough up a cool thousand dollars within three days, my bohemian sentiments would be out on the street along with my ass.

My stomach gave a little lurch.

I glanced at the microwave through the narrow door leading to the kitchen. The digital blue display hadn't moved since the last time I'd checked it. No way in hell it was still 7:22 a.m.

And then I remembered.

That wasn't the time, it was the *timer*. I'd neglected to reset it last night after a failed attempt at making wild rice in the microwave. Even half-cooked and chewy, it still beat a solid month of Top Ramen.

A worm of dread wriggled in my gut as I crossed the kitchen and pressed the reset button.

8:04 a.m. "Fuck a duck, Gilbert!"

One last check in the toothpaste-flecked mirror, then I dashed back into the living/bedroom to snatch my coat, purse, and keys off the coffee table.

"Wish me luck!" I sang to the cats as I locked my door and jogged down the stairs of the house's shared entryway.

OKAY, I MIGHT HAVE TAKEN THE CORNER A *HAIR* TOO fast. You try keeping a 1967 Ford Mustang Fastback under forty miles an hour when you're late for a job interview.

"I am *so* sorry."

I wasn't sure if I was apologizing to the owner of the gold Crown Victoria for his taste in cars, or the fact that I had just rear-ended him. Heart sinking into my guts, I had followed the other driver's lead, turning down a side street to pull over and inspect the damage. The Vic's dented bumper clung to only one side of the car, the other end leaning into the gutter like a drunk. The Mustang, on the other hand, sat perfectly, defiantly unmarred. The vehicles' respective owners stood on the sidewalk of Georgetown's quaint historic district. Candy-colored buildings stretched out behind us like a shrill rebuke to the gloomy, end-of-winter day. Beyond them, the mountains slept beneath their blanket of white, moth-eaten here and there by clusters of pine trees. It had been their silent solace that had drawn me from Denver when my marriage imploded and my life along with it.

I looked the Vic's driver over to determine how likely he was to let me skate out of this. My odds weren't good. Men with sexy, sleepy hazel eyes weren't especially benevolent, in my experience. Particularly when said eyes were paired with six feet of lean, muscled body and hair the color of brown-sugar fudge.

He glanced over at me, his gaze respectfully brief, despite a momentary detour to the scooped neck of my sweater.

Promising.

"Are you all right?" he asked.

I nodded, then shocked and horrified us both by bursting into tears.

Maybe it was the PMS. Or the hunger gnawing at my gut. Perhaps it was the realization that with this new delay, the only job prospect on my radar would be lost forever. But more than likely, it was the simple act of another human being asking me if I was okay after the long months of my self-imposed isolation.

Hands clapped over my streaming eyes, I was helpless to stop the grief gusting through me in front of this total stranger.

He cleared his throat. "Look, this is no big deal. These things happen. Let's just trade insurance information and—"

"I don't have insurance." The admission only made me sob all the harder. It was one thing privately picking through the wreckage of a once-solvent adult female life. It was another thing entirely to have to admit my sad state of affairs to a tall, pleasantly scented, grown-ass male motorist.

Cue the sound of his shoes shifting on the concrete. "Huh. Okay. Well, let's just swap numbers so—"

"I don't have a phone either." And verily, tears commenced to squirt sideways out of my eyes. "It got shut off right after the insurance."

For a moment, there was only the taste of tears in my mouth and the dull soundtrack of passing traffic.

"Divorce?"

His question surprised me enough to snap the tears off mid chest heave. I peeked at him from between my fingers. Killer grin, even through my saline-blurred vision. A disarming slash across a face just on the hungry side of handsome.

"How did you know?" I asked.

He lifted a hand and poked my recently denuded ring finger. "Tan line."

The single spot of warmth where his fingertip met my skin tingled through me. How long since I had been touched by another human? Then the answer came, and I mentally swatted it away lest it drag fresh tears in its wake.

Warmth between my shoulder blades as his hand hovered but did not land. "Look, my car's a piece of shit anyway. How about we just forget about it?"

Relief sweet and silky as spring water flooded my chest. "Are you sure? You don't want to get a police report, or—"

"Nah." He waved a hand. "Bureaucratic swine, all of them. Always better *not* to get cops involved, if you can help it."

I fought the urge to kiss him full on the mouth. Instead, I crushed him in an overzealous bear hug.

Spastic physical contact was one of the things I did best.

"You're gonna be okay, kid," he said, flashing me a devastatingly disarming crooked smile.

"Thanks," I said, releasing him and cramming myself back into the Mustang. I didn't bother reopening the door to extract my coattail as I sped the final four blocks to The Crossing, a small but reputable art gallery in Georgetown's historic district whose owner I had duped into granting me an interview.

But there had been no need to hurry, as it turned out.

When I stepped inside the gallery, I found it as silent as a tomb and equally haunted. The scent of linseed oil rocked me back on my heels—a ghost of the studio my grandmother had once painted in.

Did I have the wrong day? The wrong time? I pulled the sticky note from my purse and consulted it for the three-hundredth time.

I'd written down the details after my brief phone conversation with the gallery owner, *Mr. Mark Abernathy,* and insisted on reading it all back to him just to make sure I had it right.

Twice.

"Hello?"

My voice echoed off the exposed brick walls but found no answer beyond my own footfalls on the scarred wood floor. Dividers had been set up in the typical post-modern white box at the center of the gallery, awaiting artwork to define them and give them meaning. Today, they were empty.

Unusual. Even between shows, wouldn't they want artworks on display for the casual visitor to purchase? Abernathy had mentioned something about resident artists. Where was their work?

At the rear of the gallery, a narrow stairway led up to a heavy oak door. A slice of light filtered from beneath it, casting a warm glow across the small landing at the top of the stairs. A sign of life.

If my intention had been to slide quietly up the stairs and pretend like I'd been waiting patiently for decades, the universe had other plans. Every step released a groan of protest louder than the one before it.

"Shh!" I whispered to the stairs.

I continued on tiptoe.

The voice on the other side of the door rose in pitch, and I froze in place. I recognized it as belonging to the man I'd talked to on the phone.

Abernathy.

I ventured a step closer.

Please don't be talking about some flaky chick who's late for her interview.

"What do you mean she *knows*? How did this happen?"

Silence.

"Well, then you'd better take care of her. You understand? I don't have to tell you what could happen if she talks."

I found myself holding my breath, straining to hear over the sound of my own heart pounding in my ears.

What sort of business was this Abernathy running anyway?

Does it matter? the ever-present judgy-pants voice in my head replied. *He could be running a shop dedicated to kicking three-legged puppies and you'd take the job if he offered it.*

There was desperate, and there was *desperate*.

Then there was me.

"Don't *fucking* lie to me! If I find out you're lying to me, I'll—" A pause, then, thick with menace. "Just don't," he sighed. "Don't lie."

Lie.

The word appeared in flashing neon over my head, arrows aimed at my pointy skull as I remembered the resume tucked beneath my arm. I'd spent the last of my loose change printing it out at OfficeMax, splurging on the creamy linen paper. Were you to look for it in the library, it would be cataloged under fiction.

Truth was, despite a mostly useless master's degree in art history, I knew exactly dick about being in gallery administration and even less about being a personal assistant.

I turned on my heel to flee.

"Trying to sneak away?"

And there he was. Leaning in the doorway. Six feet and five inches—or so my ovaries estimated—of chocolate-haired, dark-eyed, expensive suit-wearing sex on a stick.

Mark Abernathy, gallery owner, in the skin.

A strange little smile lit his features as he crossed the distance between us and stepped down to the stair directly in front of mine. I resisted the urge to back away and preserve my bubble of personal space.

"You must be Hanna," he said. "You look like you sound."

Pathetic? Nerdy? Depressed? Hungry?

"Mark Abernathy?"

"Most days."

I might have peed a little when he shook my hand.

"Pleasure to meet you, Hanna." He gestured toward the door and I saw his office.

If someone detonated five pounds of C4 in the Library of Congress, I imagined this is about what it would look like. Drawers spilling their contents onto the floor in colorful piles. The shelves choking with books, folios, and folders—some dangling precariously in space, held in place by a thick layer of dust. Random objects, presumably overflow from the antiques side of the business, hidden among the debris. Abernathy kicked a path through the carpet of papers, pausing to indicate a waist-high pile of dirty laundry opposite his cluttered desk.

"Won't you sit down?"

Clutter-blindness. Turns out: totally a thing.

I glanced at the pile and tried for *light and charming* rather than *dubious and mostly awkward*. "I didn't know Armani made couches."

"Oh. Right." He swept one massive arm at the mountain, causing an avalanche of clothes and revealing part of an expensive leather couch.

I took a seat and quickly brushed away a pair of black boxer-briefs that fell into my lap. Technically, this was the most action I'd had in months.

Abernathy seated himself in a wide wingback chair behind the desk and folded his arms.

No wedding ring.

And when had I gotten back into the habit of checking?

"Your resume?" He nodded toward the paper sandwiched beneath the purse on my lap.

So much for hoping he wouldn't notice. "Yes. Sorry." I pushed myself up from the couch to hand it to him.

He took the paper and held it under a lamp that was either a Tiffany or a knock-off good enough to bluff ol' Louis Comfort himself. My fingers itched for a dust cloth. Letting a lamp this beautiful accumulate a layer of *schmutz* ought to be a felony at least.

"Hanna-laura Harvey."

"Hey! You said it right!"

He didn't look up.

"No one ever says my name right. I mean Hannalore? It's ridiculous. Of course, my mother was coming off a stint in a neo-hippie commune when I was born, and I've long suspected the ganja hadn't quite worn off when she filled out my birth certif—"

"Do I make you nervous, Miss Harvey?" Abernathy asked, glancing up from the resume.

14

Ever noticed how there's no good answer to this question?

Such as: No, my anxiety disorder does.

Or maybe: No, my face always looks like it's bracing for a shovel.

Even better: Yes, you scalding-hot dumpster fire of a man. Yes, you do. Now stop looking at me before I pull my dress over my head and run screaming from your office because I don't remember how to people.

"Me? Heck no." My answer would have been infinitely more convincing had my voice not broken on the last word of this sentence.

Abernathy nodded and resumed his leisurely perusal of the paper.

An entire civilization rose, achieved enlightenment, and fell in the time it took him to read through my one-page document. The entire time, my eyes stayed fastened on his face, scanning for the slightest sign of trouble. When his eyebrows knit together, I tensed, ready to vault over the laundry pile and make a break for it if he asked me something I couldn't answer.

"Looks good." He tossed the resume over his shoulder. It floated side to side and came to rest among its fallen comrades like a leaf on the autumn burn pile. "When can you start?"

CHAPTER 2

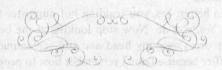

In the absolute silence following his question, I heard the tiny clicks my eyelids made as I blinked in disbelief. "Wait, what?"

"Start," he repeated. "When can you start?"

"But on the phone you said—"

"You have the skill set. I need the help. What more do I need to know?"

"Everything. What if there's someone more qualified? What if I'm not the right person for the job? What if…" *I'm the stupidest person alive?*

"Okay. I do have a question." Mischief danced in the coffee-dark depths of his eyes.

"Yes?"

He leaned back in his chair and kicked his feet onto the desk, sending a fresh flurry of papers to the floor. "If you were me, would you hire you?"

Nope. "Absolutely," I answered without hesitation.

"There you have it. If you would hire you, why shouldn't I?"

Because you hate liars. "Good point."

"So…" He yawned, the sound cavernous in his broad chest as he extended his arms over his head. "How should we do this?"

16

It took my brain a moment to register that words—
and potentially important words at that—had left
Abernathy's mouth while I was eye-humping his del-
toid through the expensive fabric of his shirt. "Do
what?"

"You're here to organize me, to cure me of my
wicked ways." Something about the way he said
wicked made me feel like I'd swallowed a lit road
flare.

"At least, that's what I understood when I looked up
personal assistant," Abernathy said. "I've never really had
one before, to be honest."

Jackpot.

I slid on my best "listen to how capable I am" voice
and tried to look thoughtful. "Naturally I *would* organize you, of course. But we haven't even talked about
the basics."

He swung one long leg over the other. "Such as?"

"My hours, my responsibilities, my salary..."

"How much do you want?"

Never in my life had someone uttered to me so
brazen an invitation. I'd thought about this long and
hard in the months following my graduation and sub-
sequent unemployment. My long years of education,
dedication bordering on devotion, a commitment to be
the best, the brightest. What was it all worth? What was
I worth?

The number in my head had more in common with
desperation than qualification.

"Well, I want to work in the arts. And this job is
more important than—"

"How much?"

"Sixty thousand." I felt myself flinch and hoped he
wouldn't see it. This was the part where he laughed in
my face and sent me packing.

"Sixty-five."

CYNTHIA ST. AUBIN

"Well, that's not quite what I had in mind but *the-helldidyoujustsay?*"

"Sixty-five thousand."

I opened my mouth to speak, but there were no words. I repeated the process a couple times before sound arrived to justify the movement. "During a negotiation you're supposed to talk me *down*," I explained. "That's how this works."

Abernathy only smiled. "If you think you're worth sixty thousand a year, then I need to pay you more. My business is complicated, and I have no desire to teach it twice. Once you're mine, you're *mine*."

I was certain he hadn't meant it the way I'd felt it.

"What do you say?"

"May I bear your children?"

"What?" he asked.

"What?" I parroted back.

"Is that a yes?"

"Emphatically."

"Do you have any questions?"

I did, in fact. *What do you look like naked?* being the chief one of them. "Let's start with the essentials." I pulled my little red notebook from my purse and dug out a pen. "As far as my job duties, what would you like me to focus on?"

"I could use some help getting organized." He glanced around his office—casual, unperturbed. "But I'm sure you know much more about this assisting business than I do. Really, I just want someone who's willing to jump in and take ownership. Create order from the chaos, if you will."

Oh, I would.

I waited for some follow-up gesture, an indication of where to begin, a lightning bolt from the heavens to strike my lying ass dead. When neither of the former options materialized, I decided movement would be

18

the best insurance against the latter. If God was going to smite me, I could at least give Him a moving target. Shoving myself up from the couch, I approached Abernathy's desk. It felt like challenging a forest fire with a squirt gun.

"Is it okay if I start here?"

"That will be fine."

"Okay then."

"Good."

Before our exchange could devolve into grunts and obscure gestures, the door to Abernathy's office exploded open. Papers puffed into the office like a brief recyclable snowstorm.

"That's it! That is *it*! I quit!" barked the room's newest occupant—a troll of a man with a fleshy red face, exceptionally round nostrils, and sizable orange mustache. He looked like the love child of Yosemite Sam and Porky Pig.

"First," Abernathy said, "you're not my employee, so you can't quit. Second, you could knock, Scott."

"Who's *she*?" asked the troll, as if I had "Typhoid Mary" cross-stitched on my forehead.

"Hannalore Harvey—" Abernathy rose from his chair "—meet Scott Kirkpatrick, one of our resident artists here at the gallery."

"The *only* artist here at the gallery," Kirkpatrick sniffed. "I would hardly qualify the rest of what's produced around here as *art*."

"You can call me Hanna," I amended, as much for Abernathy as Kirkpatrick. "Nice to meet you."

Kirkpatrick regarded my offered hand it as if I'd presented him a cockroach to hold.

"These hands," he said, cupping his own hands aloft well out of my reach, "are artist's hands. I don't *shake* with them. I *paint* with them."

They were the least artistic-looking hands I had

ever seen, short and abrupt like the rest of his body with stubby fingers like Vienna sausages.

The sausages belonged to a body dressed like an amateur fly fisherman who had suddenly been called to an impromptu business meeting. A fishing vest covered the polo shirt buttoned all the way to the crispy ginger chest hair climbing his neck. Khaki pants, penny loafers, and a floppy fisherman's hat completed the ensemble. I had an overwhelming urge to kick him in the shin.

"What is it this time?" Abernathy sighed, leaning back in his chair.

"He's watching that damnable video again. After the last time you spoke to him, I transcribed the conversation in a clearly written note and posted it on his door, reminding him that he had agreed to watch it only if I had left for the evening. I arrived this morning, and when I put my ear to the wall, I could *clearly* hear him watching it. How am I supposed to maintain my artistic clarity with that cretin banging around right next door? It's hardly the environment that I require in order to receive inspiration."

"What are the chances you're just going to get over it?" Abernathy asked.

"Get over it? Get over it!" Kirkpatrick sputtered. "Do I need to remind you who your bestselling artist is?"

"Definitely not going to get over it." Abernathy glanced at me as Kirkpatrick continued to emit unintelligible squeaks of rage. "Now's as good a time as any for you to meet the natives. Shall we?"

"We shall."

"Ladies first."

I felt a flick on my rear end as I walked past him. For one impossible moment, I thought—okay, hoped—

Abernathy had pinched my behind. When I looked back at him, he was holding up a sock.

"It was stuck to your pants."

"Thanks," I mumbled.

"Anytime." He winked at me.

I almost fainted.

WE DESCENDED THE STEEP WOODEN STAIRS FROM Abernathy's office loft single file with Kirkpatrick in the lead, his heavy, quick footsteps echoing off the floor of the empty gallery space below.

Abernathy talked while we walked. "Once a month we host a gallery event for local artists. All the in-house artists usually contribute a few pieces, but it's invitational too. A lot of the local students submit pieces."

"That sounds wonderful." Excitement let loose a burst of butterflies in my previously growling stomach. I may have lied about having gallery experience, but my lifelong love affair with art was real as shit. In a childhood devoid of siblings and marked by frequent moves, I'd sat in the corner of my grandma's studio with Time Life art books and made friends with Van Gogh, Rembrandt, Matisse, and Dali. The world within their canvas borders could be as beautiful or as ugly as I wanted it. The heavy volumes on my lap felt like a hug. When Oma took me to my first museum to meet my friends in person, it was all over but the master's thesis.

"I usually pick some pieces from the antique shop and put them out as well. I may have you help me with that," Abernathy continued.

"I can do that," I said. *I hope.*

Kirkpatrick disappeared around the corner, and Abernathy began counting out loud.

"Three, two, one."

A door slam reverberated through the gallery like a gunshot. We turned the corner and faced a hall with two doors on either side. In the center, a man wearing a leopard print bathrobe, leg warmers, and biker shorts was doing lunges.

Abernathy cleared his throat, and the lunger turned to face us.

"Mr. A! What's up?" He sauntered toward us, and he and Abernathy bumped knuckles.

"Hey, Steve, how are the quads?" Abernathy asked.

Steven was nearly as tall as Abernathy but at least fifty pounds lighter. Bird-boned and as lean as over-pulled taffy, he had a face like a baby lizard. Quirky angles punctuated with boyish dimples and a scattering of piercings. Beaky, disarming, and utterly adorable.

Steven brushed fine blond hair out of his eyes, stuck out one long, lanky leg, and flexed. "I'm finally getting some definition."

I peeked at Abernathy, whose mouth tugged to one side as he tried to suppress a smirk. Smiling was a good sign, right?

"You got a name, doll?" Steven asked.

"This is Hanna Harvey," Abernathy answered for me. "She's my new assistant. She has extensive gallery experience, so she'll be helping organize the next show."

"Sweet. Nice to meet you, Hanna. I'm Steven Franke, but you can call me *Johnny Danger.*"

"No one actually calls him that," Abernathy explained.

"They could though," Steven insisted. "It could totally be a thing."

"Totally," I agreed.

"Steve, you know why I'm here, right?" Abernathy asked.

"Yeah, I know. But I really needed to get the juices

flowing this morning, and Jazzercise is the only thing that works."

"Jazzercise?"

"Oh yeah! It has an energy, it has verve, it has..."

"Spandex?" I suggested.

"Exactly!" he agreed. "Besides, I don't think it really bothers Scott all that much."

"Yes, it does!" came a muffled reply from the door to our immediate left.

"Hey, why you no like Jazzercise?" Steven called toward the closed door.

"Troglodyte!" Kirkpatrick shouted back.

"See?" Steven smiled and held up two entwined fingers. "We're tight."

"Steve, could you at least *try* waiting until he's not here to watch it?"

"Can I at least keep doing lunges in the hall?" Steven asked.

"As long as you can do them quietly," Abernathy said.

Steven mimed locking his lips and tossing the key over his shoulder. "Now if you'll excuse me, I have an appointment with the vet."

"You have pets?" I asked.

"Just a skin tag. They should be able to nip it off in no time." Steven tipped his neon green sweatband to us and disappeared into his studio, closing the door behind him.

I turned to Abernathy. "I'm guessing this is a long-standing feud?"

"Kirkpatrick is a self-important prick of the first order, and I would personally love to tear his arm off and beat him with the wet end, but unfortunately, he is our bestselling artist as he so helpfully pointed out."

"What does he paint?" I asked. It was hard for me to imagine how an asshat like Kirkpatrick could produce anything worth buying with those disgusting little hands of his.

"Beavers, mostly." Abernathy delivered this line with a seriousness of expression that contradicted the teasing lilt in his voice.

I blinked at him.

"And otters, deer, the occasional mountain goat, or shaggy sheep's arse. The locals like his beavers, and I like their money, so we put up with him." I followed him into the attached antiques shop where I could barely make out shapes passing by the murky windows that, like the gallery's, faced Rose Street. Dust motes swam through the air where the sun managed to penetrate the gloom, as deep and thick as seawater.

"It wouldn't really help to give you a tour," Abernathy said. "I think it would be best if you just nosed around a bit and perused the place yourself."

Looking at the towering maze of shelves stretching out before me, it felt like an impossible task.

"We buy and sell objects here, so the inventory is constantly changing."

"What sort of things do you buy?"

"Oddities mostly. You'd be surprised how popular they are here." Abernathy's suit pocket buzzed. He took a pager out of it and frowned at the number.

Speaking of antiques.

"Sorry, I have to make a call." He swept back toward the gallery like a glowering thunderstorm.

I had only begun to examine a nearby mason jar full of teeth when the store's front door banged open.

The woman who approached the counter looked like she had just slithered out of an S&M dungeon. But one of the high-dollar, classy as shit S&M dungeons. Four-inch spiked Louboutins. Long, black, leather duster. Dark, silky hair with the kind of volume and texture acquired by riding some stud hard and putting him away wet.

"May I help you?" I asked.

"Where is he?"

"Where is who?"

"Abernathy. Who the fuck else?"

"I'm afraid he's stepped out for a moment," I said. "I would be happy to get a message to him for you."

"I'll bet you would." She flicked a scornful glance over my general person. "Are you his new piece of ass then?"

"I'm not *anyone's* piece of ass." I meant it to be a rebuke, but somehow it sounded more like an admission of my utter lack of sex life. "I'm his assistant."

"Do I look like a *dipshit?*" The term was especially ugly on her pretty mouth. "Abernathy doesn't have an assistant."

"No. You look like an ad for discount pleather, since you asked."

Her lips twisted into a prissy frown.

"Fine," she said. "If you won't tell me where he is, I'll find him myself." She marched through the gallery toward Abernathy's office at the back of the gallery with the confidence of a woman who had been here before. And most likely had dirty gorilla sex on every flat surface.

I caught up with her on the stairs and slid past her, grabbing both sides of the wooden railing to make myself into a gate.

"I don't know who you are," I said, "but I know you sure as hell don't have an appointment. You're not going in there. It's that simple."

"Get out. Of my way." The deadly calm in her voice made it all the more shocking when she planted two palms on my shoulders and shoved. I landed hard on my ass, the stair above me cutting into my lower back.

I captured a black, fishnet-clad ankle and yanked it out from under her as she tried to step over me. She yelped as she went down, her chin hitting the top step and splitting her perfect lower lip.

A thrill of savage satisfaction coursed through me, followed by a jolt of pure terror as she drew back to hit me.

Abernathy's door flew open, and in the next heartbeat, he was holding back her hand.

"What the hell is going on?"

I scanned his face, looking for signs that I would be summarily fired after twenty minutes of employment for tackling a woman on the stairs. But Abernathy was a book written in a language I couldn't read.

"She didn't have an appointment," I said, unceremoniously untangling myself from leather-clad limbs and getting to my feet. My would-be opponent righted herself as quickly and gracefully as an offended cat.

"Helena, what are you doing here?" Abernathy asked.

"Oh, I think you know exactly what I'm doing here." Helena's dark eyes lit with an unspoken challenge. "And a lot of other people are going to know if I—"

"Helena," Abernathy said, his eyes searching hers. "Don't."

"Are you coming over tonight, then?" Her voice dipped lower, skimming across a puddle of suggestion.

"You know I can't." His expression softened, the *I'm pretty much irritated with the entire world* perma-crease between his eyebrows vanishing. "I told you what this was."

"Fuck. You." Her dark eyes glittered with undisguised malice. "When everyone finds out what you ar—"

Abernathy's mouth covered hers as he pinned her arms to her sides, crushing her into the wall. Her energy seemed to flow outward through her lips as she crumpled into him. Her moan was a surrender.

Heat bloomed in my face and shot downward through my chest. I shifted from foot to foot on the stairs. I didn't feel like I should be privy to this scene, but I wasn't sure where else to go or what to do. Besides, aside from having Abernathy's boxers drop into my lap, this was as close to action as I'd been in way, way too long.

Helena sagged against him when he broke the kiss. Abernathy gathered her up and helped her down the stairs.

"I'm going to see that Helena gets home, Hanna. Keep an eye on the store until Rob Vincent gets in, will you?"

I gave him a half-hearted salute.

When they were out the front door, I descended the stairs, crossed the gallery, and stationed myself at the front window. I watched as Abernathy carefully deposited Helena in the passenger's side of the red Lexus parked at the curb, before walking around to the driver's side, starting the car, and speeding off.

No sooner had the exhaust from their tailpipe evaporated than the shop bell dinged and the front door swung open.

My first instinct was to hide behind one of the store's many piles until whoever it was left. Something told me this would do little to endear me to my new employer. After hearing this morning's conversation, I had no intention of being on the receiving end of Abernathy's wrath.

Taking a deep breath, I forced myself out from behind the shelf. A pencil-thin kid dipped in head to toe emo black studied an apothecary jar near the door, pecking at the glass with a black-polished fingernail. Judging by his getup, I didn't really want to know what had captured his attention so completely, especially if it might be alive.

"Can I help you?" I asked, sliding behind the shop counter.

He performed the usual scan, eyes fast down my body and up again to my face. When he broke into a sheepish grin, my tension eased a little. Goth kid, probably shy.

"Hi," he mumbled, not quite meeting my eyes. "I have something to sell."

At that moment, it occurred to me I had no idea how Abernathy conducted these transactions, where the cash would be, or how much he paid for what. Moisture abandoned my mouth and reappeared on my forehead and upper lip.

Panic! screamed the unhelpful voice inside my head. Charming, these anxiety disorders.

"Could you give me just one second?" I asked. "Feel free to look around."

I whipped around the corner to the hallway of artist's studios connecting the antiques shop and gallery and ran face first into the bony chest of Steven Franke.

"Whoa, hey, hey there," he said, steadying hands on my shoulders. He had traded the animal print bathrobe for a pair of dark skinny jeans, a well-worn Rush t-shirt, and black and white checkered Chuck Taylors. He'd drawn a variety of designs on the white rubber toes.

"Nice shoes," I said.

"Likewise," he said, glancing down at my rockabilly-red peep toe pumps. "Those kicks are a whole-ass mood." Whether Steven liked them on me or might like to wear them alone in his studio, I couldn't yet say. I was pleased to note that it didn't matter.

"Where's the fire, doll?" he asked.

28

"Someone in the shop wants to sell something."

"Ahh. And Mr. A has disappeared. Am I right?"

"It would seem so."

"Yeah, he does that. Now you see him, now you don't, the mysterious Mr. A." Steven wiggled his fingers like a mesmerist.

"What should I do? I've been employed here all of thirty minutes. I don't even know where the bathroom is."

"Oh, that's easy," he said. "There isn't one."

"You're kidding, right?"

"Nope, no toilet. We use the one at the tea joint down the street. Abernathy is a big tipper, so the owner doesn't mind."

"Any thoughts?" I asked in desperation.

"I mean, I personally don't mind walking down the block to crack a rat, but—"

"About the customer," I amended, stifling a laugh at his colorful vernacular.

"Oh! Right. I've seen Abernathy in action before," Steven said, stroking the few threads of red-blond hair pretending to be a goatee. "I bet I can do this."

"Be my guest," I invited.

I followed him into the shop, watching the studded belt around his waist catch and reflect the light in dancing squares on the walls. The young man in black waited patiently in front of an expansive oak counter, the bag tucked under his arm.

"My coworker indicated you were interested in selling an item," Steven said, assuming a curious air of formality. It fit him like jeans on an octopus.

The young man straightened up an inch or two, nodded smartly, and placed the garbage bag on the counter's scarred surface.

"Let's see what we have here." Steven untwisted the

bag, peeked in, emitted a shrill sound, and tipped backward like a felled tree.

I knelt over him and lightly slapped his cheek.
"Steven? You okay?"

His eyes popped open wide, and he stared at me in
horror.

"Sorry about that." He grabbed the counter, and I
helped him to his feet.

"Are you gonna buy him or what?" the kid asked.

I had forgotten about the bag, with its contents that
made Steven faint. Before I could make excuses about
the terribly important task I had forgotten in a distant
part of the gallery, the kid whipped back the plastic bag
to reveal its occupant.

A cat.

And not just any cat, mind you. A dead cat. A dead,
dehydrated cat with its hideous face frozen in a snarl.
The fur had long since abandoned the desiccated hide,
and what remained was leathery skin mottled brown
and gray. The eyeless sockets gaped at us, unseeing. Its
bony legs and paws stretched out straight, claws extended. It reminded me of a child's drawing, all four
legs shown in two-dimensional profile. However this
thing had died, it had suffered. If nothing else, it deserved a proper burial.

"You want to sell a dead cat?" It seemed like a reasonable question.

"It's not just a dead cat, it's a *mummified* cat. I'm
pretty sure it's ancient."

Some mummies are made by human hands, others
by nature's quirks. The likelihood that someone mummified this poor thing purposefully seemed impossible,
considering the Egyptians were the only ones on
record with a penchant for dehydrating house cats.

"How ancient?" I asked, unable to resist the urge to

see what kind of bullshit collage this kid would cobble together.

"Egyptian maybe," he said in a hushed tone.

"The Egyptians removed the internal organs and placed them in *kanopic* jars before stuffing the cavity with natrum to extract all the moisture. You see this intestinal loop here through the skin? Poor Fluffy's insidey parts are very much intact. Additionally, they would have wrapped the body in linen strips and bound them with resin." I paused to savor the bewildered stares from Steven and the kid. "Want to try again?"

"I found it buried near some Indian ruins."

God love him for trying. I shook my head no. "You found it where?"

"Under my grandma's front porch," he mumbled.

"That's a good lad," I said, and turned to Steven. "What do you think?"

"Was it a Manx?"

"I don't know." The kid shrugged. "Why?"

"It's missing its tail."

"Oh, wait." The kid rummaged around in the garbage bag, aiming his cell phone in to provide a bluish glow. "I have it right here. It sort of broke off in the car."

He pulled a withered, pencil-thin object out of the bag and held it out to me.

"Just set it...there." I shoved a stained beverage napkin toward him.

"What'll you give me for it?"

Steven considered the withered carcass and tested the sharpness of one of its front teeth with his finger. Kicking the tires.

"What do you think it's worth?" he asked the kid deferentially.

"At least ninety." The kid's protuberant Adam's apple bobbed. We all knew it was a show of weakness.

"Twenty-five," I countered.

"Thirty."

"Twenty-seven."

"Deal." He stuck out his hand to shake, but I reached for the receipt pad by the register instead. I couldn't bring myself to touch the hand that had been holding the tail only moments ago. Steven cranked open the ancient wooden register and counted out some wrinkled bills.

"Dead cat, slightly damaged," I wrote on the carbon paper. I tore off the receipt and handed the customer copy to the kid.

"Sweet! Thanks!" The bell chimed as he pushed the door open and disappeared into the street.

"Good job, doll!" Steven held up a fist, and I managed to connect two out of four knuckles. "But if I were you," he continued, "I'd hide the cat."

"Why's that?" I asked.

"If Mr. A finds it in here, you can smooch your job *sayonara*."

CHAPTER 3

"*Sayonara*? What do you mean, *sayonara*?" A rock of dread lodged in my chest.

"Mr. A *hates* cats. Freaks out when they're even mentioned."

My fingers fisted in his well-worn t-shirt. "You're supposed to stop me from doing stupid things!"

"You were on a roll. Spitting out facts like a slot machine! You should be on the History Channel or something." His cheeks were flushed pink with admiration, his eyes glowing above them like jade.

"Steven? Is that you?"

The woman hobbling through the shop doorway never lifted a foot off the floorboards. She slid along, finding the counter's base with her orthopedic shoes. Her gnarled fingers waved in the open air until they encountered the solid wood, coming to rest at Steven's elbow.

"Mrs. Kass! You're just in time to meet Hanna." Steven wrapped an arm around her bony shoulders and turned her to face me.

Mrs. Kass had more lipstick on her dentures than on her lips. She wore false eyelashes like my grandmother had, but hers wandered the wrinkled expanse of her face like nomads in the desert. One stuck to the crease in her eyelid; the other had made its way down to her over-rouged cheek. Her brows had been drawn with the precision possessed by kindergartners and large dogs. When she began petting the lump of cat jerky on the counter, I began to suspect her post-modern application of make-up might have more to do with a vision problem than a love of abstract expressionism. Frenetic application of colors and loosely organized chaos worked better on canvas than on faces, as a general rule.

When Steven introduced her as one of The Crossing's four resident artists, I did my best to keep a neutral expression on my face.

"Oh really?" My voice sounded all right, if perhaps a little shrill.

"It's very kind of Mr. Abernathy to let me paint here. He's such a nice young man," she said, her voice full of grandmotherly affection.

"Yes, he is. Very nice."

"And when did you start working here, Hanna?" she asked.

"I just started today."

"Well, welcome." Her grin revealed the shadow of an ill-fitting denture in the deeply dug corner of her mouth.

"Thank you," I said.

"I don't mean to keep you. Stevie dear, could you come help me for a moment? The light has burned out in my studio."

"Of course," Steven said, turning to me. "Will you be okay if I go help her?"

I nodded, hoping this was true.

"Back in a flash. Come along, you sexy young thing," he said to Mrs. Kass. He put an arm around her shoulder and steered her toward the stairs.

"Oh my," she giggled.

I watched as Steven took Mrs. Kass's arm and helped her up the steps into the gallery. She shuffled along beside him, her knee-high stockings bunched around the bony knobs of her blue-veined ankles below a faded floral print housedress. The overhead light in the gallery shone on her scalp through her white hair. I wondered if she had been beautiful once.

Alone now in the store, my thoughts turned to organizing—my grandmother's influence no doubt. At approximately 11:59 p.m. every December 25th, she began deconstructing her Christmas tree and whisking all the holiday trappings back into their requisite boxes.

"Vhy vait?" she asked in her brusque German way.

The antique cash register rose above the detritus like a mountain breaking through the clouds. It looked as old as some of the antiques lining the shop shelves and perching precariously in glass cabinets. Ornate leafy garlands looped across the tarnished brass faceplate over circular buttons, long since rubbed smooth by human fingers. The cash drawer opened by pulling down on a wood-handled lever. It groaned in protest as I cranked it down, revealing a drawer stuffed with wadded up bills. I pulled out a handful and began smoothing them out and sorting them into stacks.

At the back of the drawer, behind a pile of envelopes I found a stack of bills paper-clipped together. I blew the dust off them and nearly choked. Ten thousand-dollar bills. Fifty of them in all. I was holding a half a million dollars. What on earth was Abernathy thinking, keeping this much money in a register that didn't lock?

For that matter, why was I standing here like an idiot when I could be ten minutes closer to the airport by now? I fought the urge to stuff the money in my bra and make a run for it. I imagined myself back in Paris

CYNTHIA ST. AUBIN

inhaling the gloriously impolite aroma of cheese at the *Fromagerie Quatrehomme*. The luxurious feasts at Hotel Meurice. Shoes, dammit! Enough shoes to make even Imelda Marcos blush.

Truth was, I was just no good at breaking rules. I tucked the bills into an envelope and returned them to the back of the drawer.

The rest of the money, I laid in the cash drawer's wooden slots in order of increasing denomination. On a discarded scrap of paper, I began a list: WD-40, bleach wipes, Murphy's Oil Soap, Swiffer dusters, Windex, broom and dustpan, mop, and exorcist. Supplies for Abernathy's office would have to wait.

If he ever returned.

Another half hour saw the receipts sorted, the odds and ends neatly arranged in individual baskets, and the entire area wiped down with an old cloth. Satisfied with my work at the counter, I turned my attention to the store.

The floor's wood planks were stripped dull by age and use and sang a lullaby of creaks as I wandered along the aisles. The shelves and dust-fogged glass cases held objects I couldn't identify.

"Find anything?"

I started at the voice and noticed with dismay that I'd left a nose-smudge on the glass. I had also squeaked. Lame.

Abernathy crossed the space with three strides and wiped the tip of my nose with the rough pad of his thumb. "Dust."

"Thanks."

"Don't mention it."

"Did you get everything sorted out?" I asked.

"Yes, I think so. I'm sorry you had to be here for that."

Me too.

36

"She's very beautiful." It felt like offering conciliatory compliments to the family of the deceased at a funeral.

"She's also bat-shit crazy." Abernathy frowned. "I'm only sorry I didn't see it sooner."

I nodded, not knowing what else to say.

"Did anything interesting happen while I was gone?"

Between finding half a million dollars and change in his register and purchasing a dead cat... *Fuck! The cat!* I had forgotten to hide it. The black plastic bag rested on a chair behind Abernathy. I found something else to look at.

"I organized the counter."

"You did?" He looked over at the counter's clean surface, and his amber eyes brightened a shade. "You did." He circled around behind it, trailing his fingers on the battered oak border. "You even used the baskets."

Gratified, I came around beside him and began running down the locations of various objects. "Pens here, paperclips, purchase receipts in this basket, and sales receipts in the one next to it. Over here is where I put the—"

"What's that?"

"What's what?"

"That." He nodded toward the chair where the cat reclined in its black plastic cocoon.

"Oh that? It's nothing. Just some old bits and pieces."

"What kind of bits and pieces?"

"Things that were just lying around, mostly."

"Let's see." He took a step toward the bag, but I quickly scooted between them.

"Really. It's not even worth your time, I promise."

The front door swung open, and a couple of twenty-somethings in baggy jeans and death metal t-shirts wandered in.

"Look!" I pointed toward the front of the shop, in the opposite direction of the bag. "Customers!"

To my great irritation, Abernathy didn't shift his focus even a fraction. "Hanna, what's in the bag?"

I was suddenly eight years old and sitting in the cracked green Naugahyde chair in Principal Murphy's office. Having squirted Allen Fike with my juice box in the cafeteria, and on picture day no less, I passed the time waiting my turn by imagining how I would coolly deny everything. No sooner had Principal Murphy said *Hanna*, than I began to sob apologies into the sleeve of my sweater.

Pathetic, right?

"Hanna?"

"A cat," I mumbled.

"What the hell is wrong with you? That thing is probably suffocating!" He elbowed past me and tore open the bag.

"I find that unlikely," I said.

The tail dropped from the bag and bounced off his expensive Italian leather shoe.

Abernathy looked at me, the evidence of several unspeakable sentences written in his dark eyes.

"Look at it this way," I said. "At least it won't get any fur on your suit."

His brows descended his forehead, casting his eyes into shadow.

"Okay, bad joke."

"What is a dead cat doing in my gallery?"

The breath I'd been holding shot words out of my mouth as soon as my lips parted. "This kid came in and you weren't here and I didn't know what to do but there's kind of a market for animal oddities these days and I thought—"

"Are you saying someone came in to sell this thing?"

Being at the service end of Abernathy's scrutinizing

gaze was a little like staring into a canon. "Kind of."

"And you *bought* it?"

"A little."

"How much did you pay for it?"

"Twenty-seven."

"You paid twenty-seven dollars for a dead cat? Who the hell is going to buy a dead cat?"

It sounded so much more absurd when Abernathy said it.

One of the twenty-somethings looked up. "Dude, you have a dead cat? Lemme see it." He picked up the cat and turned it under the light as if he hoped to see through its stiff, dry body.

"Whoa." His friend sidled up behind him. "How much you want for it?"

I processed his features in an instant. Streaked hair, name-brand jeans, expensive sneakers. "Fifty."

Abernathy eyed me but said nothing.

The kid holding the cat put it down and began digging in his jeans pocket.

"Hey dude, wait, I was gonna buy it! I'll give you fifty-five," he said to me.

"No way, bro, this cat is mine! Sixty."

My gaze bounced back and forth between them like a tennis ball as they lobbed opposing offers over the counter.

"Sixty-five."

"Seventy."

"Seventy-five."

When his friend didn't reply, I banged the counter with my fist like an auctioneer. "Sold!"

"Dude, you suck."

"Jill is gonna *freak* when she finds this in her bed tonight." His piercings winked in the store's dim light.

Poor Jill. Was the world so devoid of actual men that vermin like this were now considered acceptable breeding partners? I looked at the pale band of skin where my wedding ring had lived. *Asked and answered.*

I took the wad of bills and handed the bag over, thinking a bow or some tissue paper might have been a nice touch. "Enjoy," I said.

When they were gone, I looked at Abernathy, who was scowling at the clean counter. Though I suspected he was already second-guessing his decision to hire an assistant, I found myself completely unable to detach the expression of abject smugness from my face.

"It was a fluke," he said. "Next time, don't buy anything unless I approve it first."

"That would be much easier to do if you were actually *here*." I regretted my words instantly. The air around Abernathy seemed to darken and chill. I waited for him to lower the axe.

"Point taken." Abernathy didn't so much say these words as force them out through gritted teeth.

The shop's door swung open with a groan and the characteristic chime. A man in ripped jeans and a faded army jacket ambled toward the counter. His reddish-blond hair was pulled into a disheveled ponytail low on his neck, and he wore the black-rimmed glasses of a coffee house poet.

"Sorry I'm late, Mark."

"Rob Vincent, this is Hanna Harvey. My new *assistant*." The last word was pronounced with the affection usually assigned to *IRS audit* or *root canal*.

"He's actually thrilled," I said. "He can't wait for me to clean out his office."

"Nice to meet you, Hanna." Rob's hand was rough like a carpenter's and strong as it closed over mine.

"You sculpt clay?" I asked.

Surprise brightened his hazel eyes. They seemed older than the rest of his face. "How did you know?"

"Lucky guess." I'd hung around the fine arts studios

in college, enjoying occasional admiration for my lengthy limbs and crazy hair. Somewhere in my ancient history were memories of a sculptor's clever hands and the deep earthen smell of wet clay. The feel of a coarse canvas drop cloth on my naked skin and his sheepish smile as he picked flakes of porcelain out of my hair afterward. Hanna Harvey, muse in the mud.

"Whoa!" Rob said, noticing the counter. "What happened?"

"Hanna happened," Abernathy sighed.

Rob set down a battered messenger bag behind the counter and crouched to examine the shelves. "This is amazing!"

I grinned at Abernathy.

"There's plenty more to do," he grumbled, stalking toward the gallery. "Hanna," barked his retreating back.

"Well, I guess that's me. Nice to meet you."

"You too," Rob nodded.

I left him wondering at the rows of clean wood shelves.

IN ABERNATHY'S OFFICE, I SQUATTED BEHIND THE DESK, sifting through piles while the wide back of Abernathy's chair ignored me.

By the time I spotted the first bit of wood floor beneath the layer of papers and trash, it had been two hours and my stomach growled in protest. My face was caked with dust and grime, a dull ache had settled low in my back, my bladder was about to explode, and I had only managed to create a few disordered piles from the chaos.

Abernathy's half of all this morning's calls had ranged from irritation to interrogation. The last thing I wanted to do was upset him further, but I was quickly approaching crisis point. I was only one dust bunny away from hacking myself into a collapsed lung.

"Mr. Abernathy?"

"Yes." It was more statement than question. He didn't bother to look up.

"Do you think I could take a short break for lunch or something?"

"What time is it?"

I had neither cell phone nor watch. Since the former had been shut off and the latter had been pawned, I had become used to telling time by the daytime TV lineup. I glanced around the office but could find no clocks to consult, digital or otherwise.

"It has to be after noon," I said.

Abernathy stuck his hand into his vest and withdrew an ancient gold relic. He popped the heavy lid open. "12:38 to be exact."

He rose from his chair and came around the desk to where I sat cross-legged, flanked by unsteady stacks of paper and books. He offered me his hand and helped me to my feet with one effortless tug.

I was close enough to feel his breath, to catch the deliciously scented currents emanating from the opening in his suit coat.

He picked a dust ball from my hair and blew it from his fingertips, considering my face like it might hide the answer to some question.

I desperately needed to swallow but didn't for fear it would echo through the room.

"Shall we?" Abernathy said.

"Shall we what?"

Not that it mattered what *what* meant. My answer was an enthusiastic and unrestrained *Please God, yes* to whatever this man had in mind.

"Get some lunch?"

My knees went all buttery and soft. "Hell yes."

CHAPTER 4

*I*f I had been less focused on Abernathy's ass sauntering toward the staircase, it might have occurred to me sooner that I had no way of *paying* for said lunch.

I paused at the landing, giving Abernathy time to get a few steps ahead of me.

"You know, I was thinking..."

Abernathy turned on his heel and faced me. "That's encouraging," he said.

I managed a courtesy laugh in lieu of donkey kicking him down the last few stairs.

"I was thinking, about lunch..." I began again.

"Don't worry about it," he said, crossing into the gallery and pausing before the hallway to the artists' studios. "Lunch is on me."

"Oh. Wait, what?"

The door to Steven Franke's studio swung open, and his head popped mole-like into the hallway.

"Did someone say lunch?"

I watched Abernathy consider what his answer might cost him. "Yes," he sighed. "Would you like to join us?"

"Does a badger like to do tai-chi in the woods?"

Steven shut his studio door behind him and tapped on Scott Kirkpatrick's.

"Hey! Captain Kirk! We're going to lunch. Wanna come?"

"Get bent!" came the muffled reply.

"Must have brought his lunch today." Steven motioned toward Mrs. Kass's door and looked at Abernathy.

"Why the hell not?" Abernathy's was a heavy sigh, full of good-natured regret.

Steven pounded on the door like a member of the SWAT team. "Mrs. Kass! We're. Going. To Lunch. Would you like to join us?"

A few moments passed and the studio door creaked open to reveal a chain lock spanning the space between the door and the jamb. Mrs. Kass's telescopic lenses glinted in the darkness. "Is someone there?" she warbled into the hall.

"Why the chain?" I asked Abernathy.

"Mrs. Kass is convinced she's being hunted by members of the Canadian mafia, among other things."

"I didn't even know Canada had a mafia," I whispered.

"I'm still not sure they do."

WE SHUFFLED DOWN ROSE STREET LIKE A PATHETIC parade: Abernathy several paces in front, hoping to prove his disassociation by lack of proximity, me waddling behind him with my knees clamped like a vice grip (wouldn't my mother be proud), and Steven and Mrs. Kass bringing up the rear at a steady hobble.

I pushed into the small crowded foyer behind Abernathy and was immediately and completely charmed. The Dusty Dahlia was not just a tea shop, but a tea *room.* Complete with chintz curtains, lacy tablecloths, and walls painted the soul-soothing pastel pinks and greens of an after-dinner mint.

Spotting the restroom sign, I made a beeline for the back of the restaurant. In my haste, I ran tits first into to a svelte, beautiful brunette exiting the bathroom.

She stopped for a moment, resting a hand on my shoulder. "Do I know you?" she asked.

Pausing, I looked into her face. Familiar. But from where?

"I don't think so."

"Oh well." She shrugged and offered up a harried smile. "Have a good one."

"You too," I said, and scampered into the nearest stall.

Afterward, thawing my hands under the tap as I washed, I considered the person staring back at me in the bathroom mirror. A face smudged with dust and dotted with smears of ink. Coppery hair strewn with fine filaments of cobweb. Layers of concealer failing to hide dark shadows born of many sleepless nights. I felt tired and sad and about a thousand years old.

I did what I could with a damp paper towel and allowed myself one fortifying breath as I walked back into the restaurant.

Abernathy, Steven, and Mrs. Kass were hunched around a table near the window. I seated myself in the empty chair across from Abernathy and shrugged out of my coat. On my left, Mrs. Kass held the menu close enough to absorb the items through osmosis. On my right, Steven was busily making a crude giraffe out of straws.

A scrim of gray hung between the restaurant and the world beyond. Condensation clung to the windows and cut streams where it pooled to the chipped windowsill. The snow lingering in the shadows between buildings and in stubborn mounds in the corners of parking lots had taken on a sickly grayish cast.

I wanted spring. I wanted the snow gone. The particles of all that surrounded me still contained the last ugly fights of my dying marriage. The snow had been on the ground when the final words were said, had stuck to my shoes as I slogged the remnants of a former life up unfamiliar creaky stairs to a cheaper, smaller apartment. The endless winter night pressed against my windows.

Abernathy folded his menu and set it down. To my great relief, he turned his gaze to the window, and I could finally concentrate my full energy on selecting lunch, for which there were many options, I was delighted to note. In addition to an expansive list of teas and dainty nibbles, the Dusty Dahlia also offered a full complement of hearty sandwiches for the greedy eater like me.

A young woman with wide oceanic eyes and cobalt blue hair approached our table, pad in hand. Tattooed pin-up girls yawned and stretched across her arms as she pulled a pen from behind her ear. "Everyone know what they want?"

"You, me, a plate of spaghetti, and some chocolate milk. What do ya think?" Steven grinned.

The girl's rosebud of a mouth turned down at the corners. "I think we've been over this."

"Repetition is the sincerest form of flattery."

"I think that's *imitation*," she said.

"Au contraire," he said. "Nothing imitation here. This is 153 pounds of pure manly splendor."

She rolled her eyes and shook her head.

"I can see you're not yet tempted by my many charms. That's okay. Because in addition to being devastatingly handsome, I'm also patient."

"Well, I'm not," she said shifting her weight. "What

will you have? And if you say 'just you, doll-face,' doll-face will dead ass stick this pen up your nose."

"Point taken. Just the usual then."

"Tuna salad on wheat, extra pickles, strawberry jam, and crushed Fritos?"

"Fritos on the side today," Steven said. "I'm feeling saucy."

"Right," she said. "For you, Mrs. Kass?"

Mrs. Kass slid her dentures around in her mouth, a gesture I would soon come to learn indicated that she was considering. "I'll have the soup of the day."

"French dip, double roast beef," Abernathy said, clapping his menu closed and handing it over.

"For you, hon?" The waitress looked at me from eyes made feline by artful eyeliner.

"I'll have the Rueben." I briefly debated the merits of requesting double corned beef like Abernathy, but social propriety won out over my typical culinary avarice.

"I haven't seen you with this motley crew before," she said, her eyes still on me. "Are you new?"

"Hanna is Abernathy's new Girl Friday," Steven announced by way of introduction. "Heavy into the organizing, and the cleaning, and the whatnot."

"Shayla." She reached across the table to take my cold hand in her warm one. "Nice to meet you. And don't let any of these characters push you around, okay? Especially this one." She jerked her chin toward Steven, who feigned a wounded expression.

"You cut me, doll." Steven pressed a hand to his heart. "You cut me real deep just now."

"I'm afraid you'll live," Shayla said, bustling off to see to our orders.

Abernathy shrugged out of his jacket, and I watched his broad torso twist beneath his tailored white shirt for as many seconds as I could steal before turning my face to the fogged window.

Abernathy, on the other hand, looked directly at me, laced his fingers, and settled his elbows on the table. "Hanna, there's something bothering me about your resume."

It's a rather unsettling feeling, the sudden relocation of your intestines three inches southward. "Oh?"

"Why would someone with your qualifications stay in such a small town? Didn't you want a PhD?"

Relief melted over me like hot butter.

"Oh, well. You know how it is." I waved a hand to sweep some lightness into the conversation. "You finish a degree, you get comfortable..." You kill a couple years and take out a grundle of student loans for your husband who changes majors six times.

"How can it be that an eligible fox such as yourself didn't get snapped up while you were in college?" Steven asked.

The dreaded question. Disgorge my sordid past? Lie through my teeth?

"I'm divorced." The first time I'd ever said it out loud.

"A nice young lady like you?" Mrs. Kass clucked. "Such a shame."

"Any offspring?" Steven galloped his giraffe across the table, where it fell afoul of the peppershaker and lost a leg.

"God no." The thought sent a ripple through my stomach. I could barely take care of three cats, much less a child—as my mother was so fond of pointing out.

"Does that mean you're back on the market then?" Steven ceased his limb reattachment surgery on the giraffe and looked at me, rosy-cheeked with boyish exuberance. "I know a great guy I could set you up with. He's a friend of mine. Austin Blade, lead singer of Kings of Karate."

"I'm good," I said. "Really. Thanks though."

"Are you sure? He just had that tattoo of his old lady's name lasered off and everything."

"Wow," I said. "Tempting. But I'm going to have to pass."

"Well, if you change your mind, I'd be happy to put in a good word for ya." Steven waggled his eyebrows suggestively.

Shayla returned and dealt out our drinks from the tray balanced on her palm.

Pouring an indecent amount of half and half into my coffee, I wrapped my grateful hands around the warm mug.

"Would you like some coffee with your cream?" Abernathy raised a dark eyebrow at me.

A feeble laugh was all I could offer. *Dad humor, anyone?*

"I suppose you drink it black?" I asked.

"I don't drink it at all."

"You're missing out. Because this," I said, hoisting my steaming mug, "is delicious." I took a gulp to illustrate my point and immediately regretted it. Scalding coffee filled my mouth and burned a molten trail down my throat. I coughed, smiled, and tried to look satisfied as my eyes watered.

"I can see that." Shadows flickered at the corners of his mouth.

Shayla breezed by and set down bowls of butternut squash soup in front of Mrs. Kass and me.

"Oh, sorry. I didn't order this," I said, hoping she might let me keep it.

"It's on the house." She winked. "You looked cold."

The intoxicating aroma of earthy sage caressed my nose. I scooped up the decorative crostini and plunged it into the soup, then into my mouth, savoring my first taste of real food in nearly a month.

"*Moh* God." Sinking down in my chair, I rode the wave of glorious velvet on my tongue.

Abernathy cleared his throat, and my eyes popped open.

"Sorry," I said. "I'm not used to eating in public."

"You have soup." Abernathy pointed to a spot on my chin. "There."

I grabbed the napkin from my lap, swiped my face, and proceeded modestly, eyes open.

The meals arrived, and thus continued my own personal culinary Renaissance.

Every layer offered a new cause for celebration—toasted rye, sharp German mustard, the crunchy tang of sauerkraut, melting Swiss cheese, then finally, tender, juicy roast beef. By sheer willpower alone I managed to keep quiet as I made my way through the wall of meat.

Steven ate quickly, pausing only to sprinkle crushed Fritos on the strawberry jam and dip his sandwich into it.

Abernathy was another spectacle altogether. I began to feel less self-conscious as I watched him push the bread out of the way and shove wads of meat into his face.

He looked up and saw me watching him.

"Mmmph?" he mumbled around a mouthful of beef.

I briefly considered telling him about the piece of beef on his chin but thought better of it.

Also, it was kind of hot.

WALKING BACK TO THE OFFICE, I FELT MY STOMACH shift left to right like the lead weight at the end of a fishing line. Abernathy's purposeful stride remained unaffected by the ridiculous quantities of cow he'd just attacked with his face. Now would have been a great time to indulge in popping open the top button on my slacks—if I had been able to button them this morning.

Once there, Steven and Mrs. Kass headed for their respective studios, leaving Abernathy and me alone in the gallery.

"Shall we continue the excavation?" I asked.

"After you." He motioned toward his office.

I trudged up the narrow stairs and tried not to look winded. Abernathy closed the door behind us and settled back at his desk while I resumed my place at the pile I had been working on, adjusting my pants to restore circulation to my lower extremities.

"What are the chances you're harboring a box of file folders in one of your cabinets?" I asked.

"Not good," he said.

"Well, I don't think I'm going to get very far without some basic organizational supplies. And speaking of organization, I have to ask. What program do you use to track the business?"

"Program?"

"You know, software. Such as QuickBooks, Quicken, something like that."

"I don't use a program. I just buy what I buy and sell what I sell."

"But how do you keep track of profits?"

Abernathy spun his chair around to face me. "I look in the cash register."

"But what about payroll? You pay Rob to run the store, don't you?"

"No. I give Rob free gallery rent in exchange for manning the shop."

"Technically speaking, I'm your only employee?"

"Yes. And I'll be paying you in cash," he said. "If that's all right with you."

It was more than all right. It was fan*fucking*tastic.

Unreported income, tax free, and un-seizable by collections companies.

"Yes, that's perfectly fine with me."

"What will you need?" he asked.

"I'm sorry?" The mere mention of the word "cash" had me envisioning frolicking slow-motion down the aisles of the grocery store, filling my cart with whatever I pleased.

"Supplies."

"Oh, right. Folders, labels, things of that nature. And I'm sure I'll need a few things to get my workspace set up."

His brows knit together as he pondered this.

"I don't have a workspace, do I?"

"I hadn't really thought that far ahead," he said.

Shocker.

"I don't need much, really. Just a desk that has room for a computer and—" Then it hit me. Abernathy's desk, with all its piles, did not house a computer. No monitor. No keyboard. Nothing with a single button, key, or LED screen. Amidst the piles of paper and assorted debris, an old rotary phone was the lone technological relic.

"Please tell me there's a MacBook hiding under there," I said.

He shook his head ruefully, his hands spread wide, palms up in a gesture of supplication. "See how much I need you?"

I sighed in mock exasperation. "What am I going to do with you?"

"I'm sure you'll think of something," he said, favoring me with a wolfish smile.

As it happened, I was already thinking of *many* somethings.

"Tell you what," he said, pushing back from his desk. "I'll give you some cash, and you go pick up whatever you need." He withdrew a battered leather billfold from the suitcoat slung over the back of his chair and pulled out a thick sheaf of bills. "Do you think this will cover it?"

Looking at the wad in my hand, I tried to blink away the stars that swarmed my vision. He had handed me eight thousand dollars.

"Um. Yeah. This will cover it."

"Good. Now take the afternoon and get set up. I have some boring business to attend to."

I had the distinct impression that I'd been dismissed, and for once, I minded not at all.

Gathering my coat and purse from the sofa, I headed for the door, trying my best not to jump and click my heels with glee.

"Hanna?"

I turned back and poked my head into his office. "Yes?"

He flapped a bill at me between two long fingers. "For this week," he said. "I'll forget otherwise."

Were my eyes bugging out of my skull? Was I drooling? Please don't let me be drooling.

"Oh, you don't have to do that now. It can wait."

Don't listen to her! insisted the little voice in my head.

"Take it," he said.

"Okay then. If you insist."

"I insist. See you tomorrow."

I skipped through the gallery and out to my old Mustang humming "We're in the Money" as bottles of Belvedere and wedges of exotic cheese hopped around like back-up dancers on the stage of my naked greed.

For the first time in as long as I could remember, I had forgotten to be sad.

CHAPTER 5

*B*y mid-morning the following day, I had commandeered the landing outside of Abernathy's office and successfully set up mission control. From IKEA, I had purchased a compact desk with plenty of shelving and ample drawer space and a desk chair with the best lumbar support Swedish engineering could offer. Additional stops at Best Buy and Staples had yielded two MacBook Air laptops and matching monitors, a printer, and enough office supplies to choke an anal-retentive horse. While at the grocery store filling my cart with every food I had not been able to afford in months, I had also thrown in a generous assortment of cleaning supplies.

Now, before the rosy glow of my twenty-seven-inch monitor, food in my fridge and rent paid, I felt almost human. I grabbed Clancy—my lucky flying pig silver letter opener—and slid him into my pencil cup.

"Now we're ready."

I scooted the remaining boxes of equipment and office supplies toward Abernathy's office door and knocked.

"Come," he called.

Don't mind if I do. I pushed the door open.

Abernathy sat behind his desk paging through an auction catalog. Crisp white dress shirt. Sleeves pushed up to the elbows. Forearms Michelangelo would have creamed his doublet to sculpt. All very sexy stuff.

"Sounds like you've been busy out there this morning," he said around a yawn. He scratched at the dark stubble shadowing his jaw.

"Indeed I have! Now it's your turn."

"My turn for what?"

I picked up the laptop box and laid it in the small clearing before him on the desk. "Merry Christmas," I said.

He blinked at the box like it was a large insect that had just lighted on his desk.

"It's a laptop," I informed him.

"I can see that."

"You know, for sending emails, organizing electronic files, keeping track of receipts. Crazy things like that."

"I don't have any electronic files."

"Ta da!" I lifted up the scanner for him to see.

"What's that?"

I blinked in disbelief. "Please tell me you're joking."

Dark eyes regarded me with guileless invitation.

"This is the Canon Pixma TR8550 compact MFD," I explained. "Only the best thing that ever happened to office equipment. It scans business cards, documents, and receipts and creates electronic copies."

"And?"

"And it does lap dances. What do you mean 'And?' It completely eliminates the need to keep paper documentation."

"Why would I want to do that?"

I gestured around at the piles on the floor and overflowing shelves. "Um. Hello?"

"You may have a point."

CYNTHIA ST. AUBIN

"First things first, I'm going to need some space here." I mimed sweeping the surface of his desk clear, a gesture that seemed to concern him.

"Fine. Just don't touch my phone."

I saluted and began to lift up a pile from his desk when his hand closed over my wrist. A hot wire of electricity shot up my arm, flashed through my shoulder, and shot straight to my heart. Lava crept into the tips of my ears and washed over my cheeks.

"I need to go through that," he said.

"Were you planning on doing that now?"

"Soon," he said.

"How soon?"

"Soon*ish*." He folded his arms and kicked his feet onto the desk. I fought the urge to pick his shoes up by the toes and slide them back off. Was he *trying* to distract me?

"Can I at least move it then?"

"Move it where?" His eyes narrowed.

"To Guam. You tell me."

He looked around the room and settled on a spot by one of the room's many bookshelves. "There." He pointed.

Negotiating the narrow path across the room, I laid the pile down. By the time I reached the desk again, Abernathy had filled the space I had cleared with several documents from another pile.

My left eye began to tic. "Mr. A, don't take this the wrong way, but I think this process would go faster without you here."

"Really?"

"Really."

Tension tightened his features. It was an expression I had seen many times before on faces in episodes of *Hoarders*.

"Look. I won't throw anything away. You get to

56

make the final decisions. I just need some space to get things set up, then we'll go through everything together. Would that be okay?"

"Why do I feel like I'm being kicked out of my own office?"

"Because I'm kicking you out of your own office."

"Huh." His face was a mélange of emotions, the chief of which seemed to be disbelief.

Incredibly, I didn't flinch.

"I'll...I'll just go check things out in the store, then." He rose and stretched and, as if for the first time, I noticed how unaccountably, staggeringly, panty-droppingly *huge* this man was. Deep-chested. Broad-shouldered. Long-legged.

I fought the sudden urge to fling myself like a spider monkey at the climb-worthy oak that he was and did some quick mental math.

Three months.

Three months since I last had a man within spitting distance of my bed. Not that that was the bodily fluid I was chiefly interested in at the present.

I bit my lip as Abernathy rolled his neck and cracked more bones than seemed appropriate for a human to have.

"Good plan," I said. "I'll come get you when I'm done."

When he was gone, I returned to my desk and gathered several boxes. A few minutes saw his entire desk clean, save for the phone he'd asked me not to touch.

Clearly Abernathy was a man who supported his own business. First the ancient cash register and now this. Still, I could see why he would hold onto it. Remarkably crafted with a polished mahogany base inlaid with a bronze rotary dialer, it was a true treasure.

Surely he had meant that he didn't want me to *move* the phone, not that he hadn't wanted me to *touch* it.

I stole a guilty glance around the office and picked up the hand piece, smooth as satin and pleasantly heavy in my hand. Out of instinct I brought it up until the cool enamel of the speaker pressed against my ear. There was no dial tone—not that I had fully expected one.

"*Hallo?*" a voice barked.

I squeaked and dropped the phone. It landed on Abernathy's desk with an accusatory thud. Wincing, I quickly retrieved it.

"Mark Abernathy's office," I said into the receiver. "May I help you?"

"Ahh. *Gute.*" For an absurd moment I thought it was the distance between the hand piece and the base of the old phone that had made the voice on the other end sound unusually far away.

"I need to speak to *Herr* Abernathy."

My heart lurched at the familiar, clipped Bavarian cadence of his words.

"Yes, of course." I glanced at the rotary dialer for a moment, foolishly looking for a hold button. "If you don't mind waiting a moment, I'll go get him."

"*Ja.*"

Carefully setting the receiver on the desk, I scurried down the stairs and into the shop. Abernathy and Robert Vincent were engrossed in conversation and didn't immediately look up when I came in. I cleared my throat.

"Done causing havoc?" Abernathy asked.

"Nearly," I said. "There's a call for you."

"A call?" A crease appeared between his eyebrows. "I didn't hear my phone ring."

"Must be the new acoustics. With my desk on the landing, I bet it changes the dynamics." It sounded plausible.

"Odd," he said.

58

"Is it though?" I shifted on my feet. "Probably should hurry because it sounded really important."

"What sounded important? What did he tell you?"

Was it my imagination, or had Abernathy's knuckles whitened as he gripped the edge of the counter?

"Nothing. I just—when he said hello—I mean, it was probably just his accent. Germans, you know?"

Without another word, Abernathy sprinted out of the gallery toward the stairs.

Rob and I exchanged a look and shrugged at the same time.

On the landing outside Abernathy's office, I shuffled papers and tried to look industrious as opposed to eavesdroppy.

"Joseph!" Abernathy boomed. *"Wie gehts?"*

Dissatisfied with the state of affairs, I invented urgent business that required me to shuffle papers inside of Abernathy's office instead of at my desk.

Abernathy snapped his fingers at me, pinning the phone between his shoulder and ear while he mimed writing. I grabbed the nearest piece of paper I could find and a broken pencil from the floor and handed them over. He quickly scratched down some cryptic notes.

Abernathy's next statement sounded like a question to me, the inflection of his words rising like a curve. He looked absently at his notes before chewing on a few words as he suppressed a dark laugh. One half of his mouth drew upward into a rogue's grin as he surveyed my profile.

I suddenly wished I had at least tried to write down some of what Abernathy said so I could translate it. Most of the German words I knew fell into the category of obscenities, courtesy of my grandmother. Further practice in grad school translating writings from art history's early German scholars yielded little that would be relevant to this conversation. I repeated a few of the words to myself and made a mental note to consult Dr. Google about them when I was done not-eavesdropping.

Abernathy returned the phone to the receiver and looked at me. "All right," he began, "I've got a proj—"

Three short raps on his office door cut him off mid-sentence.

The visitor didn't wait to be granted access. He barged in like the office might be his and he was kind enough to let Abernathy borrow it.

My eyes moved up the long khaki duster and landed on his face, with its instantly recognizable hair the color of brown-sugar fudge.

Oh. Shit.

A familiar feeling of dread settled upon me. The motorist. The one whose god-awful gold Crown Vic I had given a mechanical wedgie. He was here. And he looked like someone had cheerfully pissed in his Cheerios.

"Hi," I said, hoping to head him off. "About yesterday—"

Surprise and recognition pressed a measure of ire away from his face as his eyes found me. "Oh. Hey. What are you doing here?"

"I work here."

"Since when?"

"Since yesterday."

"Good," he said. "You should know the answers to my questions then." He reached into his coat and brought out what looked like a little black wallet, letting it drop open to reveal a badge.

"Hey," I said. "I thought you said all cops were bureaucratic swine."

The flicker of a smile softened his formidable jaw. "I did. And I meant it."

"Detective Morrison," Abernathy cast a pointed look toward me, "I didn't realize you two knew one another."

"Me and Red? Just ran into each other yesterday. Didn't we, Red?" Mischief sparkled in his hazel eyes.

I flipped through several potential responses depending on who I wanted to piss off here.

Morrison could charge me with a hit and run.

Abernathy could fire me.

With no way to please both, I pleased neither, saying nothing.

"It's been a while, Morrison." Abernathy plopped down in his chair and propped his feet on the desk. "And here I was beginning to think you didn't like me."

"And here I was beginning to think you were done killing people."

Killing people?

Abernathy ignored his comment. "To what do I owe the displeasure of this visit? Come to try to pin Jimmy Hoffa's disappearance on me? Or is this a purely social call?"

Morrison gave him a twisted smile. "Neither, I'm afraid. Last night I was assigned a brand-new homicide investigation. And guess whose name came up right away? *Yours.* Isn't that funny?"

"Decidedly not. Well, don't draw the suspense out. Who have I killed this time?"

"Helena Pool."

Helena. *The* Helena? Helena the Superslut from yesterday's stair wrestling match?

Abernathy's shirt stretched taut across his chest as he tensed.

"Anything you want to confess, Abernathy?" Detective Morrison challenged.

"Yes, I confess. Your coat looks like something out of a Mike Hammer novel."

61

"That's what I like about you, Abernathy. You've got a great sense of humor. For a murderer."

"You're half right."

Which half?

"I need to ask you a few questions." He slid a look over to me. "It might be better if we did this in private."

"Hanna is my assistant," Abernathy said. "She stays."

And oh, how my love for him did bloom. Mostly because I'd already been calculating the odds that I could not-eavesdrop on their conversation and found them decidedly unfavorable.

"We could always take a little field trip to the station," Morrison suggested. "Or I could return with a warrant. I don't mind getting my hands dirty. Of course, I'm lecturing the professor here. You've been through this before. You know how it works."

Abernathy's wide shoulders deflated a fraction, and he indicated one of the chairs in front of his desk. Morrison sat down, took off his coat, popped open an attaché case, and withdrew a manila file folder. Abernathy watched his hands.

"Hanna," Abernathy sighed. "You'll have to leave us for a moment."

Morrison looked me over unapologetically as I rose from my pile of papers.

Well, shit.

"I'll just be out here, then."

I could feel both sets of eyes on my back as I slid out the door and closed it behind me, waiting for a breath before squatting down with my eye conveniently close to the old brass keyhole.

Morrison spoke against the shuffling of paper.

"Suppose you explain to me what happened after you dropped Miss Pool off at her condo at 10:15 a.m. yesterday? The landlady saw you arrive with her, but never saw or heard you leave. She accessed the condo with the master key when Miss Pool didn't leave for work and wouldn't answer her door. I'm afraid she doesn't think too much of you, the landlady."

Abernathy remained quiet for the space of several moments.

"Why exactly were you dropping Miss Pool off at home in her car at ten o'clock in the morning? Had you spent the night together?"

"No," Abernathy answered.

"Where were you coming from then?"

"Here," Abernathy said.

"Why was she here?"

"She stopped by to speak with me."

"Yeah. *Speak* with you. I'm sure." Morrison snickered. "What were you *speaking* about?"

"We were clearing up a misunderstanding."

"What was the misunderstanding?" Morrison asked.

"Helena was under the impression that we were in a relationship. I explained to her that we were not."

"Odd, isn't it? This is the second person you're *not in a relationship* with who ends up dead. Well, second person we *know* about, anyway."

Goosebumps rose under my sweater. I listened for some note of innocence in Abernathy's voice, but he was as flat and smooth as a river-washed stone.

"Has Laura's missing persons case been labeled a homicide then?" Abernathy asked. "The last I heard, you didn't have enough evidence to prove that her disappearance wasn't voluntary."

"Not yet. But it will be. I would think that your involvement in another homicide should make that argument much more compelling."

"I imagine it would be, if I had actually killed Helena."

Morrison's words were bullets fired from a gun as he resumed his interrogation.

"Miss Pool lives approximately five minutes from the gallery. What took you so long to get back, Mark?"

"I had to walk back. I drove her home in her car. Or didn't you scratch that down on your little pad?"

"But that doesn't prove you didn't go back. What did you do after you returned to the office?"

"Hanna and I spent several hours working in my office, after which I took her and two of the resident artists to lunch. When we came back, Hanna and I resumed banging it out."

I bit down on a scoff. Hanna *and I*? What had Abernathy done other than sit at his desk leafing through auction catalogs and dumping out *ride me like a naughty pony vibes* by the metric ton?

And was it my imagination, or had Morrison's eyebrows descended ever so slightly when Abernathy had said *banging*? Hard to tell from my narrowed vantage.

"Can any of the parties you named corroborate this? I'll need their contact information." Morrison continued scratching notes on his pad.

I mentally raised my hand. "I can," I whispered.

"Hanna can," Abernathy said, glancing directly at the keyhole.

I jerked my eye away and waited for a breath before peeking through at a more obscure angle.

"Can anyone *else* corroborate this?" Morrison said.

Oh fine. You have one tiny mental breakdown in front of a guy and suddenly your corroboration is suspect? *Choosy prick.*

"I don't want you disrupting my business. And now, I'm afraid I have some things to see to." Abernathy stood—the universal gesture of dismissal.

"I have a few more questions I'd like to ask you first," Morrison said, refusing to give up his seat.

"I've answered all the questions I'm going to answer.

64

Hanna will give you the contact information for my lawyer, if you like."

"Still with Burgess, Strunkwhite, and Hawes?" Morrison rattled off the name with an ease I found distinctly disconcerting.

Hearing the scrape of chair legs against wood floor, I hauled ass back to my desk and tried to look busy. My pencil cup shot its contents across the desk as I made a desperate grab for my notepad.

Smooth, Hanna. Very smooth.

Detective Morrison glanced from me to the pencil cup to Abernathy.

"Mind if I borrow *your* assistant?" he asked.

"Knock yourself out." Abernathy kicked his door closed by way of punctuation.

Morrison pulled up a folding chair and sat across the desk from me. Extracting a yellow pad from his briefcase, he picked up one of the pens I had sent flying moments earlier. I collected my pencils and letter opener and slid them back into their cup.

"Nervous?" he asked.

"Me? Hell no." The effect would have been considerably more convincing had my voice not cracked.

A smile curved the corners of his eyes rather than his lips. "You have nothing to worry about," he said. "Aside from rear-ending the occasional cop car."

I couldn't decide if he was teasing. His face yielded no clues.

"I'm really sorry about that. Honestly, if you want me to pay for the damages, I will." *Right after I pay off my divorce lawyer, my ex-husband's medical bills, his student loan...*

"Don't sweat it, Red. The guys in the shop will take care of that for me."

"I'm glad to hear it." I breathed an inward sigh of relief.

"You're divorced?" he asked.

"How did you—"

His smirk arrested my words. I remembered yesterday's sobbing rant, and mentally slammed my head in a door.

"What does that have to do with anything?"

"It doesn't. Your boss tells me you can corroborate his alibi. That true?"

"It's true." At least, I really *hoped* it was true.

"Can you tell me *exactly* what happened when Miss Pool came to the gallery?"

"Yes," I said. "Absolutely. Helena came into the oddities shop and asked to see Mr. Abernathy. I told her he was unavailable. I offered to take a message, but she was not amenable to that course of action."

"Nice vocabulary," Morrison said. "Go on."

I smiled briefly and reminded myself I wasn't supposed to like him. He was trying to pin a murder on the man who handed me large wads of cash. Not good. Very not good.

"Miss Pool pushed her way into the gallery, but I caught up with her on the stairs and attempted to stop her from entering Mr. Abernathy's office. She shoved me down and tripped trying to step over me." That she tripped after I pulled her leg out from under her, I felt no compelling need to mention. Because: assault.

"That would explain the bruising on her knees." Morrison made another note on his pad. As he did, I couldn't help but notice his knuckles—scarred—and his nails—chewed.

You had to love a man with a potentially violent past and poor coping mechanisms.

"She didn't have an appointment." Why I felt this important to point out, I couldn't quite say.

"Mr. Abernathy heard us and came out of his office. He and Miss Pool had a brief discussion to clear up a misunderstanding. She wasn't feeling well, so he offered to take her home."

"Do you happen to remember what time that was?" Morrison asked.

"Early. It might have been around 10:00 a.m.?"

Morrison made more scribbles.

"Can I ask what the cause of death was? Have you ruled out suicide? I hate to speak ill of the dead, but she seemed a little unstable."

A sardonic smile spread across Morrison's face. I had the feeling I had just led him precisely where he'd wanted to go.

"I find it hard to believe that she would be capable of tearing her own throat out," he said. "Unstable or no."

My stomach did a modified death roll. "Torn out?" I asked. "Like by an animal?"

"I'm afraid I can't share any more information about that." He'd probably shared too much already.

"What was the time of death?"

Irritation dug a crease in Morrison's brow. "Between two and four p.m. yesterday."

"But that doesn't make any sense. Abernathy dropped her off at ten fifteen in the morning, and he was back here forty-five minutes later."

"And how exactly would *you* know what time he dropped her off?"

Because I was listening at the door just now seemed like a bad answer.

"Just a guess." I shrugged.

The corner of his mouth twitched. I suspected this was about as close as Detective Morrison came to a smile.

"What happened after he returned?"

"We spent a while organizing his office, then he took us out to lunch."

"And 'us' would be?"

"Me, Steven Franke, and Mrs. Kass."

"And after that?"

"We continued organizing his office."

"That's a lot of organizing," he said.

"You did *see* his office, right?"

"And you were with him all afternoon?"

"Yup."

Morrison blew air out his nose and slapped his pad closed. I'd clearly told him things he hadn't wanted to hear. He collected his coat and briefcase and opened Abernathy's door without knocking.

"I would recommend that you stick around town." Morrison leaned against the doorframe with the ease of a man who owned whatever space he happened to occupy. "I have the feeling you and I will need to chat again soon."

"You'll can contact my assistant if you'd like to schedule a time." Abernathy kept his eyes on the desk, refusing to acknowledge Morrison with anything more than words.

"Oh, believe me," Morrison said, firing a near-lascivious glance in my direction, "I will." He jogged down the stairs and out the front door of the gallery, leaving a trail of insinuations in his wake.

I stood motionless for several moments as I ran through memories and words, trying to piece together something that felt true.

Helena came to the gallery spoiling for a fight. Abernathy left with her, and she wound up dead the same afternoon. I tried to steel my mind against the image forming. Helena, crumpled on the blood-smeared kitchen floor, her hair around her like a corona of black flame. Elegant neck torn open and her beautiful face arrested in terror. I shuddered. I might have wished crabs on her, but not death.

"Hanna."

I jumped and squeaked (like you do. Or I do, at least), surprised to find Abernathy standing in his doorway behind me. How a man his size could move across a century-old wood floor without making so much as a creak was completely beyond me.

"Does this computer of yours allow you to make flight reservations?" he asked.

"Indeed, it does."

"And do you have a passport?"

My heart leapt. I *did* have a passport. I had gotten it two years ago when my ex-husband had promised me a Christmas trip to Dublin but decided to buy himself a moped instead. They spent evenings together in the garage, my ex-husband and his scooter, their silhouettes outlined against the door of the garage as he polished the chrome again and again with an old t-shirt. The memory caused a flame of irritation to lick my heart. *Dickweed.*

"Good," he said. "We're going to Germany."

I had to replay his words a few times to make sure I'd heard him right. "Germany?"

"Germany."

"Is this because of—" I glanced toward the door Morrison had just exited.

"No. This is because of the call I took earlier. Detective Morrison's timing is merely an unfortunate coincidence."

I wanted to believe him.

But could I really go to Germany with a man I had known for a day? A man who may or may not be involved with the disappearance of one woman and the murder of another?

"But what about your office?" I asked, grasping for straws. "I've barely started organizing it."

The office. The supplies. Abernathy had sent me

away yesterday afternoon to go purchase office supplies. Why hadn't I thought of that? *Nice going, Hanna. You just lied to the police. You could be charged as an accessory to murder.* I couldn't go back and tell Morrison now.

My palms leaked a sheen of sweat.

"I'm sure it will still be here when we get back."

"But it's only my second day."

"This is the business, Hanna. Sometimes business takes me to foreign places."

"Why take me?" My questions sounded thin and frantic, but they kept coming. Part of me, probably the same part that prevented me from pulling my dress over my head or doing cartwheels in public, hummed with an uneasy, excited energy. The kind of low-level buzz that warned against this kind of impulsive behavior.

"You *are* my assistant, correct?" Abernathy took a step toward my desk, a change in proximity I could feel against my skin.

"Correct."

"I'm going to need some assistance on this trip."

German potato salad, hinted the little voice in my head. *German sausage, German chocolate cake.* After all, I didn't *know* that he had killed Helena. In fact, there was a decent chance that he hadn't.

"Okay then," I said after not much hesitation.

"How soon can you be ready to leave?"

"Five minutes ago. Wait. How long will we be gone?"

"Probably only a couple days. This is a quick business trip. I need to meet up with an antique dealer friend of mine there."

"My cats!" A pang of guilt followed this realization. How could I have forgotten?

An expression of distaste crumpled Abernathy's face. "What about them?"

"I don't have anyone to watch them while I'm gone."

"I'll do it." Steven Franke had materialized at the top of the stairs. "I was just coming up to see if anyone had a nose hair trimmer I could borrow."

"A nose hair trimmer?" I chuckled in spite of myself. "Is that even a thing?"

Abernathy crossed the space to his desk, reached into a drawer, and produced a long slender object that he tossed over to Steven. "Here you go."

"Okay, I stand corrected."

"Thanks Mr. A." Steven scrubbed the bottom of his twitching nose with a knuckle. "I think I might have a tumbleweed growing in there. So, Hanna, how about it?"

I thought about it for less time than I would have if not motivated by the prospect of travel to Europe, even though I had only met Steven the day before. Steve definitely gave off some odd vibes, but *serial cat murderer* wasn't one of them. "Are you sure you wouldn't mind?"

"Mind? Pftt." The chain link bracelets on his wrist jangled as he waved me off. "It would be my pleasure. Give me your coordinates, and I'm on the job." He pulled a phone from his pocket and typed with his thumbs.

"I live in an apartment in a house on Ninth and Griffith."

"Dude!" Steven's eyes gleamed with boyish enthusiasm. "Is it in that big green house with all those creepy trees?"

"That's the place," I said. "I'm in number four. I could leave a key for you under my front mat."

"Cool. That's just a skip, hop, and a karate chop away for me."

"Now that minor crisis is settled," Abernathy said. "Do you want to pull some flight options for us?"

My fingers had already started sliding over the keys, remembering some of their pre-graduation efficiency. "Where are we flying?"

"Bremen. We need to be there by tomorrow."

"Roger that."

Germany! I did a covert little happy dance in my chair once Abernathy's back was turned. *I was going to Germany.*

I PACKED IN HASTE. THE TICKETS HAD BEEN $2,800 apiece for a flight that left at 1:00 p.m. that afternoon, leaving me about thirty minutes before Abernathy would be picking me up.

While I shoved clothing into an old, battered floral print carry-on bag, I offered the cats apologies and the 4-1-1 on Uncle Steven.

"He's really very nice. I think you'll like him." Stella, the youngest of the three, settled herself on top of my clothes in the suitcase while Stewie sniffed at the closet and Gilbert hopped into a drawer I had just emptied. They seemed less than concerned about my impending departure.

Litter scooped, I put out extra-large bowls for food and water. Because I was feeling extravagant, I tore up some lunchmeat and put it in a dish. Three little bodies hurtled toward my ankles at the sound of the ceramic bowl hitting the scarred hardwood kitchen floor.

Returning to the living room, I glanced out the window and was surprised to see an unfamiliar car parked at the curb—an old Rolls Royce Wraith, its long chrome lines winking in the winter light.

That couldn't be Abernathy already, could it? There was a knock at the door. *I guess it could.*

I unchained the lock and opened my door to my remarkably large employer.

"You're early."

"I pack light."

"Do you want to wait in the hall? Cats." I glanced over my shoulder toward the kitchen where the clinking of rabies tags against glass was the only sound.

"We won't be long, will we?"

"Nope, almost ready." I stepped aside to grant him entrance.

He hovered awkwardly in front of the couch but didn't sit. My living room seemed entirely too small with Abernathy in it. The random assortment of furniture that remained from my previous life shoved and jostled in the tiny space as if it too were still trying to get used to its new surroundings.

Stewie and Gilbert relinquished their pursuits and made their way over to Abernathy to have a sniff.

"Psst!" I clapped my hands. "No!"

Abernathy took a couple steps back and tried to shoo them away with his gleaming Italian leather shoe. Decidedly unimpressed with a size thirteen Ferragamo, Stewie and Gilbert hissed and scampered under the bed.

"Sorry about that. They're not used to visitors."

"Do you have any luggage I can take down?" Abernathy's eyes mapped escape routes from every door and window.

"Almost. I just have to write out the cats' schedule and throw a couple more things in my bag." Even as the words left my mouth, I wanted to reel them back in.

I had cats.

My cats had a *schedule*.

"They have a schedule?" Abernathy caught on the

precise words I had hoped would slide by unmarked. "Don't you just leave out food and water?"

"It's not for their food; it's for their medication."

"Your cats are on medication?"

Nice job, Hanna. Will you be telling him about your lucky Garfield underwear next? "Gilbert is diabetic, and Stewie is on antidepressants."

Abernathy erupted into loud laughter.

I folded my arms in annoyance.

"Sorry." He cleared his throat, regaining his composure. "I've just never heard of a house cat being on antidepressants before."

"He has separation anxiety."

Stop! The words kept coming. "His mother abandoned him at birth. He was almost dead when I found him. I had to bottle feed him for the first four weeks I had him."

His face softened. "Saint Hanna. Governess of unwanted animals."

"When the opportunity arises."

I left Abernathy in the living room and returned to the kitchen to scratch out a schedule for the cats, posting it on the fridge along with a thank you note and a twenty-dollar bill for Steven.

"Okay. Ready to roll," I said, grabbing my coat, purse, as Abernathy took my carry-on bag. "Be good," I called to the three sets of eyes watching me from the couch.

With the door closed and locked behind me, I slipped the key under my welcome mat. Abernathy's scent hung on the air in the stairwell as I descended. In the street, he grunted my gear into the trunk while I quietly inspected his muscular back.

"This is quite the car." I resisted running a finger along its sleek bumper for fear of leaving a smudge. "Have you had it long?"

"You might say that." He came around to the passenger side of the car and opened the door for me. Once I was safely settled inside, he swung it closed. It didn't so much as squeak.

I sat ensconced in buttery soft leather, gleaming metal, and glass. An enormous steel stick shift jutted from the carpeted floor and ended only inches from the bench seat. Its angle and insistence reminded me of the awkward church dances of my youth for reasons I don't care to enumerate. Next came the sensation of sweaty palms, and the memory of a large, soft boy nudged in my direction by a well-meaning Lutheran summer camp director. I missed the solid comfort of the wall at my back as he tugged me toward a spotlight under a basketball hoop. I'd never again be able to hear "Can You Feel the Love Tonight?" without blushing.

I ran my hand along the polished wood dash to the steering wheel and without thinking, reached over and pushed the car's horn. *AAHOOGA!* it screamed, at the precise moment my new employer was in front of the car's wide chrome grille.

Abernathy roared, bared his teeth, and punched the car's hood. The resulting dent could have cradled a cantaloupe.

We stared at each other through the windshield for the space of several moments before he came around to the driver's side and slid in. I could see the muscles of his jaw working as he slammed his door shut.

"I am so *so* sorry. It's a stupid thing. I've been doing it all my life. I didn't even think about it. Okay, I kinda wanted to hear what the horn sounded like. But I wasn't trying to scare you. I am *so* sorry. Did I say that already?"

"It's okay." He adjusted his tie and leaned back in his seat. "I just don't react well to being startled." We both looked at the dent in the car's hood.

That's a friggin understatement.

Abernathy cranked the engine over, and the car rumbled to life. Its throaty growl shattered the stillness of the frozen suburban afternoon and sent a vibration through the car's frame that left me feeling reckless.

He shifted the gears and gave the car some gas. We shot forward and took a sharp corner. The force sent me sliding across the narrow space of leather seat between us, and I was hip to hip with Abernathy. The corner of his mouth curved into the faintest of smiles.

The engine stilled to a purr as we gunned for the freeway. In this century-old car, with a man I barely knew, on my way to a place I had never been, I was far from myself, and I was glad.

CHAPTER 6

One of the unintended side effects of self-imposed hermitage was a keen craving for copious personal space.

I needed much more of it than was afforded to me in the cabin of the Boeing 777 traveling to Munich. The gate attendant took one look at Abernathy and upgraded him on the spot. I ended up back in steerage, smack between a man with sinus problems and a mother toting a newborn in a sling across her chest. I found myself leaning the opposite direction as my mucus-abundant seatmate oozed over the armrest and crept inexorably toward me with the infuriating slowness of a glacier.

The mother looked at me with distant brown eyes.

I laughed nervously. "They sure don't give you much leg room in these things, do they?"

She nodded and smiled. I suspected she hadn't understood a word I had said, and it was probably just as well.

The mother shifted the baby's head, and for a moment, the wet sucking sounds were amplified as the baby reattached itself. I looked straight ahead and tried to take measured breaths.

Beside me, the man's head lolled, and he began to snore. My eye twitched.

The flight attendant—a plump, pleasant English woman with a round red face—

cast me pitying glances and offered me extra wine at dinner.

By the time the plane touched down in Munich, I had finished all of Simon Schama's *Embarrassment of Riches* and four vodka tonics. In my pleasant haze, I felt suffused with affability and love for all humanity.

It took me a few tries to stand up from my seat—whether a result of the vodka or stiffness in my limbs, it was hard to say. Abernathy was waiting for me at the end of the jet way, looking irritatingly refreshed and handsome despite the ungodly hour. I felt reasonably certain that a murderer wouldn't look that refreshed.

"How was your flight?" He slung my carry bag over his shoulder.

"It was grand, thanks."

"Did we have a few cocktails?"

Had I stumbled? Had I slurred? Had God finally burned the word "lush" onto my forehead?

"No. Technically, I don't think it would qualify as a few. I was under the impression that a few was no more than three, and I had four. Then there was the wine. Would that be considered a handful of cocktails? That doesn't seem right."

"*Four?*"

"Don't judge. If you had been seated next to Snots McGee, you'd have had a few too." Clearly the alcohol was wearing off, and with it, my boundless love for all mankind.

"I'm not judging," he said. "I'm marveling."

"I'd like to marvel at a toilet. I have to riss like a pacehorse."

Abernathy snorted. "Piss like a racehorse?"

"That's what I said."

"Over there." He pointed.

I walked into the restroom and realized Abernathy was still in front of me.

"As much fun as it might be, I don't think I'll need your assistance with this, Hanna."

"Right. Yes." I slunk into the women's restroom, took care of business, and stole a moment to powder, reapply lipstick, and smooth my hair before rejoining Abernathy. We consulted the monitors and started down the hall to our next gate.

Before my liquid courage diminished entirely, I blurted out the question that had been nagging me through two flights.

"I have to ask."

"Yes?"

"I uh...overheard Detective Morrison mention that Helena's landlady didn't think too much of you. How did she even know who you were? Had you met?"

"Not exactly." He slung my bag from one shoulder to the other and scanned the overhead signs.

"Care to elaborate?"

"What are the odds you'll drop it if I say no?"

"Slim to none." It never ceased to amaze me how swiftly alcohol peeled away my layers of anxiety, leaving me with naked truth.

"I had a run-in with her at Helena's place. I assumed Helena told her about me after things with us went south."

I felt my face grow hot, which conjured a smile to his lips.

"Mrs. Clark liked to be *informed* about her tenant's business."

"What sort of run-in did you have with her?" I asked.

79

"There was a complaint from one of the neighbors while I was there."

"What kind of complaint?"

"About the noise."

"Noise?"

Abernathy glanced at me and raised an eyebrow.

"Oh." It was a sad state of affairs that it had taken this long for me to realize what he meant. It had been more than months since I had the kind of sex that engendered noise complaints. Several years, in fact. Predivorce. Pre-husband, if I'm being brutally honest. The thought of Abernathy driving or being driven to deafening screams of animal ecstasy sent a wicked flick of heat toward my belly.

"Hanna."

"Hmm?"

"Hanna, we're here."

I had been staring off into space and had walked right past our gate.

"Right. I knew that."

We settled into a couple seats with a decent view of the gate. Abernathy made notes in an old composition book. I ate gummy bears and tried not to think about jumping into his lap. Instead, I focused my energy on watching the people who wandered by.

I felt pierced by the mothers and fathers herding their little ones from place to place like tiny chicks. I envied men and women in smart suits bound for somewhere and something more. I sympathized with the many faces bearing excitement or despondency, either going to or coming from a loved one. Knowing all that I yet lacked, and worse, had failed to accomplish, made me feel old and tired.

Abernathy and I were seated together in the Volkswagen with wings that would be taking us from Munich to Bremen. As we waited to take to the skies, I leaned my head against the cool window and closed my eyes. The Dramamine I'd taken to guard against the possibility of yarking booze and airline chicken into Abernathy's lap was beginning to make my limbs feel heavy.

When I awoke, my head was no longer against the window, but on Abernathy's shoulder. And, to my abject horror, I noted a sizable dark puddle had spread on Abernathy's suit coat under my cheek.

I sat bolt upright and saw that Abernathy was awake as well. We both looked at the drool spot on his jacket.

"So that's disgusting, and I want to die. This is exactly why I *never* sleep on planes. Here. Just a second."

I pulled my purse out from under the seat in front of me, withdrew a tissue, and began dabbing at the spot. The tissue quickly dissolved and left behind a fine layer of fuzz and several white pill balls on his shoulder.

"How long was I out?"

"About an hour," he said.

"An hour? It must have been the Dramamine." *And booze.* "I'm so sorry. I seem to be saying this a lot around you."

"I could have moved you if I wanted to." Abernathy shifted and stretched his long legs into the aisle, now that he was no longer trapped by a somnolent, slobbering seatmate.

I slouched back against the seat, wishing it would swallow me whole. "I'm not usually in the habit of ruining other people's clothes."

"Clothes are overrated."

Don't picture him naked, warned the little voice inside my head. My gaze searched for a safer place to rest and landed squarely on his crotch. *Too late.*

The overhead speaker made the requisite ding, and

81

a crisp English voice came through the cabin, cutting my pervy daydream off at the knees.

"We are now making our initial descent into Bremen. The flight attendants will be through to distribute the arrival cards and gather any remaining service items."

The plane began to judder and bounce as we swiftly decreased altitude. I glued my eyes to the window to center myself and tried to focus on the carpet of glittering city lights that drew ever closer. They followed a web-like pattern that suggested the city's true age and were a marked contrast to the sterilized squares I had become accustomed to in the States. Once we were safely on the ground taxiing to the gate, and I had managed to coax my stomach back to its usual position, I inquired of Abernathy where we would be staying. He had declined my offer to find us lodgings when I had booked the airline tickets, insisting we wouldn't need reservations.

"We'll be staying in a little hotel right on the North Sea, Aparthotel Am Meer, in Cuxhaven."

Goosebumps rode the curve of my neck. *Cuxhaven.* The town of my Oma's birth. All my life I'd dreamed of visiting this place, seduced by her paintings of a bruised sky over endless swaths of shifting green and gray sea. Abernathy was taking me *here*? Over any place in the wide world?

"Cuxhaven? As in, not in Bremen?"

"Correct," Abernathy said.

"How far is it from the airport?"

"About 107 kilometers."

"It's way too late to be using those fancy words."

"Sixty miles. About an hour's drive."

I sighed heavily. I had already been in three airplanes, three airports, and two countries. So far I had been kicked and shrieked deaf by toddlers, nearly suffocated by piles of hairy flesh, narrowly avoided being blinded by a nipple, and had drooled on my boss's coat. If I didn't get myself into a bed or a shower in short order, I was in imminent danger of braining innocent civilians with the weighty art history book tucked in my bag.

"Don't worry," Abernathy reassured me. "It will go fast."

What he'd meant was *we* would go fast. In our rented Peugeot RCZ, we hurtled down the A-27 motorway like a greased rocket. The country was a maddening mystery in the darkness.

We cut through the night passing vast black plains and moon-silvered trees. I searched the flashing scenes outside my window as one might when presented with a tapestry darkened with age. The threads I could see both promised fine details and mocked my eye's inability to apprehend them.

"We'll come back this way in the light," Abernathy said, as if sensing my thoughts.

I nodded, but couldn't tear my eyes away. I felt the desperation of dreams being realized and was possessed by the fear that the moments would fly from me before I could fully live them. I had wanted to come to Europe since I was a girl. Here my deepest hopes had materialized, and I had no time to prepare. Not a second to consider. Experience it now or lose it forever.

The town took shape in the pools cast by unevenly spaced streetlights. I could make out the shapes of brown stone buildings silhouetted against the predawn sky. We pulled up in front of a three-story brick building painted the sunny yellow of Vincent van Gogh's house in Arles. The well-lit façade bore balustrades of carved stone and several rows of gleaming windows, mostly darkened.

Abernathy and I gathered our bags from the Peugeot's dollhouse trunk and trooped into the lobby. The hotel's main hall might have been grand in former days but had since settled into the kind of age that looked tired but stately. Chandeliers and lamps cast a warm and welcoming glow across worn red velvet couches and book-laden tables. Behind the wide wooden counter, we found a woman with a pleasant, motherly face and wire-rimmed spectacles.

She looked up, saw Abernathy, and clapped her plump hands to her mouth.

"Ach! Mark! *Sind Sie das?* Oh! *Komm her mein Lieber!*"

She reached across the desk and grabbed him by both hulking shoulders, pulling him toward her.

"Come here often?" I asked.

"You could say that," he grunted against the desk jammed into his belly.

She kissed him noisily on both cheeks and grasped either side of his face.

"*Lassen Sie mich dich anschauen!*" She held his face back and peered into it, and clucked "*Zu dünn! Zu dünn!*"

This I recognized—*Too thin! Too thin!*—the battle cry of German mothers the world over. She looked to me disapprovingly and shook her head. I knew I had been identified as the woman in Abernathy's life and had failed to sufficiently fatten him to German *hausfrau* standards.

"I'm not his wife," I pointed out, hoping that she, like most Germans I knew, understood English.

Now she looked at Abernathy shrewdly. I didn't need a translator to understand her thoughts. *Bring a woman that wasn't his wife to her hotel?*

"Marion, *das ist Hannalore, mein Assistent,*" he explained.

Her weathered features cast aside their sternness and relaxed into rosy-cheeked joviality.

"Hannelore!" she gushed, reaching for me and kissing both cheeks. *"Dies ist ein deutscher Name!"*

"Yes," I replied in English. *"Meine Mutter und Groß-mutter,"* I paused to pull down the words, *"kam aus Hei-delberg."*

Her face brightened. *"Das ist wunderbar!* Velcome home!"

"Danke." I smiled.

She turned to Abernathy, but spoke in a charming mix of English and German, presumably so we could both understand. "Your suite is open. *Und der* is a room next door for *die Fräulein."*

"Is that the only other room open? Isn't there some-thing on another floor for her?" The insistence in his voice left me feeling hurt and cranky.

Why did he want me on a different floor?

"Nein," she said. "We are full with *der Karneval* in town. Dese are the only two."

"All right," Abernathy acquiesced. "That will be fine."

Irritation needled my spine. Abernathy had dragged me halfway across the world, and now he was behaving as if I weren't worthy to share his hotel floor.

"You know what helps ensure you get the rooms you want?" I was far too tired to wring the sarcasm out of my voice. *"Reservations.* If only someone had offered to help with that. Oh wait..."

Abernathy glowered.

Marion wiped the smile off her face when Aber-nathy turned back to her. She handed over two brass keys. Abernathy took one and handed the other to me.

"Are you sure?" I asked. "I'm sure I could sleep on one of the couches in the lobby. Or maybe they'd let me pull up a rug on the floor?"

"Hanna, my usual suite is on the third floor, and

there are no elevators. I didn't want you to have to haul your luggage up three flights of stairs after such a long day."

"If I didn't know you were in sales for a living, I might just think lying runs in your family," I said, refusing to be charmed.

"You know," he bent to pick up my carry-on bag, "you have a real issue with trust."

"Says the man who won't let me answer his phone. I, on the other hand, came to a foreign country with a man I have known two days. And this after his implication in a murder. That sounds pretty trusting to me."

"No. That sounds reckless. And you wanted to come here anyway." He turned and headed for the red-carpeted stairwell.

I stared at his back in speechless outrage. I wasn't sure which irritated me more, that he said I was reckless, or that I had a sneaking suspicion that he was right.

He stopped at the bottom of the stairwell and waited for me. "After you."

I grabbed my bags from him, elevated my chin a notch, and took the stairs two at a time, just to show him how capable of handling three flights of stairs I really was. By the time we reached our floor, my thighs were on fire and I couldn't breathe. I set my bags down in front of room number eleven and waited until Abernathy proceeded to the next door down the hall. I smiled at him as I turned the key and willed my lungs not to explode. The lock clicked open, but only when Abernathy was safely in his room with the door closed did I fling myself, panting, to the forest-green carpet.

I thought I heard a faint chuckle through the wall.

Blood returned to my brain, and my breathing began to slow. There was a tap at my door. I willed myself to my feet and opened it a sliver. Abernathy's handsome face hovered in the gap.

"You rang?"

"We need to be at Joseph's by ten. We should leave here by a quarter till."

The bedside clock flashed blurry blue numbers. I had lost track of how many time zones I'd crossed. I gave him a half-hearted salute.

"Sleep tight." He winked at me, but I was too tired to tingle.

Exhausted though I was, I needed to wash off the travel funk before I could sleep. The en suite bathroom was characteristically European—old, small, and tiled within an inch of its life.

I stripped down and climbed under the brass shower head's steaming spray. The pipes groaned with the sounds of water running next door. First, the gurgling of water in the bathtub then the hissing, spitting sound of the shower firing up. From the closeness of the sounds, I deduced that Abernathy and I shared a bathroom wall, and that he too had decided on a shower.

Through the wall, I heard the water shift and splatter as he moved in it. I became aware that on the other side of this wall, no more than ten inches away, Abernathy was naked. *Should you really be having naked thoughts about a potential murderer?*

Three months. Three months and four days since I'd last been poured the pork.

This vision emerged at once and complete in my mind's eye. Abernathy's suit strewn on the bathroom floor, steam fogging the mirror. A wide, muscled back under the shower's spray. His hands worked through his dark hair in a practiced movement that required no thought. He'd palm the soap next, slide it across the expanse of his chest, let it ride down the rippled terrain of his stomach and follow the crease of his hip flexors.

Lower.

My eyes slid closed as my head lolled back, drawn down by the weight of the hot water soaking my hair, snaking down my back in a twisted stream.

Only it wasn't water, but fingers. Abernathy's fingers, tracing the length of my spine, finding their way over the ridge of my hips, flattening against my stomach to pull me backward against him. A rumble of male appreciation, rattling the cage that held my heart.

Moving forward then, my face shoved against tile yet unwarmed by the shower's spray, my wet hair wrapped in his fist, the force of his arm pinning me in place. Another hand splayed against the small of my back, coaxing my hips backward, open. His fingers tensed against my neck, sought purchase on my waist, bracing me as his body collided with mine in a first perfect, violent thrust—

"Hanna?" came a muffled voice.

I shrieked and grabbed the shower curtain to cover myself. I looked around the bathroom and saw no one.

And yet he was here, as pervasive in this space as the steam that clung to the tiled walls. It was Abernathy. Talking to me through the wall.

Naked.

Snapping off the water, I got out, and grabbed a towel.

Towel. How would Abernathy look with wet hair and a towel wrapped around his hips?

"Uh...yeah?"

"Thin walls, huh?" he said.

"It seems so."

From the sound of his voice, he could have been breathing down my neck. This thought gave me pause.

"Drop the soap?" he asked.

"Did I—what?"

"Sounded like you dropped the soap. Are you okay?"

"The soap? I didn—" I looked down, my body catching up with my brain. There near the drain was the lavender-scented disc I'd extracted from its polite little wrapping. When had that happened?

About the time you were thinking about Abernathy's cock.

I felt his smile through the wall.

"How's your room?" he asked.

"It's good." I reached the towel up and squeezed the ends of my hair to prevent water dripping down my back.

"Good."

"Well...good night," I called.

"Sweet dreams."

I pawed through my luggage and found my over-sized t-shirt and a pair of panties. Floral covers crawled up to my neck as I set the bedside alarm clock and clicked off the lights.

The second my skin hit the sheets, I knew I had a problem. My limbs refused to settle, opting instead to slide over and over the silky fabric, seeking sensation. My back arched of its own accord; my fingers dug into the soft-feathered pillow. A deep insistent ache settled into the space between my thighs. Flashes of sweaty, naked, tangled bodies flickered across the screen of my mind.

All these long months of isolation condensed into a singular all-consuming hunger that demanded an answer. Now.

"We can't do this," I informed the little voice in my head. "Not here. Marion would know. German women have a radar about this kind of stuff."

Just this once, something primal pleaded.

"Fine," I conceded, pulling my shirt up my stomach.

It was this or haul an unsuspecting foreigner into a dark alley and eat him alive.

"Oooooowwww!" came the hideous shriek, freezing me on the spot.

I jerked upright, scanning the darkness. Had Abernathy fallen in the shower? Was he hurt?

Another cry of pain split the air, unintelligible at first, then yielding to syllables I recognized.

"Hongraay like the wooooolf!"

Abernathy wasn't screaming; he was *singing*. Holding a note in a falsetto that could shatter glass, then falling octaves without warning like the bottom dropping out of a bucket. I shuddered, my teeth grinding against the auditory assault.

I flopped back onto the bed, disbelieving. How could a man so beautiful produce such an ungodly dissonance? It was barely human.

I had scarcely time to consider when another keen rang off the walls, forcing me to shove my head beneath the pillows, seeking the mole-like solace of sensory deprivation. Sounds were blessedly muffled, then eventually ceased.

Somewhere beneath the layers of feathers and cloth, in the absence of desire sent fleeing by shower karaoke from hell, sleep found me at last.

CHAPTER 7

" anna."

"Hanna."

"*Hanna*, get up. We're late."

I felt a heavy hand on my shoulder. The last wisps of dream evaporated, and I yawned and indulged in a delicious stretch.

"Mmmm." My voice was a sleep-heavy purr. "I knew you'd come. After our shower last night…"

"*Our* shower?"

My eyes snapped open. Abernathy loomed over me, larger than life in a freshly pressed suit and shirt. His dark hair fell around his eyes as he leaned forward. He'd shaped his stubble into a rough goatee.

Breakfast anyone?

My own state came to me in spastic bursts. I was in a hotel room. I was in Germany. I was in a t-shirt and underwear, in the presence of Abernathy. I sat bolt upright and pulled the floral comforter to my chest.

"What are you doing in my room?"

"You weren't answering your door. We're late."

"But my door was locked! I bolted it myself last night before I went to bed. How did you get in here?"

"I'm due at Joseph's in fifteen minutes," Abernathy

said, glancing at the digital clock on my nightstand. "We should be leaving right now."

I rubbed my eyes to clear my head and felt smooth naked skin under my fingertips. No makeup. If I didn't have make-up on then...*dear God, my hair!* I had slept on my hair wet. I reached a trepidatious hand up to assess the damage.

Most days, with the aid of several styling products and small artillery of electric devices, I could persuade my hair to look like something that belongs on a human head. Without my usual post-shower ritual, it had assumed the shape it took when I crashed onto the pillow. A shape that would likely have pleased De Kooning. Scattershot brushstrokes grappling for the edge of the canvas. And it was big. Arkansas beauty queen big.

Abernathy grinned at me.

"What?"

"I like your hair natural. It's sort of..." He paused, searching for the correct term.

"Frightening?"

"Wild."

I was grateful for the blush that warmed my cheeks. It would help to dispel the Queen of the Undead vibe I tended to emit in the morning.

I pushed myself up under the comforter and glanced at Abernathy. "I'll need ten minutes to put myself together."

"Feel free." He made no move to vacate the premises.

"Alone."

"Even after *our* shower?" His mock wounded look was a little too sheepish. Not so good with the jokes, my boss.

"Out!" I pointed a stiff arm toward the door.

"Of course. I'll meet you in the lobby."

A brief shower, then I rushed through my normal makeup routine. Eyeliner was sacrificed as a nod to the gods of punctuality as I went straight for the mascara and blush. I dampened my hair with a little water and tried to shape it into waves instead of a five-alarm squall.

Having no idea what this day would entail, I opted for professional wear to mirror Abernathy's. I selected a black blouse, gray pencil skirt, lacy tights, and four-inch heels. Under all of it, I had wriggled into my newly acquired spandex body-shaper to smooth out the lingering jiggly bits from my recent months of inactivity. If luck held out, I could breathe just enough to avoid an attack of the vapors.

Down three sets of stairs I teetered, using my purse as a counterweight and grasping the wooden railing for dear life. In the lobby, I found Abernathy leaning across the desk chatting with another one of the hotel's employees—a weather-beaten man in a Cosby-loud sweater and a fishing cap.

I tapped Abernathy's shoulder. The four-inch heels put me much closer to his height. When he turned to face me, I could see in his eyes traces of amber and gold I'd never noticed before. Of course, it had nothing to do with my seeming inability to maintain eye contact with Abernathy for any length of time.

"You clean up nice." His gaze traced over me from head to heels, leaving me with the sensation of being touched.

"Likewise."

Although, Abernathy *not* cleaned up was just as dangerous. Perhaps more so.

"Ready?" he asked.

"Lead the way."

Outside, rain clouds crowded the sky overhead. The rush of waves breaking on the shoreline behind the hotel and the distant cry of gulls were the morning's song. Air settled heavily on my skin—cool, damp, pregnant with the mingled moisture of sky and sea. Abernathy beeped the Peugeot and held the door open for me to get in.

Murderers don't open doors for people, I reassured myself. Beads of rain drew paths down the windshield as we pulled out into traffic.

In the daylight, the city was a captivating mix of old stone buildings and newer shop fronts and stores. On the North Sea at the mouth of the Elbe river, Cuxhaven lived up to its reputation as a port town founded and maintained by those who wrestled their living from the sea. The rain-soaked streets were occupied by men in slickers and fishing boots. Everywhere I looked I saw hard faces stained ruddy from salty winds. In the part of the town where we were, bicycles and pedestrians far outnumbered cars. We gathered stares as we wound down the narrow streets in Abernathy's purring, efficient machine.

We slowed to a stop in front of an old stone building flanked by the canopies of an outdoor market. People marched toward it in umbrellaed streams.

"Here we are."

"Is this where we're meeting Joseph?"

"No," he said. "This is where the auction is."

I conjured the details of my previous conversations with Abernathy but found them laced with vodka and jetlag-induced perforations. "Auction? What auction?"

"The one you'll be attending."

"But I thought we were meeting up with your gallery contact, Joseph, this morning."

"Well, you're half right. *I'll* be meeting up with Joseph this morning. You'll be going to an auction."

"You didn't mention anything about an auction." Panic honed an edge in my voice. The prospect of being alone in an unfamiliar city and shoved into a situation where I would be competing with a crowd of strangers was enough to set my bowels squirming.

"I did tell you I would need your assistance on this trip. That *is* why I brought you, is it not?"

"You're saying it wasn't just for the pleasure of my company? I'm crushed." *Logic, sub-par. Sarcasm, intact. Systems nominal.*

"I'm afraid not. I need to meet with Joseph, or I would go to the auction myself." He leaned forward in the seat and pulled a battered auction catalog out of his back pocket.

"There's something I want you to buy for me." He flipped through a few doubled pages, folded the catalog back, and handed it to me. I glanced at the picture he'd circled and read the item description. *Moonstone pendant carved with woman's profile. Precise provenance unknown. Dated to 14th century Britain.*

"I've never been to an auction before. What if I do something wrong?"

"Really? With all your gallery experience?"

Fuck a whole flock of ducks. I had forgotten about that little fudge on my resume. Okay, *large* fudge on my resume.

"What I meant was—" Have there ever been four more obvious words to announce an impending lie? "—of course I've been to an auction before. Just never one in *Europe*. They may do things differently than the ones I've been to."

"I see," Abernathy said. I could tell he was humoring me, and for once, I felt no compulsion to argue. "It's very simple, Hanna. I have an account with Bonham's auction house. I've informed them you will be coming in my stead today. They'll give you a bidding number linked to my account. When the pendant comes up, you bid on it. That's all there is to it."

"What if I get outbid?" I asked.

"Don't." His one-word answer failed to inspire confidence.

"But what if I do?"

"You won't."

"But what if—"

"Hanna, there are no ifs. Bid on the pendant, no matter the cost."

Must be nice to have an endless supply of money to play with. But then, today he was letting *me* play with the endless supply of money. A girl could get used to this.

"If you say so."

"I say so."

"How long will you be at Joseph's?" I asked.

"Not long. I'll swing by here to pick you up as soon as we're finished."

I looked at the unceasing crowd filing into the building. "How will you find me?"

"I'll find you. Here." He reached into his pocket and withdrew a handful of Euros in various denominations. "In case you get hungry."

I felt like a kid getting dropped off at an unfamiliar babysitter's house and bribed with treats. I took the money, sorted the bills, and stuck them in my wallet.

"All right then," I sighed. "See you later." I got out of the car and turned to follow the stream of people.

"Hanna!" Abernathy called.

Why is it he could never remember what he had to say to me until I'd left the desk/office/car?

"Yes?" I leaned toward the open window on the passenger side of the Peugeot.

He handed out an umbrella. "Wouldn't want your hair to get wet. This is an event attended by professionals, after all."

I narrowed my eyes at him and snatched the um-

96

brella. "You better get going. I'd hate for you to be late for another time of death."

His laugh was completely disarming, I noted with irritation. He rolled up the window and drove off.

I stuck the unopened umbrella in my purse and walked as slowly as I could to the auction house's front door.

IN THE VESTIBULE, I MADE MY WAY TO WHAT LOOKED LIKE a registration desk. A woman with a sleek platinum bob and killer red suit waved to me.

"Excuse me. I was wondering if you could help me."

"Hanna?"

"Yes. How did—"

"Mr. Abernathy called in to tell us you would be coming." She spoke in the erudite, endearing English accent shared by Hugh Grant and his ilk rather than the brusque German I had been prepared for.

She pushed her chair back from the table and slid up to a credenza bearing file boxes and bins. While her back was turned, I performed the requisite perfunctory assessment exchanged by females of breeding age. Shapely legs wrapped in black stockings, trim waist, ass annoyingly unaffected by gravity or doughnuts. I resisted the urge to conclude that she probably had a hideous STD and kicked puppies in her spare time.

Her delicate fingers walked a stack of cards.

"Ahh, here it is. Abernathy. Looks like we're 119 today."

"And 119 would be what exactly?"

"That will be your bidding number." She reached into a basket behind her and withdrew a paddle bearing the aforementioned numbers and handed it to me.

"I hate to be a bother, but I'm afraid I don't know exactly how this works. Is there someone that could give me a quick run-through?"

"Why, of course! Surely you didn't think we'd leave you all by your onesie. I'll be with you throughout the auction, love."

Relief washed over me. Of course, in that silky accent, she could have asked to take a crap in my handbag, and I would have handed it over with my compliments.

She turned back to the two men in dark suits standing at the registration desk.

Security?

"I'm off now."

They nodded.

"I'm Penny Bailey, by the way." She offered me her hand.

"Nice to meet you," I said. *Penny Bailey.* Her name was the phonetic equivalent of her perfect bottom. My name sounded like a horse sneeze by comparison.

She linked arms with me, and we joined the crush of bodies wandering through the doors.

"This way."

The layout was in line with the auctions I'd imagined when I fantasized about being a wealthy patron of the arts. Stage and podium at the front for the auctioneer, seating in the center of the hall, and objects on display behind ropes as glass cases flanked the sides and back of the building. A wide path for circumambulation stretched around the space before the objects.

"Is it a particular object he's sent you for?"

"A moonstone pendant." I opened my purse to look for the auction catalog.

"I know the one," she said. "Let me take you to it."

We ambled down the walkway, passing a scattered assortment of people. The truly wealthy, unassuming and surrounded by satellites of minions in dark suits; the eccentrically rich in furs, pearls, and tuxedos; the lookey loos speaking in reverent whispers; and the assistants like me, representing people too important to be here in person.

"Is this your first visit to Cuxhaven?'

"Yes. My first time in Germany, actually."

"How delightful! Are you staying nearby then?"

"We're at the Aparthotel Am Meer." I squeezed past a cluster of bickering tweed coats to keep up with Penny's crisp clip.

"Wonderful. Is this your first auction?"

"It's certainly my first auction in Germany." Wonderful when the truth works.

"I imagine it's rather similar to any other auctions you've been to. When the auctioneer announces your object, you wait for him to open the bidding. You simply raise your paddle to make a bid. If someone else is bidding against you, the auctioneer will set the increases. If you are willing to keep increasing the bid, you keep raising your paddle. That's all there is to it."

"That sounds simple enough," I said.

"It is, love. Don't worry. You'll do fine."

"I hope so." I could only imagine the conversation I would have to have with Abernathy if I failed to win the pendant.

Penny nodded and swapped pleasantries with some of the people we passed. In between these exchanges, she spoke to me from the side of her mouth. "You have to tell me," she said in a confidential tone. "What is he like?"

"What is who like?"

"Abernathy, of course."

"Oh, yes." Dragged to the surface from my swimming thoughts, I struggled to come up with something satisfactory. "Well, he's very...dynamic." It seemed suitably vague and yet still accurate.

"Mmm," she purred. "I'll bet he is. You're so lucky, working closely with him. He's a myth around here, he is. No one's ever seen him. But that doesn't stop everyone from speculating. What does he look like? We're just dying to know. I've only spoken with him on the phone. Wicked voice, hasn't he?"

Abernathy's voice was low, resonant, deeply smoked like scotch. The sort of voice you could easily imagine breathing threats or promises of violent physical consequence.

"Yes, he has. As far as what he looks like," I scratched for the right words, "he's huge. Not huge as in fat, but *big*. Dark hair, dark eyes. Fit."

"Fit. Yes. And hung like a stallion I'd wager." She nudged me with an elbow.

Wouldn't I like to know, I thought. If only the walls of our hotel were a mite thinner, I'd be able to tell her what religion he was. I fanned my face with the paddle.

Penny captured my wrist. "You won't be wanting to do that during the auction, love. They'd count that as a bid, you know."

"Oh. Right." I tucked the paddle in my purse.

Penny slowed in front of a glass case set back from the aisle. "Here we are."

I approached slowly, careful to allow plenty of room to lean forward without smudging the glass with my nose. The pendant glowed as if lit from within, bright as the moon itself on a sea of black velvet. It reflected flashes of blue and white fire as I adjusted the angle of my head to minimize the glare of overhead lighting. The carving revealed itself gradually. A woman's profile, impossibly delicate for the pendant's size, was carved in low relief on the pendant's gleaming surface by a deft hand.

"They say the profile is of the goddess Diana," Penny explained. "That's another name for—"

"Artemis. The goddess of the moon."

"Yes," she said, seeming pleased.

I tore myself away from the pendant's hypnotic glow, and we wandered around to peek at the other objects. For a history nerd like me, an antiques auction represented complete sensory overload. Objects fought for my attention from every conceivable direction—paintings, tapestries, books, sculptures, clothing, jewels, curios, cabinets, dishes—everything imaginable. I longed for enough hours to sift through them one by one, to imagine who had owned them, to discover where they'd come from, to postulate how the lives they'd lived had come to intersect with my own.

Through a brief clearing in the jostling crowd, I caught the flash of marble across the room. I wove a path through the herd and approached the creamy white bust of a young man on a stone plinth. It was labeled only with a number. Sparks flew across long-neglected synapses in my brain. The sereneness of the facial features bordered on the Greek Classical. And yet, the softness of its details suggested a fondness of retrospection that only the passage of time could produce. Neoclassical most likely, late 18th or early 19th century.

Because it was in an auction and not in a museum, I suspected it came from the School of Antonio Canova, but not from Canova himself. His had been the hand that smoothed sculpture into the graceful, clean arcs after Bernini's Baroque stone dramas. I loved them equally for different reasons.

For the briefest of moments, I imagined the sensation of pressing my lips to the marble. It would be cool, even in this room of lights and bodies. This was likely the face of an aristocrat's son. Someone who could afford to have his likeness carved in the style of a civilization long dead.

"Remarkable, isn't it?"

"It's beautiful." I meant it, though it seemed an unsophisticated thing to say. I felt like a beggar at the feast, only aware I had been starving now in the presence of a richly laden table.

"Ooh. It looks like we're about to begin. Shall we sit?" Penny placed a hand at the small of my back and steered me to a cluster of empty chairs in the third row from the stage.

The auctioneer shuffled to the podium, sniffed, and cleared his throat into the microphone. I winced at the amplified sound of phlegm rattling around in his ancient pipes. The roar of conversation dropped to a hum as everyone found their seats.

Penny spoke close to my ear. "That'll be Basil Hackett. Been around since Bonham's was founded, best I can tell."

"When was it founded?"

"1793."

I stifled a snort as the room fell silent, drawing a disapproving glare from Basil. One gray caterpillar of an eyebrow crawled toward the expanse of his sparse, slicked hairline, giving him a puzzled expression. The gesture was performed with such slow precision that I wondered if the auction might last another couple of centuries.

"Ladies and gentleman," he drawled, "please take your seats. The auction will begin presently."

He straightened his bow tie, emitted a dusty cough, and the words erupted from his ancient mouth like a bullet out of gun. "Our first item is lot 7442, an Edwardian mahogany sideboard. We'll begin the bidding at four hundred pounds. Who will start us off?"

Paddles sprung up like spring tulips as Basil lithely

swung a gnarled finger from one person to the next to call the bids.

In time he brought the gavel down, sending a heavy clack through the hall to punctuate the transaction. And so, the process was repeated through paintings, portmanteaus, and pins. The dry sound of pages turning and people scraping tensely in their chairs formed the chorus after each resounding gavel shot.

"Lot 7483. The moonstone pendant." Basil sniffed and ran a hand over his lacquered hair.

I straightened and looked to Penny, who nodded her encouragement. A fine sweat coated my palms as I gripped my paddle at the ready.

"We'll begin the bidding at twenty thousand pounds," Basil announced.

"Twenty thousand pounds?" I hissed to Penny. *"Twenty. Thousand. Pounds?"*

"Shhhhh!" several voices chastised.

I recalled Abernathy's directive. *Bid on the pendant, no matter the cost.* Why on earth did he want this so much? The man didn't even own a cell phone but would pay a tidy forty grand for a pendant. The more time I spent in Abernathy's service, the less I knew about him. The impossibility of it affronted the stuffy academic in me. *Research,* the academic suggested. Yes. A concerted investigative effort was what this situation required. The thought provided small comfort.

But for now, I would do as I'd been bidden.

"Who will start the bidding?"

I saw a paddle sprout from the row to my right. It was held aloft by a young blonde wearing enough mink to populate a zoo habitat. An octogenarian husband was her only other accessory.

"Twenty thousand from the lady in mink. Am I bid twenty-five?"

I extended my arm to its full length.

"Twenty-five from the ginger miss. Am I bid thirty?"

She was the "lady in mink" and I was the "ginger miss"? The dusty old fart.

Again, the blonde's paddle went up. She turned and gave me a saccharine smile.

Oh it's on, Goldilocks.

"Is there thirty-five?"

"Thirty-five!" I confirmed, flapping my paddle at Basil.

We volleyed bids back and forth until at sixty thousand pounds, the aged husband snatched his wife's paddle away. She folded her arms and aimed her surgically narrowed nose skyward.

"Sixty thousand pounds."

"Sixty thousand going once, going twice..." Basil paused, giving my competitor one last opportunity. "Sold to the ginger miss down front!" He brought the gavel down, sealing the transaction.

I jumped up from my chair. "I did it! I won!"

The blonde heaved a disgusted sigh and stomped off down the aisle. Her husband hobbled after her like an ancient but still dedicated dog.

Penny caught my wrist and tugged it gently. Descending from my cloud of exultation, I observed that Basil, along with the rest of the assembly, was staring at me in open-mouthed, slack-jawed disbelief.

"Sorry," I whispered to Penny.

"Not at all."

"What happens next?"

"Mr. Abernathy's account is already well established. The funds will be wired automatically. The object will be shipped with Box Brothers. Insured appropriately, of course."

"Of course," I repeated.

The men in suits had materialized in the aisle where

we sat. One of them bent and whispered to Penny, who nodded.

"Well, I should dash." Penny gave me a harried smile. "Will you be all right?"

"I should be, yes." Abernathy would, in theory, show up for me at some point. Nothing left to do but wait.

"It was lovely meeting you. Give us a squidge." She leaned in and gave me brief squeeze. Her skin and hair were smooth against mine. "If you ever catch a glimpse of the bits and pieces," she whispered, "will you send us a post?"

I laughed, shocked and delighted by her cheek. "I highly doubt I will, but if I do, you'll be the first to know."

"Thanks, love. Ta!" She blew me a kiss, ducked out of the row, and was gone.

When Basil closed bidding on the next object, I made my way back toward the doors. To my surprise, Abernathy was already there. Whether he was leaning against the wall, or the wall was leaning against him, it was impossible to say.

How long had he been there? Had he seen me jump around like a housewife on *Price is Right*?

I glanced at his face to get a read as I approached speaking distance. Grinning. *Fuck a duck.*

"Howdy," I said.

"If I had known you get so excited at auctions, I would have stayed."

"I like winning."

"I could see that." He rolled his body effortlessly away from the wall and gestured toward the doors.

I scanned the foyer for Penny as we walked through, but she was nowhere to be found. Pity. She'd have gotten quite a kick meeting Abernathy in the flesh, so to speak.

"How did your meeting with Joseph go?" I asked.

"Good." He held the door open for me, and we emerged into the cool, damp daylight. The air felt clean and fresh on my face after sharing not enough space with too many people. I let it wash into my nose and lungs.

"Just good?"

"Yes."

"Why was it you needed to meet with him again?"

"To pick something up." He didn't have to push through the crowd. They saw him and moved.

"What something would that be?"

He paused to beep open the Peugeot and opened the door for me, once again. Once I was

safely closed inside, he walked around the front of the car.

My eyes drifted to the Peugot's horn. My hand twitched. I gave it a stern look. *There will be none of that.*

Abernathy slid into the car, turned the engine over, and navigated through the maze of pedestrians into the street.

I looked at him expectantly. "So?"

"What?"

"What did you come all the way to Germany to get from Joseph?" Had he really forgotten that I'd asked him a question in the time it took to walk around the car? Or had he been hoping *I* would forget?

"Spoon," he mumbled.

"A spoon?"

"A spoon."

"We came all the way to Germany to get a spoon." I repeated the words as a statement, hoping they would compose themselves into something that made sense.

They didn't.

"Couldn't you just have had him mail it to you?"

"No."

"This whole stony silent type thing isn't helpful for our working relationship, you know."

"There's my business," he said, "and then there's *my business.* This happens to be the latter. Not the former." A smug smile slid onto his profile.

It was a good line, and we both knew it.

Damnable huge, sexy man and his stupid brilliant wordplay. I huffed and turned my face to the window, determined not to utter another word. Maybe I wouldn't speak to him until we got back to the hotel. Hell, maybe I wouldn't speak to him for the rest of the *trip.* I would be cool, aloof, my silence impenetrable, my stillness unmatch—

"Hungry?"

"Hell yes!" Okay, maybe I was not so good at the stony silent act. Particularly when food was involved.

"Good," he said, "I know a place."

I suspected that Mark Abernathy knew *all* the places.

CHAPTER 8

*A*bernathy ordered an impressive assortment of knockwurst, weisswurst, and sauerbraten but had touched very little of it. I politely relieved him of the burden of over-ordering by taking seconds, then thirds. For the space of several blissful moments, I was back in my Oma's kitchen. Biting through the crisp skin of sausages burnished mahogany by the grill, I closed my eyes to savor and found her there reflected in the space between matter and memory. My grandma standing at the sink washing dishes in her iconic German way, her hands red from the steaming water and slick with iridescent suds. Better to risk scalding your hands than to leave a trace of grease on the plates.

It was around my third stein of Schneider Weiss that my brilliant plan for conducting covert academic research on Abernathy really went off the rails. My observations began to focus themselves around the way his shirt strained around his biceps when he leaned on his elbows rather than on his endless supply of funds and command of several languages. In the course of placing our dinner order, he'd discovered our waiter was a Latvian transplant and had easily slid into a conversation.

The restaurateurs stopped by the table to welcome Abernathy personally. He spoke with them first in German, then in rapid French.

"Why does everyone know you?" I asked.

Abernathy loosened his tie, shot his cuffs, and shoved his sleeves up to his elbows before using his napkin to pat away a fine sheen of sweat from his forehead.

"They don't," he said, an ironic smile twisting his lips. "But I've stopped through here now and then over the years."

"How many years would that be exactly?"

"I haven't counted." He picked imaginary crumbs from the tablecloth and stared through the scarred wood floor. His eyes took on the glassy, impenetrable sheen of marbles. A gray pallor stole the color from his cheeks.

He would give me nothing, I knew. I felt heaviness in my chest for him. Abernathy the island, Abernathy the iceberg.

"Are you okay?" I asked. "You don't look so good."

"I'm fine," he said.

"Are you sure? I have some Tums in my purse if it was the food." I sincerely hoped it wasn't the food, considering that I'd just eaten three times more of it than he had.

"I'll be fine."

"You don't know how to let anyone help you." It felt like a profound insight, but it might have been the hefeweizen talking. "If you won't tell me anything, I won't know anything. And if I don't know anything, I'm going to keep making ill-fated attempts to organize you and improve your life in ways that probably bug the ever-loving crap out of you."

He managed a small, amused smile. I much preferred it to the sip of his loneliness I'd just tasted. "Maybe that's a good thing."

"Maybe it is."

"Do we need to leave?" I looked at the food with undisguised longing.

"No."

And so, over the expanse of plates bearing the last remnants of German meats, salads, and dark bread, I recounted the details of my day at the auction.

Abernathy interrupted my rhapsody over the marble bust to say, "You should have picked it up." As if "it" were a loaf of bread or a stray cat.

"Call me crazy, but I have this little hang-up about not spending a quarter of a million dollars of someone else's money without their advance permission."

"Is that what it went for?" He glanced at the windows, the door.

I helped myself to the last slice of moist pumpernickel and spread it with a thick layer of creamy white butter.

"You have good instincts. I trust your taste."

"Please. You don't even trust me to buy a thirty-dollar item for the shop."

"I reserve the right to decline purchases of roadkill. Roadkill and silver. Terrible investment, silver. Never keeps its value. Anyway, I trusted you to buy the pendant for me, didn't I?"

"You're completely missing the point."

"Enlighten me."

"You had me buy something you already knew you wanted. And, don't take this the wrong way, but money doesn't seem to mean a whole lot to you. When it comes to information, you're tighter than a gnat's chuff. It doesn't do much to improve this whole boss-assistant thing we're trying to get off the ground."

He was quiet for a few beats. "Perhaps."

After a moment, he leaned back in his chair and stretched his arms behind his head, cracking several joints. His chair mirrored his efforts with small pops and groans. He consulted the tab our waiter had left with the last round of beer and stuffed it into his shirt pocket, then stood, pulled out his billfold and left a sizeable wad of cash on the table. "What time does our flight leave tomorrow?"

"6:45 a.m. See? Isn't it nice to let someone else keep track of a detail once in a while?" I rose and slipped on my coat, pausing at the table to drain the last few swallows of my beer.

"I suppose. I'll work on getting used to it."

"That's all I ask. Well, that, and that you start keeping track of your receipts." On the brazen wings of rapidly absorbing alcohol, I reached into his shirt pocket and nabbed the curl of paper, my knuckles grazing the warmth of his chest in the process. I smoothed the receipt and stuck it in my purse.

He gave me a crooked grin and squeezed my shoulder, opening a luminescent well of pleasure in my chest. "One thing at a time, Hanna. One thing at a time."

WE BOTH ELECTED TO CALL IT A NIGHT EARLY, OWING TO the obscenely early hour of our departure. The flight would put us back home by dusk.

I thought of my little cube of space in a century-old house across the sea. Was that home? It contained everything I had in the world, and I supposed that meant something. I stretched my legs out to the end of the hotel bed, empty of the three cat bodies I had become accustomed to. Did they miss me? A hand that fed was a hand that fed, whether attached to Steven Franke or me.

The longer I was away, the more the small new life I'd cobbled together felt like trying to remember a dream after waking. Slowly, the details submerged themselves into the shifting gray, until I was no longer sure they had ever been real at all.

Fishing my laptop out of my shoulder bag, I flipped it open. I had turned my cell phone off before I left New York to avoid roaming charges, but if I could get wireless, I could get Facebook. For the first time I could remember, I harbored the hope that my mother had left a well-intentioned but vaguely demeaning comment on my feed.

The Mac popped up a list of available wireless networks and allowed me to connect.

My mother didn't disappoint.

"Dearest Daughter," I read aloud. *"I just wanted to let you know that I'm here for you during this difficult time in your life. I know you must be feeling lonely now that you live alone again. Call me."*

She had commented on her own post. Twice.

"I'm not judging you for being divorced." And also, *"Women are having kids in their 40s these days."*

I smiled in spite of myself. This conclusively proved that I existed, if nothing else.

The Mac's speakers chirped, announcing an instant message. I glanced at the flashing box.

Dave: *were r u?*

Dave? My ex-husband Dave? Really? I blinked and rubbed my eyes, hoping this might be a temporary jetlag induced lapse in visual acuity. No such luck.

Which of a hundred answers to give him?

Best to suss out the reason for this communication before committing the facts. *Why?* I typed.

Dave: *I stopped by ur apt and ur new fuckboy answered the door he said you werent there*

His spelling and punctuation had gotten worse. *Because you're not constantly correcting him anymore. He hated it when you did that.* This last thought did nothing to endear him to me, much less his inference that Steven Franke was my "fuckboy." Not that Steven was a bad sort of chap, but my feelings for him orbited sisterly affection.

He's not my fuckboy. Not that it's any of your business. He's looking after the cats while I'm out of town.

Dave: *Sure he is*

Is there a particular reason you elected to grace my apartment with your presence, or was it purely motivated by concern for my well-being?

Dave: *u left ur wedding drss at the back of the closet when u moved out. I thought u might want it*

Skewered.

Six months ago, we'd still been sleeping side by side every night. Six years ago, we'd been newlyweds. It was his smile I remembered best, looking over at me while I performed some mundane task and smiling like he'd seen some secret meaning in it. I had never asked him what he was thinking in those moments. I didn't want to know. I only wanted it to remain something better than I could guess.

My fingers hovered over the keys. I began several apologies and deleted them all.

Dave: *hello??*

I'm still here, I typed, unsure of sure how I meant it.

Dave: *so what do I do with it???*

I used the excessive punctuation to work up enough irritation to answer.

I'll be back in town tomorrow. Just leave it outside my door.

Dave: *k*

I closed the chat window, then the laptop. I didn't want to see the green dot by his name. I didn't want to know he was at a computer somewhere and available to talk, and that this was all we had to say to each other.

Tension clung to me as I shoved myself off the bed and stretched my arms skyward. This short conversation had been enough to tangle knots into the muscles of my neck and shoulders. I changed into an oversized t-shirt and yoga shorts, refolded my clothes, and packed as much as I could.

Darkness had fallen outside my window. I pushed back both sets of curtains and looked out upon a full moon endlessly reflected on the waves of the North Sea. The water moved like a living thing, the slivers of moonlight growing ever slimmer as they rocked toward the empty shoreline.

A crash, the sound of breaking glass, then a muffled groan on the other side of the wall I shared with Abernathy.

A cleansing bolt of adrenaline sizzled along my nerves.

Sliding my feet into my pink pig slippers, I shuffled down the hall to pound on his door. "Mark!" I shouted, surprised at the sound of his first name. I had never before used it, but four syllables seemed like far too many at a time like this. "Are you okay?"

No answer. What if he'd fallen and hit his head and couldn't get to the door?

"Shit." I tried the doorknob and found it unlocked.

I knocked again, inching the door open a crack. "Mark?"

Still no answer. I peeked through the opening and saw legs sticking out from behind the bed. Time seemed to stretch and slow as I moved across the space between us.

I found him crumpled in the small space between

his bed and the wall. The nightstand had been turned over, and the lamp lay in shards on the floor beneath one massive bare arm.

He was shirtless and limp but breathing.

"Mark!" Something sharp bit into my knee when I knelt next to him. I put a hand on his shoulder and gently shook it. When his eyes opened a fraction, I felt a rush of relief.

He blinked and looked up at me, then glanced at the pig slipper mere inches from his face. A weak smile curved his lips.

"Here," I said, "let's get you up." I wrapped both hands—*both hands*—around his bicep and tugged him upward. "Watch your other arm. There's glass."

Was I depraved for noticing the way sweat trickled down his abdominals at a time like this?

Abernathy pushed himself up and fell back on the bed. I perched next to him on the edge of the mattress, brushing glass fragments off his arm while trying—and failing miserably—not to ogle his bare chest. Not the artificially symmetrical physique of a gym bro, but the rough-hewn muscle, bone and sinew of a man. A real man in a world he fought with his wits and sometimes his fists. Strange for such strength to be yielded to my hands. His face naked of its usual scowl. Dark lashes against high cheekbones. The tender crease of his eyelids. The bridge of his nose, so fine, so proud, somehow vulnerable.

"Should I call someone?" I asked.

Abernathy shook his head, his tongue-dampening lips gone pale. "No."

I pressed a hand against his damp brow. No fever. Quite the opposite. He felt cold, clammy. "Does your stomach hurt? Do you think it was the food?"

"No. Had these since I was a kid," he sighed. "I'm fine."

CYNTHIA ST. AUBIN

"Yes, I can see that. The very specimen of good health."

"Like the *David*."

"Like the *Death of Marat*."

"Should have bought it," he said.

"Bought what?"

"The bust. You should have bought it. Nice guy, Canova."

Stretching one of his eyelids open with two fingers, I saw his unfocused, dilated pupil. "I don't think we're all here, are we?"

"He was a nice guy, Canova," Abernathy repeated. "Didn't like tomatoes though."

"Mark, what the heck are you talking about?"

He looked petulant and boyish for a moment. "Canova. Had dinner with him once."

"You had dinner with *the* Antonio Canova, 18th century sculptor."

He nodded. "Didn't like the pasta. Allergic to tomatoes."

"Okaay. Whatever you say, boss."

I wondered if I should call an ambulance despite his protestations.

He dropped a giant hand on my bare knee. "You're bleeding."

It was the first lucid thing he had uttered, and I spoke quickly, hoping to anchor the conversation.

"I think a bit of the lamp got me. You must have knocked it over when you went down."

"Must have. Nice slippers."

The pigs' glassy black button eyes stared up at me from plush pink paces. "I like them." I shrugged.

His hand came to rest on my inner thigh, the contact crackling through me like a downed power line. Thank God I'd shaved.

"Nice," he sighed.

116

Were we still talking about my slippers?

With no warning, he yanked his arm away and sat bolt upright, nostrils flaring. "You have to go," he said. "Now."

A split second later, there was a knock at the door.

"Who could that be?" I wondered aloud. Perhaps another guest had heard the crash and informed the hotel staff. I rose to answer the door, but before I could get around the bed, Abernathy was already in front of me.

"How did you—"

"Don't." All traces of vulnerability had utterly vanished, leaving behind his typical granite-faced certitude.

"Mark, really. Please lie down." I looked over his shoulder and gasped. "Oh my God!"

He jerked his head around, and I used the opportunity to dash the last couple of steps to open the door.

This time my gasp was real.

"Penny?"

$\mathcal{S}$he had traded her red suit for a black silk sheath dress. It dipped low enough to allow a generous view of creamy white cleavage and clung to every graceful curve. I couldn't help but notice the juxtaposition of my pink piggy slippers against her black patent leather stilettos. In my t-shirt and shorts, I felt like a swamp frog to her swan.

"Why, Hanna. Pleasure to see you again, love."

"Penny, what are you doing here?"

She didn't answer, and instead, looked past me. I read Abernathy's position behind me from the flash of hunger in her eyes.

She spoke not to me, but to him. "I've come to speak to Mr. Abernathy, actually. I'm afraid there was a problem with the transaction this afternoon."

"Problem? What kind of problem?"

"That's a confidential matter. I'll need to discuss it with Mr. Abernathy. In private."

The chill in her tone sliced through my confusion, and I understood. She'd come to try and have a go with Abernathy. How could I have been so stupid? All that friendly banter. I'd told her where we were staying. All it would take was a simple question at the front desk about which room was Abernathy's and *Bob's your uncle, Fanny's your aunt.*

"How helpful of you to come all the way to his hotel room at nine o' clock at night to address it," I said, attempting to conjure some of her chill. "Are all the employees at Bonham's as *dedicated* as you are?"

"Quite."

We locked eyes, and I knew at once that she'd correctly taken my meaning.

"Mr. Abernathy is not feeling well. You'll have to call our office on Monday."

"That's not possible," she said. "Mr. Abernathy and I have to settle this matter right away."

I felt Abernathy's hand on my shoulder. "It's okay, Hanna. I'll speak to her."

"I don't think that's a good—" The words died away on my tongue as I saw him over my shoulder. Every muscle of his torso and arms was carved with perfect tension. His color had returned, and his dark eyes were fastened on Penny with unblinking interest. I resisted the urge to look for a telltale bulge in his pants.

You have got to be kidding me.

"She could always join our discussion," Penny said to Abernathy. Her eyelids lowered a fraction. I noticed the hard buds of her nipples rising under the thin silk of her gown.

"No," he said firmly. "Hanna was just leaving." He gave me a warning glare.

"Of course. Far be it from the lowly assistant to get in the way of your *discussion.*"

I brushed Penny out of my way and marched—judiciously, I thought—back to my room. Of course, the effect was significantly compromised by the bouncing snouts of my pig slippers. I didn't look back but heard Abernathy's door slam and the lock slide home.

I slammed my hotel room door in reply.

Un-fucking-believable.

I paced the meager length of my hotel room, working myself into a fine lather. My core was a molten mix of anger, confusion, and disbelief.

This was the second time in one week I'd come between Abernathy and a rabid lady fan. I was beginning to understand what beef Helena might have had with him. *Helena who got herself dead.*

Had he not a shred of discretion? He'd never even met Penny.

And *Penny*, the two-faced walking mattress. Had she planned this out from the moment that Abernathy called in? I'd bet she hadn't even been assigned to help me. Probably just saw the opportunity and weaseled her way in.

Abernathy—he was no longer Mark—had recovered quick enough, hadn't he? Or had he been expecting her?

I flung myself down on the bed and tore open one of the German chocolate candy bars I had picked up while we were out. Even the creamy sweetness of it on my tongue was not enough to dispel my bitter humor.

Maybe I was being unreasonable. For a moment, I considered the *very* remote possibility that I might be overreacting. Tiptoeing over to our shared wall, I pressed my ear to the faded floral wallpaper and was rewarded with a violent impact on the other side.

A primal growl then, and another crash, this time knocking one of the hotel-issued seascapes off my wall.

A rough, low moan. Feminine, throaty, ending in a growl.

Something thumped hard on the other side of the wall. Thumped again.

Then again, and again, and again. The sound moved down the wall, then resumed where Abernathy's headboard met the wall.

Bang. Bang. Bangbangbangbang.

I pounded the wall with my fist as hard as I could.

"Hey! *Hey!* Get a room!"

Then, realizing that they already *had* a room, elected to amend my suggestion.

"Or get *another* room! I'm right!" *Bang.* "Fucking!" *Bang.* "Here!"

Abernathy roared again, a sound that could have been pleasure or pain. Maybe both. A final crash, punctuated by the staccato of breaking glass.

"Animals!"

Eerie silence followed.

I waited for a few beats, expecting to hear mumbled words or sighs to mark the end of their frantic exchange.

Nothing.

What did people usually do after a good bout of anonymous shagging? A quick handshake? A friendly wave goodbye?

I couldn't imagine Penny would be sleeping over. She would have to leave sometime.

So I sat on the bed, and I waited.

Minutes passed into an hour without so much as a peep from next door. No doors opening or closing. No muffled voices. Not a sound.

Fitful sleep found me plagued by visions of Abernathy, Penny, and Dave. Tangled images filtered through the unreality of dreams. Fear-soaked and strange.

The alarm woke me at 4:00 a.m.

I showered and dressed in comfortable clothes. Remembering Penny, stunning in her black silk, I spent more time than I had planned on my hair and makeup.

One final check around the room to make sure I had everything, and I wrestled my bags downstairs to the empty, silent lobby where I settled on one of the couches to wait. Irritation turned to worry at around a quarter till five. I approached the registration desk and gently tapped the silver bell.

Marion wandered out from a connecting room looking rumpled and tired.

"Ahh, Hanna. *Guten morgen*." She yawned.

"*Guten morgen*, Marion. Have you seen Mr. Abernathy?"

"Only last night." My own worry reflected back to me from her kind face. "Not yet today."

I frowned. "We were supposed to meet here to leave for the airport."

"When do you fly?"

"6:45 a.m.," I said.

She consulted a wristwatch of faded gold. "You must leave soon."

"Yes, I know. I should go see what's keeping him. May I leave my bags here?" I asked.

"Yes, yes. They will be safe."

I took the stairs two at a time, fueled by nervous energy. It was one thing to fuck around with some random tart the night before you had an early flight. It was quite another to miss your flight entirely for it.

I knocked briskly on the door. "Abernathy? Are you ready?"

No answer. *Déjà vu.*

"Hey! Mr. A! We need to leave."

Again, nothing.

I tried the door and found it locked. Either Abernathy was still in there, or he had left and locked the door behind him. I intended to find out which.

Another sprint up and down the stairs and a near-asthmatic attack later, I slid my borrowed key into the lock and opened Abernathy's door.

I didn't know what I had been expecting, but it wasn't this.

The room was in pristine condition. Bed made, surfaces clean, not a bag in sight. As if Abernathy had never been there.

Stranger still, the lamp that had lay in shards on the floor last night now sat on the nightstand. A closer inspection revealed nary a crack. I stooped and pulled up the coverlet to look under the bed. No shards on the floor. Not even a dust bunny.

Peering out the window, I saw the Peugeot hunkered down at the curb in the pre-dawn darkness.

Wherever Abernathy was, he had gone without a car and had taken his bags. I could think of only one explanation, and I didn't like it.

He'd left with Penny. They had decided to take off on some little spree together, and Abernathy hadn't so much as left a note.

I descended the stairs slowly, considering my options, and returned the key to Marion. "Are you sure he didn't check out? All his bags are gone, and the room looks like it's been cleaned."

"Mr. Abernathy does not check out always. He pays in advance. He leaves the room clean though. Don't vorry." Her voice was warm, reassuring. "This is not unusual. He comes and goes. Like the weather."

"Like an inconsiderate dickhead."

I judged by her expression that "dickhead" was not one of the English words in her vocabulary.

Damned if he was going to make me miss our flight. I didn't have enough money to buy another ticket, and I'd had about enough of this disappearing shit. When I got back, I would hit the pavement. Look for another job. I doubted McDonald's cashiers got ditched in foreign countries as a regular part of their duties. And there might be free French fries. There's a lot a girl would do for free French fries.

Or this girl, at least.

123

"Marion, he was my only ride to the airport. I don't have the keys to the car. Do you know a cab or taxi I could call?"

"Oh no, not so early." Her expression brightened. "*Meine sohne*, Stephan! He can take you in the hotel van. I will go get him."

"I could take you," a voice offered as soon as Marion was out of sight. "I'm headed there anyway." The accent was difficult to place.

Over on the red lobby couch, a leggy brunette folded the newspaper she'd been reading and set it in her lap. Even in the dim lamplight of pre-dawn, I could see she was lovely. Dark hair and eyes, lips painted blood-red to match her coat. Had I seen her before? At the auction perhaps?

"I couldn't ask you to do that."

"You didn't. I offered. I have a flight to catch myself. Business." She glanced toward the briefcase at her feet.

A strange woman always seemed a safer bet than a strange man.

"Well, if it wouldn't be too much tr—"

"Here he is!" Marion interrupted.

Judging by the peculiar angles of Stephan's jutting blond hair, he'd been awakened from a sound sleep.

"Oh," I said, looking to the brunette. She now stood, briefcase and car keys in hand. "Actually, she's headed to the airport and—"

"No," Marion said firmly. "Stephan takes you." She cast a withering look at Stephan, who grabbed my luggage and headed out the door. He loaded my bags into the van while Marion hugged me to her matronly bosom.

The brunette walked past us to a Porsche and took off at breakneck speed.

Perhaps it was a good thing Marion had strong-armed me into riding with her son after all.

"Take care, Hanna. We will see you again, I hope."

Not bloody likely.

"Thank you," I said. "It was nice to meet you."

We rocketed to the airport at a speed that would have put Abernathy to shame. Whether Stephan drove to get me there in time to make my flight, or so he could get back to bed sooner, I couldn't tell. It worked for me either way.

At the airport, Stephan helped me unload my bags. I took the remaining wad of Euros out of my purse and handed them over to him. It felt vaguely satisfying to waste Abernathy's money.

"*Danke! Danke schoen!*" Stephan said, wide-eyed and grateful.

The attendant at the counter rushed me through, and I made it to the jet way just as they were beginning to close the door.

Settling into my seat, I leaned back, and closed my eyes. I'd made it. I was on my way home.

MY PROBLEMS DIDN'T END WHEN I TOUCHED DOWN AT the Denver airport. I had come with Abernathy and once again had no way of getting home.

When I turned my cell phone on, the onslaught of missed text messages and calls lit it up like a Christmas tree.

My mother had called eight times; Dave, four; and Steven Franke once. They would have to wait.

A brief inspection of my wallet revealed twenty-four dollars and change. Not enough for a shuttle home from the airport. It was either walk seventy miles or call someone to come get me. I scrolled through my list of contacts. Mostly grad school friends I'd lost touch with and married friends that had been part of my life

B.D.—before divorce. I was down to Steven Franke or Dave.

I held my breath and dialed. He picked up on the first ring.

"Pirate's Cove, this be Long John Silver! What be yer business?"

"Hi, Steven. It's Hanna."

"Hanna! Back from the land of liverwurst and lederhosen?"

"Sort of." I stepped out of the way of a family marching along the sidewalk with luggage in tow. "I'm at the airport."

"Nice. I love the airport. Great people watching there. Lots of wind suits. Agents of the outer zipper, if you know what I mean."

In fact, I did not. "Right, well, the reason I'm calling is—"

"You want to know how the cats are doing, right? *Die katzen* in German, that is."

"I didn't know that. Actually..."

"They're doing great. We had a fiesta last night. Watched the *Three Amigos* and ate quesadillas. Totally extra."

"That's amazing. Hey, listen. I was wondering if you could do me a favor. It's kind of a big favor."

"Talk to me."

"I'm a little bit stranded at present. Abernathy missed our flight this morning, and now I don't have a ride back. Do you think you could come get me?"

"That crazy Abernathy. What a guy, huh?" Steven laughed.

I wasn't sure "guy" was the word I would have chosen at that particular moment.

"I know it's a lot to ask."

"No worries, doll. I'll be there in thirty."

"Thanks a million, Steven. Call me when you're

close. I'll meet you in the pick-up lane."

"10-4, little buddy."

While I waited, I read through the texts. Several cat pictures from my mother, followed by three texts marked urgent, asking why I wasn't responding. How did one mark texts urgent, anyhow? Two texts from Dave in the early morning hours. Drunk dialing no doubt.

whose that guy at ur appt???

And then: *were r u?????*

He'd sent them before finding me on Facebook.

Bags in hand, I wheeled myself out to the pick-up curb where the night air on my skin felt refreshing and familiar. I considered going to check if the Wraith was still where we'd left it in the parking garage but decided I was too tired to care. Abernathy was on his own.

After what felt like a near eternity, Steven puttered up in an old Volkswagen bug. The faded black exterior had been embellished with hand-painted metallic red stars. It occurred to me I had never seen Steven's work at the gallery, nor any of the resident artists' work for that matter. What kind of art did Mrs. Kass of the severely impaired vision make, exactly?

On the cracked leather dashboard, a monkey in a hula skirt wobbled to and fro suggestively as we motored off.

Goose flesh raised on my arms at the sound of the engine.

My father had traded in his shiny yellow Trans-am for a tan Volkswagen Beetle when he had married my mother. I'd made my debut into the world ass-first—an omen if there ever was one—nine months later. Some of my earliest memories of cars were framed by these words, what they meant, and how they sounded in my father's voice. *Trans-am*, the way it buzzed off his tongue like an exotic rocket. *Volkswagen*, rounded, comforting, tasting like black licorice and feeling like road trips.

I remembered the distinctive tattoo of a VW bug's engine rattling into our driveway, announcing my dad's arrival home every night. Until one idle evening halfway through my fourth year of life, when the sound failed to come. I sat on the back of the couch watching for him through the front room window until the police cars came. The walls of our living room flashed red-blue, red-blue in time with their lights. I'd answered the door when they knocked and led them to the bedroom where my mother had been stationed all day, too sick to move.

They had news.

"How was the trip?" Steven asked.

I blinked away the sheen that filmed my eyes. "It was...interesting."

"I bet."

We rode in silence for a few moments. Passing headlights filled the car's interior like an oil lantern. All the houses looked like little campfires in the distance.

"When is Mr. A coming back?" Steven asked.

"Beats the hell out of me. All I know is we were supposed to meet to ride back to the airport this morning, and he never showed."

"Mr. A can be a little unpredictable."

"You think?"

"I'm sure he had a good reason for not coming. Something must have happened."

"If by 'something' you mean a blonde with a butt like Baryshnikov, then yes, *something* happened."

"Come again?" Steven asked.

I launched into an account of the entire trip, beginning to end.

"I wouldn't be so sure," Steven said after I'd finished my tirade. "There could be another explanation."

"If it walks like a duck and talks like a duck, it's probably a duck," I recited. I slid down into my seat, exhausted and empty.

"Unless it's a guy in a duck suit," Steven pointed out. "We've all been there. Am I right?"

I snorted. I didn't like that he was offering excuses for Abernathy, though his loyalty was endearing.

"How long have you known him?"

"Oh, for a while. He saw my work in a gallery once and invited me to join the resident artist group at The Crossing. The rest, as they say, is history."

"How long has everyone else been there?"

He toyed with his lip piercing as he thought. "I think Mrs. Kass and Rob Vincent have been around the longest. They were there when I moved in. Kirkpatrick has been there about a year."

"Kirkpatrick is a turd," I diagnosed. My filter had clearly evaporated somewhere over the Atlantic.

"He's not so bad once you get to know him." Even Steven's optimistic tone couldn't float the weight of that claim.

Getting to know Kirkpatrick sounded about as fun a recreational vivisection. I felt something poking me in the hindquarters and readjusted to feel around behind me. My hands closed around a tube. I brought it forward to look at it in the light. Dentucream.

I held it out to Steven. "Yours?"

"Ha!" he said. "Mrs. Kass has been looking for that. Must've fallen out of her bag. Do you want to shove it in the glove box?"

I did as asked. "How did her denture cream get into your car?"

"She rides with me to the gallery every day," Steven explained. "She was taking the bus when I first met her. Has a little trouble seeing."

"That's really lovely of you, Steven." An inexplicable

surge of warmth filled my chest.

"She's an interesting bird."

"Speaking of animals, how did it go with the cats? Did they give you any trouble?"

"Not a lick. Gilbert was pretty upset though."

"He's got some temperamental issues," I said. Like crapping in my shoes. "That's why he's on the anti-depressants."

"Yeah, we sorted it out though."

"Sorted what out?" I asked.

"His issues. We had a little pow-wow. Turns out he was feeling bummed because he didn't have any high stuff to jump on anymore, so I picked up one of those little platform deals and set it up in the kitchen. I hope you don't mind."

I blinked at him. "Say what now?"

"My man Gill was missing all the high stuff he used to jump on. That's why he was depressed."

This brought me up short. Gilbert's issues had started shortly after I moved out of my and Dave's apartment with its built-in shelves and fireplace mantel. Gilbert used to spend hours perched there.

"I had assumed it had something to do with the divorce," I mumbled.

"Nah. Gilbert didn't think he was good for you anyway."

Steven said all this as if it were the most natural thing in the world.

"Anyway, it's all good now. I don't think he needs the meds anymore."

"Oh. Right. Okay."

"Welp, here we are," he said, pulling up to the curb in front of my house. He'd left the living room lamp on for me. The window cast a square of warm light on the snow-covered lawn. "Good to be home, huh?"

I smiled at him. "You know," I said. "It really is."

CHAPTER 10

I awoke to a changed world. The snow had melted under an early rain, and the streets were wet but clean. I pried through several layers of paint to open a window and let the scent fill my apartment. Concerned about lead paint in older houses and knowing Gilbert's propensity to snack on non-foods, I carefully swept up the paint chips and disposed of them.

A good night's sleep in my own bed with cats warming my feet had done wonders for my mood. As had stuffing my wedding dress in the dumpster at the back of the house.

Gilbert was a cat reborn. He snuggled, played like a kitten, and left my shoes virtually un-assaulted. As I went through the routine of making coffee, he watched me from his newly acquired kitchen perch. Steven had to be some sort of cat whisperer. He ought to have his own show on Animal Planet. Who could be more fun to watch than Steven?

Abernathy.

Ugh. Don't say that name to me.

Unwelcome images pressed their way into my thoughts. Abernathy with Penny up against a wall.

Abernathy and Penny tooling around together in her car, footloose and fancy free somewhere in the German countryside. I could have forgiven being evicted for a good rogering. God knows I needed one. But *ditched*? Hell no.

Still, little details worried the edges of my foregone conclusions. Abernathy had seemed genuinely ill that evening. He'd collapsed and taken out a nightstand and a lamp. That much I knew. And the growling, the breaking glass. His picture-perfect room the following morning. The swarm of discordant facts hummed in my brain like locusts.

But then, discord of all kinds and colors seemed to be status quo in Abernathy's world. Steven had certainly confirmed that these kinds of random disappearances were a pattern where "Mr. A" was concerned.

I knew about patterns.

Patterns could be *changed*.

Perhaps this simply called for a little more persistence on my part. Maybe this wasn't a *rejection*. Maybe this was a *challenge*.

I turned this idea over in my head as I lingered over a second cup of coffee. Maybe Abernathy thought if he were enough of a nuisance, I would give up and let him go back to the way things were before he hired me.

The idea shot a jet of fire to my belly.

Abernathy had paid me for a week, and a week he was going to get, by God, whether he wanted it or not.

I thought it unlikely that he had returned to the country overnight and would be back at the office this morning.

The office.

The office that I never finished organizing.

And no Abernathy here to tell me what I couldn't touch. *Damn shame, that.* I guessed I would just have to do my humble best to organize the office without him.

Picturing his irritation brought me the morning's first smile.

Showered and dressed, I packed myself some Stilton, clementines, and flatbread for lunch. Opening a can of tuna and dividing it among three plates, I reassured myself I wasn't doing it to make sure the cats liked me better than Steven Franke.

Bundled up against the bone-chilling rain, I navigated my '67 Mustang over to The Crossing. Driving, like eating, was one of the few pleasures I could count on, and the chief reason I'd refused to part with the Mustang even in the face of eating ramen noodles after the divorce.

No Wraith waited at the curb when I arrived, not that I had really expected it to be there. Rob Vincent waved as I passed the shop and crossed the gallery to the stairs. I hooked my laptop into mission control and flicked on my lamp. Open for business.

I gathered some empty boxes and an armful of cleaning supplies and made a game plan. Empty first, sort second, scan and file third.

My quest began with loose paper. I dug through the layers like an archaeologist. With each new level, the dates on the papers reached further into the past. When I came across an auction receipt from 1987, I was forced to pause and take in a couple facts.

How old was Abernathy exactly?

If this receipt was indeed his, it meant he'd acquired it when I had been approximately two years old. Was he old enough to be doing business then? I had assumed he was older than I, but never considered by precisely how much. Could he really be over forty? The very idea seemed ludicrous. And yet, here was the evidence.

I chewed on this information as I filled a lawn bag with the pile of Abernathy's clothes I'd moved to the corner earlier this week. He had refused my offer to take them to be dry cleaned, and as I sorted through them, I discovered why. These clothes didn't need a dry cleaner; they needed a priest to perform the last rites and let them go. *I'm sorry, we did everything we could.* Almost every shirt was stained or missing buttons. Several pairs of pants were torn out at the knees and their cuffs caked in mud. And every last item was *covered* with fur.

Abernathy hadn't mentioned having a dog. He'd said he was allergic to cats. Where had it all come from? I made a mental note to bring a lint roller in to work, tied the bag, and rose to take it out to my desk.

Mrs. Kass stood in the doorway.

"Mrs. Kass." I rested my hand over the heart leaping like a gazelle in my chest. "You startled me!"

Today, she sported a faded mustard-yellow muumuu and dark knee-highs. Her cotton candy hair hid beneath the ubiquitous floral print scarf worn by old ladies across the globe when the air was damp or the wind was high.

"Oh, is that you, Hanna? I was looking for Mr. Abernathy."

I tossed the bag of clothes past her toward my desk. They landed with a soft *whump* near the railing.

Mrs. Kass looked over shoulder. "Stevie, dear?" When *Stevie* didn't answer, she turned her attention back to me.

"Mr. Abernathy isn't back yet, I'm afraid. Is there something I can help you with?"

"Oh, I don't know. I'd hate to bother you."

"You could never bother me." I motioned toward the couch. "Why don't you come in and have a seat?"

She sat herself on the nearest stack of cardboard boxes.

"My, Mr. Abernathy likes a firm sofa, doesn't he?"

She wiggled her hind end like a duck settling on its nest.

I didn't have the heart to tell her that she'd missed it by several feet.

"He sure does," I said.

She blinked at me through her massive lenses and smiled. Magnified to an obscene size, her eyes looked like they belonged on an insect or nocturnal animal.

My, Grandma, what big eyes you have.

At this close distance, Mrs. Kass emitted a scent I'd encountered in the nursing homes where my mother had worked as a nurse's aide. Cleaning chemicals, medicinal creams, boiled food, and the musty smell of afghans residents' families brought in to remind them of home. Before grandma had come to live with us, I went to work with my mother and stretched out on the plastic-covered sofa in the TV room. There I ate sunflower seeds from the vending machine and listened to the soft moans of those they wheeled out to the hallway for a change of scenery. I had decided right then and there that I'd sooner chew a handful of razor blades than end up in a place like that. Mrs. Kass reaffirmed this commitment in my mind.

"What can I do for you?" I asked.

I knelt on the floor by her orthopedic shoes and started separating Abernathy's documents by year, using manila folders as makeshift dividers.

"Well, it's about the show next week. I'm afraid I don't have a thing finished."

"I'm sure that's fine," I said, only half listening until the words sank in. "Wait, what?"

"We have a gallery show every month. Mr. Abernathy likes us all to put our finished pieces in it."

Abernathy had mentioned this the day I started, but I hadn't given it much thought since.

"It's next week?" I hoped I had misheard.

"Yes, dear. It's the second Thursday. I thought you would know, on account of you being the organizer."

"Me? The organizer?"

"Why yes. At least, I think that's what Mr. Abernathy told us."

"He did, did he?"

"Oh yes. Of course, that nice young lady of his organized the last one. Took care of the food, the invitations, everything really. I don't suppose she's been around in a while though."

"I don't suppose she has." Too busy being dead. "So, there's food and invitations, what else?"

"Now let's see." Her giant eyes floated to the top of her goggles as if looking for the answer somewhere in the great beyond. Her dentures slid side to side in her mouth like a person pacing.

"Well, I think she collected all the pieces and decided where they'd go and such. Hung the paintings, put the other things on pedestals. And if I remember it right, she wrote up the labels and prices for everything."

"Oh, is that all?"

"That's about it, I think."

"Sounds like I've got my work cut out for me."

"I'm sure Mr. Abernathy will help you though, this being your first time and all. When is he due back anyhow?"

"I'm afraid I don't know."

"But I thought Stevie said you and Mr. Abernathy were in Greece together."

"Germany," I said. "But he...he didn't make the flight."

"You mean to say you came back all by yourself?" she asked.

"Something like that."

"Well, that wasn't very nice of him, was it?" Her tone was motherly and disapproving.

"No, not very. But I'm sure he had a good reason." Had I actually just said that? Out loud?

"Yes, he usually does."

Before I could ask her what she meant, I heard the fall of heavy footsteps on the stairs. My stomach did a dead roll. *Abernathy?*

The figure filling the doorway was equally surprising and twice as problematic.

"Detective Morrison." I pushed myself to my feet and hoped he didn't hear my knees pop as they begrudgingly unbent. *Must. Not. Groan.*

"Red." The couple days that had passed since I'd last seen him hadn't been kind. He looked wrung and tired. The hollows under his eyes deeper, his jaw sanded with stubble. He might have slept in his clothes.

"A detective? I don't think we've been introduced." Mrs. Kass pivoted on her box and stuck a gnarled hand into Morrison's crotch.

He jerked instinctively but not quickly enough. Direct hit to the nuggets. Morrison stumbled backward a step, bent at the waist, coughed, and leaned one hand on the doorjamb. After a moment, his other hand reached out and closed around Mrs. Kass's bony knuckles.

"Detective Morrison," he grunted. "Nice to meet you."

"Rosemary Kass. And this is Hanna." She gestured to a dead office plant to my extreme right.

Morrison gave me a querulous look. I shrugged.

"Pleasure, Hank," he said.

I angled a snotty smirk at him.

"What brings you to our gallery?" Mrs. Kass asked.

Morrison took a deep breath and gave Mrs. Kass a wide berth as he walked into the office. He rolled Abernathy's wide wing-backed chair from behind his desk and plopped into it.

Marking territory.

I seated myself on the edge of the coffee table by the couch.

"I came to chat with Mark," Morrison said.

"He's not in at the moment," I said.

Mrs. Kass looked surprised to hear my voice behind her rather than coming from the corner. She squinted in my general direction.

"Oh?" Morrison asked, one eyebrow raised.

"That's right," Mrs. Kass chimed in. "He's still in Greece. Left poor Hanna to come back all by herself."

"Is that true?"

"Not entirely," I said. After my last session with Morrison, I was determined to count every word carefully before I spoke it.

"Which part is inaccurate?"

"The Greece part. We were in Germany."

He wagged his finger at me. "And after I told him not to leave town. Very suspicious. Very naughty."

"It was a matter of professional responsibility. We went to an art auction." Technically, this wasn't a lie. We had both *gone* to an auction. Abernathy just hadn't gone inside.

Status: defensible.

"Will his professional responsibility be bringing him back at any point? I have a few questions for him."

"I expect it will." Truthfully, I had no idea what to expect. Awful lot of women in the world. He'd only screwed half of them, as far as I could tell.

"Questions? What kind of questions?" Mrs. Kass asked. If she'd had better control of her slackened facial muscles, they might have showed concern.

I directed a look at Morrison, wondering how much information he'd be willing to part with.

"Questions regarding the de—questions regarding Helena Pool."

"Helena Pool. Helena Pooool." Mrs. Kass repeated the name as if to trigger a memory. "That name sounds familiar."

"I understand she and Abernathy were *involved*." He put more meaning into the last word than I thought could likely be picked up by Mrs. Kass's hearing aids, regardless of their gargantuan proportions.

For my part, I knew a little too much about what Abernathy's *involvements* looked like. Sounded like, for that matter.

"That's right," Mrs. Kass said. "Now I remember. That was Mr. Abernathy's young lady. I was just telling Hank that she organized our last gallery show. Haven't seen her since. That's not unusual though. He's quite the ladies' man, you know."

There's the fucking understatement of the century.

Morrison's features, sharpened by interest, suggested the keenness of a hunting dog.

"Abernathy's been involved with quite a few women that you know of?"

"My, yes." She laughed. The tops of her dentures were visible against the line of her gums through her broad smile. "None of his young ladies seem to last very long though."

Morrison laughed mirthlessly. "That's been my impression as well."

I mentally palmed my face. Oh, Mrs. Kass. No good could come of this.

"I've told him it was about time he settled down with a nice girl. But a handsome young man like that. I suppose he likes to keep his options open. Doesn't he?"

"Do you happen to remember any of their names?" Morrison asked.

"Goodness no. My memory's not so good these

days. And there's been so many over the years. Who could keep track of them?"

At this, Morrison looked irritated. The scent was lost as quickly as it had been discovered. He dug around in his shirt pocket and located a tattered business card, handing it to Mrs. Kass. "Call me if you think of anything else."

Mrs. Kass pinched the card between the thumb and index finger of each hand and brought it close enough to brush the tip of her nose.

"I'm sure Hanna would be glad to dial the number for you if you needed it."

I gave him a look that said, *Hanna is about to throat-punch a detective.*

"Let Abernathy know I stopped by for him," he said, turning to me. "We're going to need to chat."

"Will do," I said. If he happened to come back before my remaining forty-eight hours of employment expired, that was.

Detective Morrison rose from the chair and sauntered to the door. As he did, I caught a glimpse of his wrinkled trousers from behind. No trench coat this time. I had to admit, for a dickhead detective, he had a pretty nice ass. He turned back just in time to catch me looking.

A grin worked at one side of his mouth. "See you soon."

I nodded a little too vigorously. "Uh huh."

When he was gone, Mrs. Kass turned to me. "Well, he seemed like a nice man, didn't he?"

"Nice," I agreed.

"Well, I better get back to work," she sighed. "Maybe I can try to finish something after all."

I stood and offered her my hand. Beneath her paper-thin skin, the veins shifted under my palm like fat, warm worms. The delicate bones of her hand felt like they might crush like chalk in my grip. I let go as soon as she looked stable.

In her absence, I turned my attention back to the office and reviewed my progress. Clutter-free floor, clean desk. Abysmal bookshelves and cabinets containing unknown horrors. Addressing the cabinets first would let me know how much storage room might be available for extra books.

Just as I stooped before the first set of shelves, an avalanche of papers slid into my lap, sending a tsunami of dust into my face.

Pushing the pile aside, I pulled out the leather-bound ledger tucked at the back of the cabinet. A fine snowfall of debris fell from the cover as I opened it. The yellowing parchment was covered with the looping script of the kind I imagined a quill might produce.

I scanned the first line to the column marked for date. *July 8th, 1768.*

Butter my butt and call me a biscuit.

There would have to be a market for this kind of old memorabilia. So why would Abernathy bother to collect it if he was just going to shove them into cabinets? My museum training came back in a sudden burst. These should be in acid-free sleeves at a minimum. Temperature and moisture-controlled storage would be even better.

Unless he wasn't collecting them.

I looked over some of the names in the ledger entries, but only recognized one: Wedgewood. The rest seemed familiar in a maddeningly vague way. Halifax Bank of Scotland, C. Hoare & Company London, Grieves and Hawkes, Rowland, Gröditz, Haig, L. Cornellison and Son, Ede and Ravenscroft, and Allens of Mayfair. I jotted the names down on a sticky note, deciding this merited further research.

As I stacked the papers the best I could and slid them back into the cabinet, my fingers brushed across the cool slick surface of polished wood. I peered into the inky pocket of shadow and could make out light reflecting dimly along a straight edge. With a crab-like wandering hand, I coaxed a box of delicate inlaid wood out of the shadows. Not a speck of dust marred its gleaming face.

"And what are we hiding in here?"

The lid eased open to gentle pressure. Unlocked.

Inside was a picture, yellowed with age, cracked, and stained. God but her face looked familiar. Dark hair tied back in a knot at the back of her neck, high cheekbones, wide-set dark eyes. How did I know this face?

Under the picture, I found more paper. Only this paper had been folded neatly into a sheaf and bound with a black satin ribbon. It looked to be every bit as old as the other documents I encountered, only in much better repair, protected by its wooden casket.

I tugged a corner of the knot, and the bundle slid open with a sigh of dry pages. My heart thudded in the perfect silence of the room.

"Hey, doll!"

My hands jerked, snapping the lid of the box shut as I shoved it back into the cabinet.

I turned and peered over the edge of Abernathy's ponderous desk. Steven Franke slouched in the doorway.

"Hey, Steven. How's it going?" I hauled myself to my feet, spanking the dust from my pants.

"Good. Splendid. Über. Just stopped by to see what you were up to."

I gestured to the newly cleaned floor. "That, mostly."

Steven looked at the floor as if seeing it for the first time.

"Wood floor huh? Nice."

"The papers," I said. "I cleaned the papers."

"Oh yeah! Wow."

I suspected he didn't have the faintest idea what the floor looked like before. Steven seemed to exist largely on another plane. One where leopard print and unicorns were as common as khakis and Pomeranians.

He flung himself down on Abernathy's sofa and propped his arms behind his head.

"Bad day?" I asked.

"Blocked."

"Must be catching. Mrs. Kass was telling me something similar earlier."

"It's like there's a disturbance in the force or something. I can't figure it out. I've tried all the usual things that get the mojo going. Jazzercise, headstands, I even sacrificed a chicken."

I raised an eyebrow at him. Steven didn't look like he would be capable of sacrificing a housefly.

"Okay, well, I ate at KFC. I thought that would be close enough."

"Only if you got extra-crispy. Anything less doesn't count."

"Of course I got extra-crispy. This ain't my first time at the rodeo, doll."

"Right," I said.

"Anyway, it's really getting me down. I don't know if I'll have anything for the show next week. Mr. A gets real cranky about that."

"At this rate, I don't think you have to worry about that, with Mr. A being AWOL."

"Oh, he'll be back," Steven assured me. "He's always back by show time."

"I hope you're right."

He considered the ceiling in a shared and companionable silence.

143

"Steven, can I ask you something?"

"Lay it on me." He let his head drop to the side and met my gaze.

I settled myself on the floor by the couch, gathering my thoughts.

"Have you ever noticed something kind of...strange about Mark?"

His fine blond brows drew toward his creased forehead. "Like what?"

"Oh, I don't know. It's just...well. He has all this money. He's always disappearing. He has papers from three hundred years ago in piles on his floor and stuffed into his cabinets." *He gets sick during the full moon. His dry cleaning is covered in fur. He moves faster than I can see. His most recent girlfriend ended up with her throat torn out. He reads my thoughts on occasion.*

What was I saying? What was I *thinking*?

Steven shrugged. "Yeah, he's kind of eccentric, I suppose. I always chalked it up to the business."

"I suppose."

"You think it's something else." It was a statement of fact.

"Maybe."

He looked thoughtful for a moment. "What do you think it is?" His normally hazy green gaze locked onto mine with surprising intensity.

"I'm not entirely sure."

"You think he's a werewolf?"

"What?" I half-coughed/half-laughed.

Just where in the hell had he pulled that from? Perhaps he read the minds of crazy cat ladies in addition to those of cats.

"A werewolf, a lycanthrope, a humanoid member of the lupine family."

"No! That's crazy! I would never—"

"There are tests you know."

144

"No shit?" I asked, completely derailed from my righteously indignant denial.

"Yeah. It just so happens I have a friend who's an expert in the matters. He has a pamphlet."

"You're shitting me. A pamphlet?"

"Seriously. I could bring in a copy tomorrow."

Was I really considering this? I looked at him with eyes beseeching him not to think of me as a total crackpot.

"Only one way to find out."

I swallowed around the golf ball that had suddenly found its way into my throat. "I mean, if it wouldn't be too much trouble…"

"Nah, no trouble at all."

"Thanks, Steven."

"My pleasure, doll." Steven pushed himself up from the couch and stretched, looking like nothing so much as a strange featherless bird. All tendons and long neck. "Holy shit!" he gasped.

"What?"

He loped from the room and took the stairs two at a time. "I think I'm unblocked," he called over his shoulder. "Gotta run."

I sincerely hoped he was speaking about his art.

IN THE QUIET OF ABERNATHY'S OFFICE, I WATCHED THE first fat raindrops turn into sleet, exploding like clumps of wet sugar against the glass. My attempts to psych myself up to put out my flyers for the gallery show had failed spectacularly.

A quick conversation with Rob Vincent had armed me with the knowledge that Abernathy eschewed any kind of social media advertising (shocking) in favor of —I shit you not—*flyers*. I'd spent three hours redesigning them, correcting and comparing my work to Helena's. Leave it to me to obsess over outdoing a dead woman.

Mine *were* better though.

I turned from the window and considered the day's work. All the wood surfaces had been polished with lemon oil. They gleamed softly in the gloaming. Every paper had been filed and the boxes neatly stacked in a corner. For the third time, I rearranged the decorative throw pillows I'd purchased for Abernathy's leather couch. At last, I had to admit there was nothing left to do.

Time to go home.

Still. *The box.*

Steven and Mrs. Kass had left earlier. The shop was closed and dark. Scott Kirkpatrick, the ginger troll, had been thankfully scarce. No one to interrupt me this time. Though there was no one there to see me, I tiptoed over to the bank of cabinets and bent down. My hand crawled blindly among the papers to feel for the box, but found nothing.

I ducked my head and squinted into the cabinet's depths. No box. Had I put it back in the wrong place, perhaps?

A quick check of the cabinets on the other side quickly disproved this theory.

Nothing.

"Ze plot theeckens," I said to the empty room, offering up a mental apology to Agatha Christie and Hercule Poirot for my atrocious Belgian accent.

I tossed this newest development onto my pile of unanswered questions and hit the lights. I'd done enough damage for one day.

THE TEAKETTLE WHISTLED MERRILY ON THE STOVE. I wrapped my wet hair in a towel and turned the burner off as I crossed the kitchen on the way to the living room.

A long, hot shower had banished the chill from my bones and the exoskeleton of dust from my skin. Wrapped in my black silk robe and my thickest, wooliest socks, I collected my steaming mug of Earl Grey and enhanced it with a goodly slosh of whiskey. Thus reinforced, I curled onto the couch.

As if sensing my proximity, the old brass radiator groaned and knocked in protest. It seemed to kick out heat grudgingly and only on a timetable of its own making. Time for plan B.

I considered the old brass-mouthed fireplace in the corner of my living room. The century-old, jade-green ceramic tiles were chipping and its mirror crazed, but its effect in the room was cozy and bewitching. Only I wasn't even sure if it was still functional.

After wrestling off the soot-caked cast iron cover, I forced open the ancient flue. Its rusty whine drew the attention of my three feline roommates, who had been dozing nearby on the couch.

"Trust me. I learned how to do this at camp." Come to think of it, I'd never completed that merit badge.

Still, there was something rather satisfying about the *whoomph* that consumed the crude teepee I'd constructed out of Duraflame logs and collections notices.

No sooner had I settled back onto the couch when a bracing knock rattled my front door and caused me to slosh hot tea into my lap. My heart leapt up to my nostrils and plummeted back down in my chest with a sickening slap.

"Shit!" Clunking the mug onto the coffee table, I peered out my window into the street below. An unfa-

CYNTHIA ST. AUBIN

miliar car was parked at the curb. Not Abernathy's. Not Steven's. Not my ex-husband's.

My front door had no peephole. No telling who it might be.

Options were limited. Open it, or pretend I wasn't home. They had probably already seen my lights on.

Another forceful knock.

"Who is it?" I called in the least serial murder victim voice I could muster.

"Morrison."

Was it dread, or something else that released a skittering flood of insects in my stomach?

I popped the lock and opened the door.

"May I come in?" Morrison asked.

May I. Correct grammar and everything. I subtly shifted my hips to make sure my panties hadn't spontaneously dropped around my ankles.

Thus assured, I stepped out of the way and motioned toward the couch. He breezed past me, carrying in the scent of damp night on his coat before collapsing onto the sofa and scrubbing his face with his hands. He glanced toward my mug on the coffee table.

"Can I interest you in a mug of Cinnamon Splendor tea?" I asked.

"I don't suppose you have coffee?"

"As it happens, I do."

"I'd love you forever."

"I'd settle for thirty minutes." Had I said that out loud?

Three months, six days, thirty-seven minutes.

That's how long it had been since my ex guilted me into a "one last time" boning.

I say boning, but I've met unbaked biscuits that were harder than he was that night.

"You and me both." Morrison looked me over then, perhaps to see if the innuendo might contain a genuine

148

prospect. Hazel eyes starting at the top and working downward, taking in the wet hair, the robe, the socks, and inevitably, my pig slippers. His mouth slashed upward on one side.

"I wasn't planning on entertaining this evening," I said. "You take your coffee black I'm guessing?"

"Guilty. Walking cop stereotype right here."

"I'll see your cop and raise you a crazy cat lady."

I shuffled into the kitchen, scooped some coffee grounds into my French press and poured over the still-steaming water from the kettle. "It will be just a few minutes," I called.

"Fine," he called back.

Then, opening and closing cabinets under the pretense of domestic industriousness, I leaned over the kitchen counter to subtly scope out the detective on my couch.

He sat hunched over his phone, blue light reflected in the wet surfaces of his eyes. Thumbing the screen with one hand, massaging his temple with the index and middle fingers of the other.

And about those fingers.

I allowed myself the time I hadn't had for unhurried appreciation.

Long, thick at the knuckle. Callused, I'd wager.

Detective Morrison had been in his share of scrapes. And had drawn his share of blood.

No doubt about that.

And here he sat on my couch. Not entirely civilized. Ready for violence with minimal provocation. Closer to my bed than was advisable.

Clearing my throat to warn him of my impending intrusion, I nabbed a mug with one hand and the coffee press with the other.

"You might want to let this cool down for a few minutes," I said, setting the goods down on the table.

Morrison reached forward and pushed down the plunger, forcing the grounds to the bottom of the press. He decanted the rich brown liquid into his mug and took a slurp.

I winced for him.

"Ahh," he sighed. "This is good."

"Is your throat made of asbestos?"

"Something like that." His laugh was coffee-warm and husky. "You drink it this strong?"

"My grandmother's coffee would dissolve a spoon. She'd consider this puppy shit."

"I think I'd like your grandmother."

I settled myself at the opposite end of the couch and shucked off the pig slippers, tucking my feet underneath me and tugging the silky robe over my knees.

"She would have liked you too." My throat constricted around the past tense, so I loosened it with a sip of spiked tea. "She had a thing for cops."

"Oh yeah?"

"Yeah. Well, at least, she had a thing for Walker, Texas Ranger. Never missed an episode." Nor had I, though my participation had more to do with snacking on grandma's potato pancakes and homemade applesauce. I drew a deep sip of my tea and reveled in the warmth spreading in my belly.

"Got any more of that whiskey?" he asked.

"How did you—"

"You're a deep exhaler."

Face burning, I rose from the couch and returned with the amber bottle of Jameson, which I set on the table before him.

"Much obliged," he said, unscrewing the lid and dosing his coffee with a goodly glug. He lifted it to his lips and sipped. "Better."

"I would hate to seem inhospitable," I said, "but may

I ask why you're randomly stopping by my apartment after business hours?"

"Reasonable question." He set his mug back on the coffee table and folded his hands.

"I thought so."

"Red—"

"Hanna."

"*Hanna.* You seem like a nice girl. I don't want to see you get mixed up in this."

"You really are a walking cop cliché."

He smiled tightly. "Abernathy is trouble, Hanna. I would ask you to steer clear of him, but I know you won't. So instead, I'm going to ask you to be honest with me. There's a woman lying dead in the morgue with her throat torn out. My duty is to her. I feel like you know something you're not telling me. I want to know what it is."

I flashed back to my earlier conversation with Steven. *Werewolf.* The word hung in my head like an accusation against my own stupidity. There was no way in hell I would mention that angle to Morrison. I wasn't anywhere near sure I believed it myself.

"I only started working for Abernathy a few days ago. I don't know a thing about him."

Mostly true.

Morrison scratched his darkening stubble. Most men had to artfully cultivate the kind of rough, sexy shadow that covered his jaw, the kind of facial hair that suggested he might have decent recommendations to offer up on outerwear or aftershave.

"I don't buy it, Hanna. I can respect that you're being loyal to Abernathy because he signs your paychecks, but in this case, that loyalty is misguided. He abandoned you in a foreign country. He obviously doesn't care what happens to you. Do you really want to throw your lot in with a guy like that?"

The implication stung. He was good, this Morrison. Poking an expert finger directly into a dark, squishy bruise on my ego.

"This is not about loyalty. If I had anything concrete, I could give you, I would."

"I hope that's true. For your sake."

"It is." *So long as it didn't incriminate me.*

"Good. Speaking of concrete, do you have anything you can give me to prove you and Abernathy were in Germany, as you have alleged?"

"*Alleged?* I'll give you *alleged.*" I shoved myself to my feet and took a step toward the kitchen to retrieve the receipts I had tucked away in my purse. Only...my legs wouldn't work. Someone had swapped them with wooden pegs from the knee down. I felt them buckling underneath me, deprived of blood while I had been sitting on them. In horrifying slow motion and at a disembodied remove, I watched myself fall toward Morrison. There went my jutting elbow, knocking his coffee cup into his chest. And oh hey! There's my hand, planting itself on his shoulder. Would you look at that? My ass has charted a direct and incontrovertible trajectory towards Morrison's lap!

"Oof!" he grunted.

I struggled to disentangle myself, gushing apologies.

Morrison dabbed at the coffee stain on his shirt with a wadded-up tissue from his pocket. "Hey, it's not every day a woman throws herself in my lap."

They would, I thought, if they knew what you were hiding in those rumpled khakis. Speaking of, I quickly banished thoughts of pole-vaulting myself into the lap I'd just vacated.

"Let me get something to clean that up."

In the kitchen I soaked a towel with warm water and a few pumps of soap and grabbed a second towel to dry.

Scooting in next to him on the couch, I scrubbed at the spot with my rag.

"I think it's coming up!" I said triumphantly.

"Easy," he admonished.

"It's not like you're going to break or anything."

"Really, that's enough," he said. "You're getting me all wet."

"Trust me, this works better while it's still warm."

He leaned back and glanced down at his shirt. "You're pretty good at this."

"I oughta be," I said. "As often as I do it to myself."

"You too, huh?"

"Embarrassingly often. I could go faster if you would stop squirming."

"I'm not squirm—"

My door exploded open without warning, splinters showering inward.

"Just what the fuck is going on here?" Abernathy. In my living room. For the briefest of seconds, his eyes weren't brown, but molten bronze. Pouring over Morrison, then me. His hands tightened into fists as his shoulders squared. A vein pulsed at his temple.

"Mark?" Though I wasn't sure why, I jumped away from Morrison. Why did I feel like a high school kid getting caught playing hide the salami on her parents' couch? This was *my* apartment dammit.

"Where the hell have you been?" Purifying anger boiled out of my brain and singed its way into my limbs.

"We'll get to that later." Abernathy's eyes narrowed, nostrils flaring.

"Actually, I'd like to get to that now." Morrison shifted forward on the couch.

"Fuck off, Morrison," Abernathy said.

"What are you doing here, anyway?" I asked.

Abernathy glanced from me to Morrison accusingly. "What am *I* doing here? How about Fuckchops McGumshoe? What is *he* doing here?"

"It's none of your business what he's doing here. Were you listening at the door?"

"I didn't need to listen at the door. I could smell the distinct aroma of stale coffee and desperation from a mile away."

"*He* stopped by to wheedle me for more information about *you*, and I told him I don't know one goddamned thing! Beyond that, I was going to provide him receipts that confirmed what I told him about us going to Germany together for an art auction."

I strode into the kitchen and dug the receipts out of my purse. Back in the living room, I shoved them at Morrison. "Here!"

"Why are you turning on me all the sudden?" Morrison asked. "I'm not the one who left you in a foreign country."

Abernathy glared at me. "We tattled about that, did we?"

"For your information, I did *not* tell him about that. Mrs. Kass did!"

"Right. Next thing you'll be telling me that you weren't just giving Morrison a knob job."

I hauled back and punched Abernathy as hard as I could in the solar plexus. It felt like cracking my knuckles on a brick wall.

Abernathy didn't flinch. I, on the other hand, blinked back tears.

"Listen you overgrown, oversexed meathead! I was getting up to get the receipts to help save *your* ass, and I fell down. I spilled Morrison's coffee on him, and I was helping him clean it up. End of story."

"And I'm supposed to believe that? Come on, Hanna. If it walks like a duck and talks like a duck..." Abernathy trailed off.

Now this was sounding vaguely familiar.

"You don't have to believe me," I said. "I don't give a furry pink rat's ass what you think. And anyway, who the hell are you to criticize me for what I do in my own apartment, Mr. I'll-screw-anything-with-tits-that-wanders-into-my-hotel-room!"

"What the hell are you talking about?"

"Don't give me that big dumb and innocent act. Penny Bailey! That's what I'm talking about. Happy Tits the Wonderslut!"

Recognition softened his features.

"Hanna," he said. "You don't know what you're talking about."

"I, for one, would love to know what she's talking about," Morrison added. "She didn't mention any of this when we had our little chat earlier."

He had been sitting back casually on the couch taking in the action like a kid at the circus. Now he was fanning the flames of Abernathy's rage purposefully, trying to get one of us to slip up and say something he could use.

"Get out," Abernathy growled to Morrison.

"Hey, this is *my* apartment," I snapped. "If anyone kicks anyone out, it's going to be me." I turned to Morrison. "Get out."

"What about those thirty minutes?" Morrison feigned a wounded expression.

"Out!"

Morrison rose and chugged what was left of his cold coffee. "I'll be back around to talk with you tomorrow," Morrison said.

"Splendid," Abernathy grunted.

We waited in silence to hear the front door to the building shut. I raked over my rage to ready myself for the impending onslaught.

Abernathy sighed, throwing water over my fire of indignation.

"Look, Hanna. I overreacted. I heard what you and Morrison were saying, and I lost it."

A man that admits he's wrong? They make those? Clearly I'd been shopping at the wrong store.

"It's okay." My breath had mostly returned to its normal cadence. "Nothing happened though, just so you know."

"I know. And anyway, it's none of my business. I came over to apologize, if you can believe it."

"For what?" I asked.

"I shouldn't have left you to come back alone. You have to believe that I had no choice."

Now that my eyes were no longer clouded with red-hot rage, I saw his contrite and tired face. Fading pink scratches traced across his forehead, cheeks, and throat. Either Penny was a serious sadist, or Mark had recently lost a fight with a roll of barbed wire.

"What happened?"

"I can't tell you that." A shadow passed behind his eyes, darkening them with words he wouldn't speak.

"And why not?"

"I just can't."

"Oh, well in that case..." I shook my head. "You know, Mark, you're not making this easy for me."

"I know. This probably hasn't been what you thought you were signing on for."

"You are whole-ass correct."

"What I'm trying to say is that it's up to you whether you want to keep working for me. But... I homfrm-mumble." He looked away.

"I'm sorry, what was that last part?"

He exhaled and looked me in the eye. "I hope you will," he said. "Keep working for me."

I would be damned if the worldly, sophisticated

Abernathy didn't look like a lost little boy at that very moment. In the end, it was this that unstitched my anger and righteous indignation.

"As if you could get rid of me that easily."

"You'll stay?" The vulnerability in his voice drove down past my defense nets to a place of shared spiritual topography. He needed me; I needed to be needed.

"Yes, I'll stay. On two conditions."

He folded his arms and gave me a look of mock shrewdness. "Yes?"

"First, I get free rein to organize your office—provided I don't throw anything away without your permission."

"Deal. What else?"

A wave of relief washed over me. *You heard it here first, kids. Hanna is off the hook for unauthorized cleaning.*

"Second," I ticked off a finger, "you're going to get a cell phone."

"A cell phone? Why?"

"I know this sounds crazy, but sometimes when people have to change their plans last minute, like for example, missing their flight back from a foreign country and leaving their assistant to drive to the airport alone with the hotel owner's kinda creepy son, they use these things called cell phones to call and give them a heads up. It's the damnedest thing."

"Okay. I accept the terms."

"Actually, there's one more condition."

He narrowed his eyes, even as a grin worked at the edges of his lips. "You said *two*."

"Three," I insisted.

"Very well," he sighed. "The third?"

"You bust into my apartment like that again, and I'll brain you with my grandmother's cast-iron frying pan."

"Madame," he replied, "you have a deal." He offered me his hand, but instead of shaking mine, he held it.

157

"You have chosen wisely," I assured him.

"Why do I feel like I've just lent the firing squad a handful of bullets?" His thumb traced over my knuckles.

The room was suddenly, unbearably hot.

"If it walks like a duck and talks like a duck..."

"It's probably a duck," he finished for me.

Unless it's a werewolf in a duck suit.

wo items were waiting on my desk the following morning: the first, a werewolf pamphlet from Steven Franke; the second, a steak.

And not just any steak. This was perhaps the most beautifully marbled ribeye I had ever seen in my life. Hand-cut, one-and-one-quarter-inch thick.

I resisted the urge to kiss it passionately, stuff it in my bra, and growl at anyone who came within ten feet. Instead, albeit reluctantly, I read the note scrawled on a scrap of butcher's paper.

"Hanna, Sorry for last night. I hope this will meat your needs.- A."

I mean, God love him though.

A sudden rush of affection for Abernathy flooded my heart. Who had ever heard of sending apologetic meat? Flowers maybe, or chocolates. But meat?

His office door was closed, but a sliver of lamplight glowed in the crack between the bottom of the door and the wood floor.

Shit. I had hoped to beat him in this morning so I could gauge his reaction to his newly cleaned office. Still, the meat was a good sign. He could have taken it back if he was mad at me.

I tapped on the door.

"Come." His harsh command held me back a moment.

My intestines crawled a few inches south as I eased the door open and stepped in.

"Good morning," I said.

The tension gripping my stomach eased when he looked up from his desk and smiled. "Morning," he said. "I see you were busy while I was gone."

"Well, you had paid me in advance. I was just making sure you got your money's worth."

"That, or you were royally pissed at me and felt the need to indulge in a bout of revenge cleaning."

Was I that transparent?

"Everything is still here." I gestured to the boxes in the corner. "Just alphabetized and filed. Some of the older things I put in acid-free plastic sleeves."

"Huh."

"Was that a 'huh' like 'I really wish I hadn't given her that steak,' or a 'huh' like 'I should have bought her a whole tenderloin'?"

"It's a 'huh' like 'huh,'" he said.

"Do you hate me?"

Abernathy emitted a cross between a laugh and a sigh. "Hanna, I don't think that's humanly possible."

Infinitely debatable, that.

"Thanks, by the way," I said. "For the steak."

"Oh. Yes. It was nothing, really. I just wanted to say...you know."

"I do," I said. At least, I hoped I did.

"I trust you won't dishonor the cow by cooking the steak anything more than medium rare." Abernathy leaned back in his chair, turning a pen end over end on his blotter.

"Are you kidding me? I grew up in Texas. Mostly I

just trot the cow past the grill to scare it, then lead it to my plate."

"My kinda girl," he said.

Was I?

"What's on the docket for today?" he asked.

I pulled out my pad and pen from my coat pocket and flipped to the list I had for him. "I hope that wasn't a rhetorical question."

Abernathy's mouth slid into an amused smirk.

"Scott Kirkpatrick wanted to see you about an urgent matter."

"Everything is urgent with him. Next."

"Donald Ivy called asking about the Capuchin monkey skull he had discussed with you a couple weeks ago."

"I'm still waiting on the owner for that one," he said. "Last I heard from her, she felt that the monkey's spirit didn't want to sell."

Monkey spirit doesn't want to sell, I noted on my pad. This job had officially become responsible for some of the strangest sentences I had ever spoken, written, or thought in my life.

"Okey dokey. I'll give Donald a call back and let him know. Next item, Amy Grayson from the Art and Frame shop called and asked if there were any pieces that needed to be framed and prepared for hanging for the next show."

"Shit. That *is* next week, isn't it?"

"So I hear."

"We'll need to check with Mrs. Kass, Steven, and Scott to see if they have anything that needs framing. Rob is the only non-painter."

"I can do that," I said.

"We'll also need to get mailers out, and flyers up in some of the local places."

"Already done." I slid a flyer across his desk. "I got

the mailing list from Rob and sent them out yesterday. I also checked the gallery guest register downstairs and compiled a list of email addresses, which I saved into a spreadsheet. We have a subscriber list and sent out a note to everyone with the show information as well. The only thing I have left to do is call the caterer."

He blinked at me, astonished. "Oh. Good then. Yes. Well."

I might have enjoyed his look of befuddlement just a shade too much.

He cleared his throat. "Was there anything else?"

"Just one thing." I came around the back of his desk and produced a brand-new iPhone from my coat pocket. "For you."

"What's this then?"

"This would be the phone we discussed."

"Ahh."

When he showed no signs of taking the phone, I turned his hand palm up and slapped the phone into it.

Before I could blink, Abernathy had my hand sandwiched between both of his, the phone trapped under my palm.

"Your hands are cold," he said.

"Cold hands, warm heart. Isn't that a thing?"

He rubbed a rough palm over the back of my hand and released it. An instant white-hot jolt tingled up my arm and into my chest, forcing blood into my face, fingers, and feet—among other places.

"Well, anyway." I fumbled in my coat pocket and dropped the instruction manual on his desk. "Here's this. For the phone. I programmed my number in there. And my name. Hanna. In your contacts. Are we good? I think we're good."

I could feel his smile in the back of my neck as I turned on my heel and tripped toward my desk.

Seating myself, I slipped on my nerdiest pair of

reading glasses in hopes of channeling an air of librarian-like prim respectability. The lenses fogged instantly. I picked up Steven Franke's werewolf pamphlet and fanned myself with it. When the blush passed, I scrutinized the cover.

"Werewolves and You," it was titled. On the front page, someone had drawn a crude illustration of a werewolf, though honestly it looked more like an exceptionally aggressive Golden Retriever, gnawing on a young lady's arm. She seemed rather upset by the proceedings, as was indicated by the speech bubble hovering above her head, bearing the words "Oh noooooo!"

At least the artist had refrained from using multiple exclamation points.

Maybe there would be something in here about magic wolfy blood-warming powers or bad puns. I flipped to the introductory page.

Concerned reader,

You will find herein a list of characteristics by which you may identify the common werewolf. These methods have been proven by several independent experts in the field of lycanthropology.

Somehow the words *common* and *werewolf* didn't seem to comfortably share much real estate. I leafed past the intro and came to a stop at "Ten Common Signs of Lycanthropy."

"Bingo," I whispered.

1. Has unusually hairy hands and/or palms and may have conjoined eyebrows.

This I dismissed immediately. Though Abernathy wasn't overly fussy, he almost certainly engaged in occasional manscaping. He was too well groomed not to. Too easily concealed to be any kind of effective indicator.

2. Has small pointed ears or unusually sharp canine teeth

in human form.

I snorted. No, and no. *Why, exactly, was I entertaining this notion again?*

3. May exhibit sweating, shaking, clammy skin, and suffer lapses in memory during week leading up to full moon.

Right then, my mind wandered back to Germany, to the fearful tableau of me bent over Mark as he sweated and shook. I swallowed hard.

4. Often displays naked aggression in confrontational settings. May snarl or bare teeth when upset or startled.

The hair on my scalp prickled. *Mark's face last night when he'd burst in on Morrison in my apartment, the look of killing rage pushing blood into the pulsing veins at his temples.* I read on.

5. Urine may adopt a purplish or maroon hue owing to consumption of raw flesh and blood.

Flesh. I looked at the steak warming on my desk, Abernathy's gift of apology. The fat was turning translucent under the warmth of my lamp. A greasy lump slid down my throat.

"Hanna?"

With my characteristic grace, I shrieked and flung the pamphlet over the railing behind me. Abernathy blinked at me from his doorway.

"Lord almighty," I gasped. "Do I need to put a bell on you?"

"That, or you could lay off the Starbucks."

I laughed nervously, hoping to God that the pamphlet had landed face down.

"Do you want to have Kirkpatrick come up?" he asked. "I might as well swallow that particular frog."

"Sure thing, boss."

I pushed back from my desk and walked downstairs, taking advantage of the opportunity to scoop up the pamphlet and tuck it under my arm as I crossed the gallery to the artists' quarters.

I fortified myself with a deep breath and knocked on Kirkpatrick's door.

He didn't answer. I heard scuttling movements beyond it.

I rapped again, trying to work in a measure of the irritation I felt.

"What do you want?" came the muffled reply.

"Mr. Abernathy is free now, if you would like to see him."

A small rectangular panel abruptly slid to the side at chest height, revealing a cross-section of Kirkpatrick's face. His piggy eyes blinked at me through the gap. I glanced around at the other artist's doors. Kirkpatrick's was the only one with a peephole. Had he installed it himself?

"What is this, the Emerald City?" I bent to meet his eyes at the slot.

"I'm busy now," he said. "Come back later." The slot jerked closed, nearly relieving me of the tip of my nose.

I pounded the door.

"Go away!"

"Open up and talk to me like a civilized human being, you ginger jerk!"

No answer came. *Time to up the ante.*

"Okay, have it your way. I guess I'll just have to scrap that piece about you I put in the *Daily Herald* for the show."

The door opened a fraction. Before he could shut it again, I wedged my boot in the gap.

"Gotcha!" I poured myself into his studio through the narrow opening, rolling his body off the door with a quick shove.

"You can't come in here! Get out!"

"Listen, you have no right to—" My breath seized in my throat, and my tirade dissolved away, caught up on a sudden current of disbelief. I saw the painting Kirkpatrick had been working on before I'd interrupted him.

It was me.

Me, but not me. The painting had something of the Pre-Raphaelite nostalgia. Dreamy, soft brushstrokes like the longing of an ancient paean—the rendering a worshipful love song in paint. My hair was a loose mass of auburn fire set against a cloak of deep emerald satin. And within it, the serene white field of my face, bearing an expression I couldn't identify. I followed the line of sight to my cupped hands, where in the cage of my fingers, a delicate gray bird had made its bower.

I felt the warmth of its feathered heartbeat against my skin and saw the implicit trust in its shining black marble eyes. And oh, the unbearable weight of that trust. This tiny life in my hands. Tears stung a sheen to my eyes, and in blinking them back, I could finally look away.

But they were all around me, those haunted black eyes. Kirkpatrick's work lined the walls of his small studio. From every angle, their plight raked at my soul. A deer with her fawn, otters stealing a playful moment in the sun, ducklings bobbing on the surface of an onyx pond. Impossible, fragile life.

"These are beautiful," I whispered. I felt the sudden humility of one whose worldview has recently shattered. Everything I knew about Kirkpatrick had to be wrong.

"Of course they are." His pointy nose angled toward the ceiling as he sniffed. "I painted them."

Well, maybe not *everything*.

"You could at least be a *tiny* bit chagrined, you know. I did just discover that you've secretly been painting a picture of me, which, by the way, is creepy as hell."

He snorted. "You *would* think that. I was painting a

166

picture of the bird. You're immaterial. Just a background. Of no consequence whatsoever."

"If that's true, why were you trying to keep me from seeing it? Why would you care?"

His eyes sought out the pennies winking up from his loafers. "I don't care. I just don't want people in here. I don't like people." Something flickered across his downturned face. Pain?

"Thus the paintings of animals that are more human than most humans are," I observed.

His reddish eyebrows bunched together. He hadn't expected me to understand this. I wished I didn't.

"Is Abernathy free or not?" He stalked out of the room.

"Hey!" I called after him. "We were having a moment!"

His stout back made no sign of acknowledgment.

Alone in his studio, I considered the painting. However much I wanted to hate the ignoble little prig, he had chops. His manner called to mind the Dutch *little masters*, each item in the painting material evidence of unashamed specificity: feathers, satins, the glassy surface of a wet eye. Detail like this required a kind of attention most people had neither the inclination nor skill to achieve.

Reconciling these contradictory parts of Scott Kirkpatrick's person was too much work for eight o'clock in the morning. Better to cling to my comfortable stereotypes for the moment and save the deep, tricky bits for analysis later.

My attention returned to the pamphlet clamped under my armpit. In the presence of these painted animals, the idea that Abernathy was something other than human seemed patently ridiculous. How had I even allowed myself to consider it?

Back at my desk, I shoved the pamphlet in my

bottom drawer beneath the stack of menus I'd acquired from local caterers and restaurants. Picking hors d'oeuvres for the gallery show—now that was a task I could sink my teeth into. I pulled the top menu from the stack and perused the items leisurely, savoring each description.

Smoked Gouda Beggar's Purses with Mushroom Duxelle. "Come to momma."

Abernathy's door flew open, and Kirkpatrick waddled past me and down the stairs. Abernathy came to the door as if drawn in the wake of Scott's hasty exit.

"Guessing that didn't go well then." I didn't glance up from my menu.

"Does it ever?"

"Not with that little weasel."

"He's not so bad, really, once you get to know him." Abernathy looked over the balcony to where Kirkpatrick's rotund little body had pounded across the gallery.

"I understand the Marquis de Sade's mother said precisely the same thing."

Abernathy chuckled—a rich, welcome, warm sound.

"What is it that has you so enthralled?" he asked, peering over my shoulder.

"I'm looking at menus for—ooh! Brie en croute with rustic fig jam!" Abernathy's features migrated into a pinched, dubious expression. "Figs?"

I rolled my eyes at him. "Don't make that face, mister," I said. "I'd love to let you pick the menu, but I get the feeling our patrons might be interested in something more than Cheetos and beer."

Now Cheetos and wine, on the other hand...

"Oh, my tastes are *much* more exotic than that." Abernathy's eyelids dipped to half-mast.

"Right. Cheetos, beer, and *steak.*" I glanced at the warming meat in the Styrofoam boat on my desk.

"Speaking of which," he said, "we ought to get that on ice. Shall we pop next door to the deli? Shayla will let you borrow a spot in their fridge until you head out for the day."

We. My stomach gave a happy little lurch.

"PLEASE TELL ME YOU'VE COME TO COLLECT HIM." Shayla shifted her tray from her hip to her shoulder and looked down at the end of the counter, where Steven Franke screwed up his features in a mock wounded look.

"Hey, I thought we had something going here."

Steven was seated on one of the Dusty Dahlia's many bistro tables, nursing a cup of coffee. Judging from the debris of coffee creamers and empty sugar packets, he'd been at it for a while. His angular grasshopper's legs swung sideways, too long to fit underneath.

"That something would be *irritation*." She loaded the tray balanced on her arm with plates of food slid through the short-order cook's window.

Today, her cobalt hair was twisted into chunky knots and pinned at the nape of her neck.

"Nice to see you again, Hanna." She nodded at Abernathy and slid around us to deliver the food.

"She's this close to falling for me." Steven held up his thumb and forefinger in a tight pinch. "I can feel it."

"But can she?" Abernathy followed Steven's gaze to Shayla, who hip-checked a chair out of her way.

"How could she help it?" Steven gestured up and down his lengthy torso with two braceleted hands.

Shayla brushed by us with a load of dirty dishes and pushed through a swinging door to the back of the house. She returned, wiping her hands on her apron.

"What can I do for you kids?" She looked directly at Abernathy and me, deliberately avoiding Steven, who had taken to flexing his bicep while lifting his coffee cup.

"I was wondering if I might borrow your fridge," I said, pulling the steak out of my purse.

"You keep steak in your purse?" Shayla laughed. "You just became my new favorite person."

"Not under normal circumstances." *Under normal circumstances, it's cookies.*

"Sure, no problem," she said, reaching for the steak.

I hesitated. "You don't happen to have a marker, do you? Can you put my name on it?"

"Sure." She dug in the drawer beneath the cash register and produced a Sharpie.

I took it and carefully wrote my name on the cellophane.

Four times.

Abernathy grinned.

"Don't judge me," I said. "Is it okay if I stop by to pick it up on my way home today?"

"You bet," she replied. "If I'm not here, just wander back and grab it. I'll put it in the walk-in."

"Thanks, Miss Shayla."

"If you'll excuse me," Abernathy said. "I'll make use of the facilities while we're here."

"Good call," I echoed, trailing him to the restrooms.

I heard him whistling in the tiled expanse next door, then a splash and the unmistakable sound of a steady stream of piss hitting porcelain.

Urine may adopt a purplish or maroon hue owing to consumption of raw flesh and blood.

Oh lawd, this was happening.

I waited until I heard Abernathy wash his hands and the bathroom door close behind him, counting out the crucial seconds it would take for him to return to the foyer to wait for me.

A quick scan of the urinals revealed only the requisite cakes and no trace of any urine, purple or otherwise. I laughed at my own stupidity.

Right up until the intestine-liquefying moment when the door swung open to reveal Abernathy. He stopped short, surprise, dismay, and utter incomprehension warring for supremacy on his features.

"Hanna?" he asked, as if it were more likely that I had a twin who lurked inexplicably in men's bathrooms than it was that I would wander seconds after he'd left.

My eyes darted around the bathroom searching for something, *anything* that might justify my presence here. *Bingo! iPhone, corner pocket.*

I reached out and snatched it up from the brushed steel shelf above the sink.

"I heard an iPhone ringing in here. I thought you might have left yours." If I kept this up, I'd need to carry around a shovel in my purse.

"Oh," he said. "Guilty."

Aren't we all? I handed the phone over to him, and he slid it in his jacket pocket.

The bathroom door erupted inward, and Steven rushed in, looking pale. He glanced from Abernathy to me and past us to the toilet stall.

"I don't wanna break this up or anything, but I've had eight cups of coffee and I got a pot of trouser chili on the back burner." He shifted from foot to foot.

I threw my hands up to allay any further detail. "Just leaving," I said.

Abernathy followed me out.

We nodded to Shayla on our way to the front door. I wondered at Abernathy's ponderously large back as he preceded me down the walk. It looked like a wall of linen holding back a deep pool of unguessable history and unknowable thoughts.

Were any of them about me?

Probably. He just caught you hanging out in the men's room. Because you wanted to check for purple werewolf pee. He's probably thinking you're crazy as a shithouse rat.

A twinge of gratitude for Steven Franke, Mrs. Kass, and even, I was chagrined to admit, Scott Fitzpatrick expanded in my chest. Compared to the regular cast of characters inhabiting Abernathy's life, I wasn't all that odd. What was a little trip to the men's room compared to trouser chili and midgets with anger management issues?

Right?

CHAPTER 12

*A*bernathy's rib cage pinned me face first to the wall as he panted against my neck.

"Yes." His gasp sent a warm current of air toward my sensitive ear. "Now."

I ducked under his arms and looped around behind him, admiring.

"Is it straight?" he asked.

"What? Oh. Yes. Perfect." Tearing my eyes off Abernathy's arms was a considerable effort, particularly when they were stretched to perfect tension, holding up one of Mrs. Kass's near machine-sized paintings.

After hanging the first two, Abernathy had shed his button-up shirt. I, apparently, had shed any sense of decency along with my shoes.

His white undershirt clung to the planes of his back and shoulders like God's own tablecloth. A single bead of sweat left the dark hair at the nape of his neck and slid down his smooth, tanned skin.

For one ludicrous second, I wondered what he'd do if I chased it with my tongue.

"Hanna?"

He'd said something. "Sorry," I said. "What was that?"

"I said, is that good?"

Was that a trace of amusement in his voice?

"Actually." I stepped back, evicted from my appreciative trance. "The left side needs to come up just a titch."

Abernathy shifted, and once again, my gaze was drawn to the change of shadows carved into his bicep by the track lighting overhead. *Not just good for paintings.*

"Juuust a titch more."

Another flex.

"There! Perfect."

He backed away and joined me where I stood considering the wall bearing Mrs. Kass's three gigantic paintings. I'd decided they were non-representational, but with her visual acumen, they might have been portraits or even still lives. Who could say?

"How on earth does she paint these things?" I asked. "She's all of five foot nothing."

He shrugged. "I've never watched her work."

"Are her paintings usually this size?"

"They vary. She sells surprisingly well."

"Really?"

He nodded. "Not as well as Kirkpatrick. But yes."

I glanced over to the wall where we'd hung Scott's five framed paintings. I still had difficulty looking at them for any length of time.

"I'm a little surprised he sells as well as he does," I commented. "If I had one of these on my wall, I'd have to fight the urge to leap from my window every morning. There's so much pain in them."

"I suspect not many people pick up on that. They just want something that won't clash with the sofa."

"What about Steven?" I asked. His work was stacked against the far wall, awaiting our attention. Like Kirkpatrick, Steven painted animals. Only his were portraits. Ascot-wearing badgers. Rabbits with reading glasses. Wolves in suits. Whimsical and wonderful, like the artist himself.

"He has his own following. Some of his smaller works sell locally. He has a few out of state collectors from larger markets."

I looked from wall to wall, amazed at how present these artists all were, though they had long since gone home. Their work spoke for them in this silent space.

Abernathy and I alone remained, hanging madly in preparation for tomorrow's gallery show. Winter's early darkness pressed against the windows of the gallery. It was time to get moving.

"Shit," said Abernathy, lifting the first canvas. "Do you want to hold this while I fix the hanging bracket?"

"Sheesh. This is heavier than it looks."

"I think he uses lead paint."

I suppressed an eye roll.

He pushed the hair out of his eyes and bent forward, staring at the offending bracket. His fingertips worked against the back of the canvas millimeters from the curve of my breast.

A slick of sweat bloomed beneath my fingers where I grasped the frame. I tried to readjust for better purchase, but the painting slid from my hands and darted downward.

Abernathy had it sandwiched between us in a flash. His thigh, bearing the canvas's full weight, was wedged between my legs as his big, warm hands closed over my upper arms.

He looked at me from beneath dark lashes, the world quieting around us so it too could hear the sounds of our breathing. "Close call."

"Uh huh."

I waited for him to release me and grab the painting. He didn't.

Had it always been such an effort to force air into my lungs?

His gaze wandered down the length of my face, stopping at my mouth.

What little air I managed froze in my chest. Even drawing a breath seemed like it might be enough movement to break the spell.

His head lowered toward mine in impossible increments. *He was going to kiss me.* Mark Andrew Abernathy, murder suspect, possible werewolf, ridiculously beautiful globetrotting multi-millionaire, was going to kiss *me.*

My eyelids fluttered closed as I felt the heat from his lips through the fraction of air that separated us.

"I should have known it wouldn't take you long." The mocking voice sliced through the red haze of lust curtaining us.

Mark jerked away, grabbing Steven's canvas in the split second before it clattered to the floor between us.

Dazed, I looked around to find the source of these unwelcome words, even as my brain summoned recognition of their familiar sound.

Dave. Now available with douchey blond highlights. Lady boner officially lost.

"We're closed." Abernathy squared his shoulders to him.

"The door was open." Dave nodded his gel-slicked spikey head toward the oddities shop.

"Dave, what are you doing here?"

"You know him?" Abernathy asked.

"Oh, believe me, she *knows* me."

The suggestion in his voice threatened to resurrect my afternoon snack. A disgusted sigh worked its way up instead. No avoiding it now.

"Mark, this is my ex-husband, Dave the fuckstick. Dave the fuckstick, Mark Abernathy, my boss."

Abernathy looked him over but didn't offer his hand. He turned away and resumed his work on the painting to give us some privacy.

"Boss, huh? Looks like you're working some *overtime.*"

I grimaced. "Did you have a particular reason for stopping by, or are you just here to resume your tireless pursuit of ruining my life?"

"Funny thing to say to the best thing that ever happened to you."

"I reiterate my previous question. What do you want?"

His features arranged themselves into the mask of self-satisfaction I had grown to detest before the end. He reached into his jacket and withdrew a folded sheaf of papers.

"Read it and weep," he said, flourishing them dramatically.

I snatched the bundle and flipped through a few pages of legalese.

"Petitioner is contesting custody of cats jointly acquired during the marriage?" I stared at him, aghast. "You've got to be fucking *kidding* me. You didn't even want them. No. Out of the question." I shoved the papers into his bony sternum.

"It's come to my attention that you've been neglecting them. Leaving them in that shoebox of an apartment while you take off for days at a time..." His manicured hand trailed through the air is if underscoring a dozen more accusations he thought but wouldn't say.

I fought a sudden and inexplicable urge to bite him. Imagining the abject shock wipe the arrogant smirk from his face as I clamped my teeth into his palm-meat brought me a surge of sudden pleasure. "I had someone taking care of them. I told you that."

"But the judge doesn't. The way I see it, if I have the cats, my upcoming request for spousal support will be so much more compelling."

"You—*what*? Spousal support?"

"I worked while you finished your degree. I think it's only fair that you contribute while I'm finishing mine."

"Are you out of your mind? You worked part-time because you dropped out. I worked too. While I went to school full-time." Salt stung my eyes.

He shrugged. "My lawyer seems to think I've got a good shot. Particularly since I'm living in a house these days, and you've got those poor little cats cooped up in a tiny apartment."

"You live in your mother's basement. It's not even your house!"

He sighed overdramatically. "Look, babe. Let's not do this. You can't afford a lawyer. I hate all the ugliness. Why don't we just arrange a monthly payment, and we can avoid the whole thing. You keep the cats. I go to school. Everyone wins."

"You're blackmailing me with my own *cats*?"

"Don't think of it as blackmail, think of it as—"

But he didn't have time to finish. Or perhaps it wasn't time, but air, he lacked. Abernathy's hand was around Dave's throat, driving his back two feet up the gallery wall. Dave's eyes bugged out of his head like glassy marbles. I couldn't tell if it was the pressure from air caught in his trachea or just pure, good old-fashioned shock.

Abernathy's voice was a low growl. Picking out words was like trying to grab stones from a rushing river.

"Ever...near her... will find you...keg for death."

Or was that *beg*?

Dave jerked a compliant little nod and slid to the

ground like a string-less marionette as Abernathy abruptly released his grip. It took Dave a moment to stack his joints back into a standing position.

He bolted. If this had been a cartoon, he would have left a little jet of smoke in his wake.

Dave's departure left us in a bell jar of sudden, stifling silence. Abernathy snagged me in his gaze, his eyes the exact shade of scotch on the rocks.

The moment was there, but I chickened out. He read it in my face.

"Right." He reached down, grabbed the canvas, and hung it neatly on the wall.

Perfect the first time, I noted with disappointment.

"Are we about good?" I asked. "Because I have a date with a certain steak."

"Far be it from me to get in the way of carnivorous pursuits." Abernathy bent to retrieve his button up shirt and mopped the back of his neck with it.

"Thanks," I said. "For...for before. You really didn't have to do that."

"I *wanted* to."

Goosebumps danced up my arms. *Wanted.*

"Get some rest," Abernathy said before I could make a tension-annihilating joke. "We have a big day tomorrow."

And we did.

Bigger than either of us knew.

IN TERMS OF DISASTROUS PAIRINGS, MRS. KASS'S HIGH-heeled shoes and Rob Vincent's delicate ceramics were right up there with cabernet sauvignon and dog food.

She had a real Mrs. Havisham thing going on tonight in her faded floral print gown, mink wrap, white gloves, and tottery velvet pumps.

179

Between my shifts of supervising the food tables and welcoming gallery guests, I had become her unofficial babysitter.

More than once I'd steered her gently from near disaster as she alternately backed into and tried to introduce herself to the clear plastic pedestals.

In the throes of desperation, I slid up to Steven when he was between groups of admiring patrons.

"Looking good, doll," Steven said, giving me the once-over.

I had gone with my go-to little black dress and added red patent leather peep-toe pumps for a splash of color. Dried naturally and curled within an inch of its life, my hair was big enough to yank a small star system out of planetary orbit.

Steven had selected a black tuxedo print t-shirt, bright yellow plaid pants, and black Chuck Taylors.

"Looking good yourself."

He did a little tap dance by way of acknowledgment.

"I really hate to ask this since it's really your night and all. But I need your help. Mrs. Kass…" I trailed off, trying to locate her through the crowd.

"Gotcha," he said, thumbing invisible suspenders. "Johnny Danger is on the case!"

"Thanks, Steven. I owe you huge."

"All in a day's work." He bowed and sauntered off in Mrs. Kass's direction.

I ducked through the crowd and paused in front of Scott Kirkpatrick's door, the little slot, his portal to the world, firmly shut. I pecked on the metal, hoping the sound would carry into his studio.

"Scott," I said to the door. "Could you please come out?"

"No!"

"Everyone is asking for you." A lie, technically, but a well-intentioned one.

"I don't care."

The desire to take the door off its hinges and drag him out by his piggy nostrils was overwhelming. Instead, I dug deep for whatever was left of my three-day stint as a daycare lunch lady. It was impossible to bargain with a three-year-old. But you could tell him the nap monster would come and eat him if he was not lying down on his cot in ten seconds.

"Now Scott, if you don't come out, I'm afraid I'll just have to tell everyone your paintings aren't for sale. You don't want that, do you?"

Silence.

"Okay then," I sang. "Here I go to take the price tags off."

I clomped my stilettos on the wood floor, softening the pressure every couple steps.

"I know you're still there!" Scott shouted. "You won't take the tags off. Abernathy wouldn't let you."

My bluff was being called by a rotten little Oompa Loompa of a man with a fly fisherman's vest and a narcissistic personality disorder.

"Fine, stay in there. But just so you know, your fingers look like Vienna sausages." I stepped away to indulge in a modest panic attack. Bending over, I put my ears between my knees and squeezed my eyes shut. That was supposed to do something, right?

"I'd lend you my paper bag, but I left it in the car."

From the space between my calves, I saw Morrison slouching against the wall behind me.

"Aww, shit." The world turned itself right with a dizzying rush as I stood up.

"I think I'm hurt," Morrison said, raising a hand to his chest. A chest that, I had to admit, was filling out his crisp blue button-down shirt rather nicely. He looked decidedly un-coplike in jeans.

I peeked around the corner and saw Abernathy and

CYNTHIA ST. AUBIN

Rob Vincent chatting up a handful of assorted groupies. Why hadn't I noticed that the gallery's subscriber list was about 85% female when I was sending out invitations? At least they were occupied for the moment.

"Please," I said to Morrison. "Please just turn around and go back to your cop car. Or to a bar. Or a strip club, or pretty much anywhere on Earth but right here, right now."

"What?" he said, his face a convincing mask of angelic innocence. "Aren't I entitled to be a patron of the arts?"

"Right. If you can name four artists who were not also Teenage Mutant Ninja Turtles, I'll eat my shoe."

"Chagal, Matisse, Kandinsky, Rodin."

"Fluke. Who's your favorite Impressionist?"

"I don't like Impressionism."

"Nice try," I said. "*Everyone* likes impressionism."

"Really. I'm not into masturbatory, sun-dappled, pastel puke. But, Post-Impressionism? Dark. Twisted. Gritty. Why jerk off when you can fuck dirty?"

Something rabid broke loose and ripped through me like a hook. I did my level best not to climb him like a tree.

"I kind of like proving you wrong." Morrison grinned. "But I'll ask you not to eat your shoe. That would be a terrible waste." His gaze traveled down my leg.

"Okay, fine, you know art," I conceded, gathering my wits. "But we both know that is *not* why you are here."

"Perhaps not."

"Look, I'll level with you. I've got one artist locked in his studio pouting, another talking to houseplants, hordes of women trying to hump my boss, and a caterer who can't find his ass with either hand. The last

182

thing I need is a pissing contest right in the middle of the gallery. This is my first show, and if you ruin it, I am going to beat the ever-loving shit out of you with a wooden spoon, so help me God."

"Promise?" He smirked.

Steam erupted from my nostrils, and my left eye began to twitch.

"Relax," he said. "I'm not going to make trouble for you. I'm just here to observe."

I eyed him suspiciously.

"Have you given any thought to our conversation the other night?" He leaned in a shade too close for comfort.

Which part?

"I got some pretty interesting DNA results back from Helena's body. The area around the neck wounds in particular."

"Good for you," I said.

"The DNA was *canid*." He watched my face to see how this last word landed.

"Canid?"

"Canine."

"It might not have been a murder at all then. Maybe she was attacked by dog or a—"

But the words were gone. Goosebumps rose on my skull and took a roller coaster ride down my spine.

Wolf.

"Pretty talented dog that can close and lock the door after himself."

"So, what? You think someone used a dog as a murder weapon?" I asked. "That seems like a bit of a stretch."

"Maybe. Or maybe someone purposefully left non-human DNA at the crime scene to muddy the waters. There was a farmer who murdered his wife a few years back. He slaughtered a pig in the same spot to ruin the blood evidence."

"Well it obviously didn't work too well, if you know what happened."

"He didn't count on his eight-year-old daughter watching daddy feed mommy's body to the pigs."

I shuddered.

"But speaking of DNA." Morrison shifted his weight as he changed gears. "I've politely asked your boss to come in and provide a sample."

"I can't imagine that went over well."

"Indeed not. In fact, I believe he suggested a couple orifices where I could store my polite request."

A smile crawled across my face.

"I don't suppose you know where I might find any of his DNA. Say, on a tissue, a coffee cup, something in the trash, perhaps?"

In fact, I knew about fifty places Morrison could find it, but that was entirely beside the point.

"You're not seriously asking me this."

He didn't blink.

"You are out of your fool mind, Morrison."

"That may be true, but it doesn't change the fact that I need his DNA, and I know you can get it for me."

"Let me guess. You can't muster enough evidence to get a warrant for it, and you don't know where he disposes of his trash. Am I right?"

His silence answered for him.

"Oookay." I held up my hands and slid around him. "I think I'm done here." I turned to walk away, but he snagged me by the upper arm.

"Want to know how many ladies Abernathy has been *involved* with in the last year?" His heated whisper hit my ear with staccato bullets. "Care to know how many of them have disappeared?"

I shook my head, wanting to empty it of suspicion.

"I don't have time for this." Wriggling away, I pushed my way into the crowd, scanning for Steven and Mrs. Kass.

I found half of what I was looking for. Steven—standing in front of one of his canvases, a shock of bright blue hair visible between passing patrons. *Shayla.*

"There you are." Abernathy took my elbow and steered me behind a secluded divider. He began to speak, but stopped abruptly, his nostrils twitching. Darkness passed over his features like the shadow of a predatory bird circling overhead. "Where is he?"

I blinked up at him, wondering how the hell he knew Morrison was here, and who had stapled my eyebrows to my hairline. "Who?"

"Morrison."

I threw on the mental brakes and took a hairpin turn away from the cliff. "Oh, Morrison." I laughed, about as casual as an undertaker. "Mrs. Kass invited him to stop by, I think."

Abernathy's eyes searched my face, which now bore a smile that felt like it was being propped up by toothpicks.

"As long as he behaves himself, he can stay. But I won't have you chatting with him, Hanna. This is work. While you're here, you belong to *me*."

A chill spilled down my spine.

"And is this why you dragged me away from my *work*? To tell me not to chat with the patrons? Last time I checked, that was part of my duties as hostess." The three anxiety-soothing glasses of white wine had finally caught up with me, it seemed.

"No." He folded his arms across his broad chest. "I wanted to tell you this is the best turnout we've ever had. We've sold almost everything."

"Really?"

"It's all your fault," he whispered close to my ear.

We were standing almost on the very spot where we'd been last night, when the painting on the other side of this wall had been sandwiched between us.

A crash echoed through the crowded space.

Mrs. Kass.

"If you'll excuse me." I nodded to Abernathy.

I found her planted butt-first on a tray of prosciutto and melon, her bony legs twitching in the air like a geriatric beetle. One of the glass water pitchers lay in shards on the floor nearby, where a white-shirted server mopped at the mess with a tablecloth.

"Oh, Mrs. Kass," I clucked, pulling her to her feet. "Let me help you."

"Goodness. Why on earth is there a bench right in the middle of the room where a body can trip on it?"

"Poor planning, I suppose." Next time I would be sure to rope off the food table with parking cones, road flares and a foghorn.

I grabbed a handful of napkins from the table and dabbed at the back of Mrs. Kass's dress. "It looks like you've got a little balsamic reduction here."

"A duck?" She squinted through her lenses. "Where?"

"Stay right here," I said a little louder. "I have a Tide stick at my desk!" I pointed both fingers to the floor.

Steven caught my eye as I loped toward the stairs and mouthed an apology. I waved a hand at him and gave him a thumbs up.

A flash of white paper on the printer/fax/copier by my desk caught my eye as I plucked the Tide stick from my drawer.

Impossible. I'd only set up the machine this morning. I hadn't printed so much as a recipe for brie en croute.

I lifted the sheet out of the tray and glanced over it. It looked to be a photocopy of a newspaper article. My knees gave way as the picture and byline shifted into focus.

"Local antiques dealer found murdered, maimed in coastal German town."

It was Penny Bailey.

CHAPTER 13

A fog of unintelligible noise drifted up from the gallery below, the discordant din of too many conversations. I didn't remember sitting down but felt the wood floor beneath my palms. The world began to widen beyond the circle of black that telescoped my vision.

Out.

My entire consciousness rearranged itself around this one goal. I scrambled to my feet, grabbed my purse and keys, and flew down the stairs.

Steven was saying something. I looked through him, tracking Abernathy.

My face felt numb, detached, composed of dead meat I could not move. My lips jerked, twitched, tripped over words. I hoped I'd managed to complete an apology, to excuse myself.

Free in the icy night air. Cold droplets settled onto my face, my arms. I'd left my coat.

The Mustang slept under a thin blanket of frozen mist. I slid behind the steering wheel and puffed irregular clouds into the car's familiar air. The keys were clumsy in my hands, shards of metal some ancient civilization had left to befuddle me. Numb fingers finally managed to turn the engine over.

The car slammed into gear and fishtailed as I took the first of many wrong turns on the way home.

BLISSFUL NUMBNESS: I HAD FOUND IT AT LAST. A delicious heaviness settled into my limbs as the vodka worked its way into my bloodstream.

Somewhere on the edges of my shrinking awareness, a prim, irritating voice lectured me. *"Drinking is not a charactered adult response to emotional distress, Hanna."*

"Well, if my husband wasn't sleeping with our marriage counselor, maybe I wouldn't haff to," I answered her, about six months too late.

"Seriously," I slurred to the cats. "What kind of marriage therapist sleeps wither clients? That's what I wanna know. He wasn't even good in bed."

I counted seven more sips of rubied liquid from my glass. That ought to shut her up.

"Feeling is overrated."

Six more sips. Another wave of blessed warmth settled over me. "I do think I'll have another."

The ice clinked as it danced into my glass, followed by a gurgling waterfall of vodka. "Who says I'm not an optimist?" I giggled. "See? Half full."

On the couch, I counted down eleven sips. "This is probably a bad idea." My cats looked at me through a scrim of fading pink at the glass's bottom.

Penny's face surprised me in the darkness behind my eyelids. "Leave me alone," I whispered.

All thought evaporated. Time was liquid. The universe reeled. Hunger gnawed at my empty gut.

I staggered to the fridge and ate propped against the

open door. My hand froze midway to my face at the sound of rustling in the bushes below my kitchen window. *Scratching. Growling.* I parted the kitchen curtains and met a flash of green, the brief reflection of animal retinas. Then nothing.

"Uh oh." I burped.

The bathroom lurched toward me, and I gripped the cold porcelain, evacuating the whole guilty mess of vodka, cranberry, cheese, and the last few shreds of my carefully chosen appetizers.

The shower's handle squeaked toward scalding under my palm as I crawled fully clothed into the claw-footed tub. There I sat with hands dug into the mass of my wet hair as tears and the shower's spray mingled in a common stream down the drain.

"OH GOD," I MOANED, PULLING THE PILLOW TIGHTER around my head.

Please make it stop, I begged, sending the lush's age-old prayer to the heavens. *I swear I will never drink again. I'll help orphans. I'll go back to church. I'll stop saying fuck so much. Anything. Just please—*

Bangbangbang!

I sat up straight in bed, realizing the pounding was not, in fact, just in my head.

The sand of drunken sleep and unwashed make-up glued my eyes together. I stumbled to the front door and pried it open a crack.

Morrison.

Was there no end to the humiliation? I unlatched the chain and stood in the narrow gap.

"Jesus H. Christ," he muttered, looking me over foot to head in a single sweep.

"But can you tell me what the 'H' stands for?" I

yawned, wandering away and flopping face first back down on the bed. "No one seems to know that," I mumbled into my pillow.

"Rough night?"

A grunt was the most intelligent answer I could manage.

He sighed deeply. I heard the rustle of his coat dropping onto the couch, his footsteps receding into the kitchen.

The combined smells of coffee, eggs, onions, and potatoes slid their silken fingers into the gray hell of my coma. Morrison cleared his throat, and I peeked out from under my pillow to find a full English breakfast basking in resplendent sunlight on my coffee table. Deciding it was a dream, I retreated back under the covers.

Morrison laid a hand on the small of my back and gave my hips a little shake. "Rise and shine."

With considerable effort, I rolled myself into a sitting position.

He held out his hand and dropped four ibuprofen and two Dramamine into my palm. Steam curled from the dark, creamy coffee he offered to wash down the meds.

"You've done this before." The rich, warm liquid sluiced down my throat, warming my belly.

"Once or twice."

I scooted to the edge of my bed, looked down at my lap and froze, confused.

"When I answered the door, was I, uh— did I…?"

He shook his head in the negative.

"Sorry," I said. "I usually wear pants." My blanket became a makeshift toga as I padded over to the couch.

"You don't hear me complaining." He plopped down next to me, and we ate in silence.

"This is good," I said around a mouthful of hash brown and toast. "Garlic and basil?"

He nodded.

"Knows about Post Impressionism and can cook. You're just determined to blow my stereotypes all to hell."

He shrugged. "I like to eat."

"We have that in common."

"Among other things."

"I'm too hungover to blush."

"Good to know."

I drained the remainder of my coffee and used my toast to mop up the last of Morrison's perfectly over-medium eggs. "I may live."

"Good." The thump of his mug on the coffee table marked a clear line in the conversation. "Where the hell did you go last night?"

I sighed and slumped back against the couch. "So, this breakfast has ulterior motives, then."

"I wouldn't be much of a cop if it didn't."

"I just felt like leaving."

Exasperated, he shoved himself up off the couch and walked to the window.

"You pull Rosemary's ass off the hors d'oeuvres, run upstairs, grab something at your desk, then toss your—"

"Wait. Rosemary?"

"That's Mrs. Kass's first name," he clarified. "We've been in touch."

"Touching."

"What was it?" He turned and pinned me with his stare.

"What was what?"

"Quit being cute."

I smoothed the blanket over my thighs and tucked a

crazed wisp of hair behind my ear. "I didn't think that was an option in my present state."

"You know what I mean."

I stared at the floor. My adventures of the evening previous hadn't afforded me much chance to process what I'd seen. I didn't know what to tell myself, let alone anyone else.

"Look. You and Mark have a history that doesn't involve me. What happened with him and Helena is none of my business. She stopped by the gallery once while I was there."

"On the day she was murdered."

Murdered, maimed.

I shuddered involuntarily.

"Chilly?" he asked.

We both knew better.

Morrison's pocket vibrated and belted out a tinny version of Neil Diamond's "Cracklin' Rosie."

I raised an eyebrow at him.

"Morrison." He pronounced his own name like a threat.

Silence while he received news from the other end.

"I'll be right there." He snapped his phone closed and dropped it back in his pocket.

"Get dressed. We're going on a field trip."

"Uh, thanks, but I'll pass."

"It wasn't a request."

"Someone has a slightly over-inflated sense of his influence in my world."

"You have two options." He held his thumb and index finger for emphasis. "You can go get dressed, or I can drag you out to my car in your blanket. Or, *I* could always dress you. That could be fun. So, three options, I guess."

I inspected his face and determined he wasn't kidding. This was not a fight I was going to win.

"Five minutes," I said. I gathered up my blanket and shuffled over to the closet, where I snagged a pair of jeans and a sweater.

In the tiny bathroom, I scrubbed my face at the sink and smoothed my hair back into a braid. Five minutes gave me time for some quick concealer, blush, and mascara. Ten minutes, and I could have knit him a scarf.

By the time I made it into the kitchen, Morrison was finishing the last of the breakfast dishes and loading the drainer. The sight of him at the sink hit me like a sucker punch to the gut. A man in my kitchen. A man with a broad back and a damn near perfect ass, washing my dishes. He ran a hand through his thick brown sugar-colored hair and slung the dishtowel over his shoulder.

I wanted to ride him to Timbuktu and bake him a pie when we got there.

"The domesticated male. Rare to see one in the wilds."

"You should see me do laundry. I even use fabric softener."

"Gold star for you." I dug through my sock drawer and decided on my thickest, coziest pair.

"And what does a gold star earn me?" he asked.

"My respect as a human being."

"Not exactly what I was hoping for."

"A cookie then?"

"Closer."

I spent a little extra time shrugging into my coat and pulling on a beanie. There would be no fixing the hair after this.

"You must be feeling better."

"Why is that?"

"You're blushing."

I narrowed my eyes at him and pointed to the door.

"Out." Locking the door behind me, I followed him down the stairs.

"I hope they pay you extra for driving that," I said, appraising the familiar gold Crown Victoria parked at the curb in front of the Mustang. At least they'd paid to have the bumper fixed after our little run-in.

"This is my personal vehicle."

Open mouth, insert foot.

"Oh."

"It has a V8. And it's roomy," he added.

"Right. And damn near indestructible, if I remember correctly."

It was a little stale, but then, it had been a while since I dusted off the "repair the wounded male pride" chops.

He took a moment to shovel papers out of the passenger's seat before crossing around to the driver's side.

I climbed into the car and into air intensely Morrison. Layers of scents I couldn't identify, but what I suspected were cologne, laundry detergent, and something altogether his.

The back seat was littered with fast food wrappers and discarded gas station coffee cups.

"Spend much time in here?"

"On occasion." He cranked the engine over and turned toward town.

My phone chirped inside my purse. I glanced at the clock on Morrison's dash. 9:48 a.m. on a Friday. Abernathy would be sitting at his desk by now. I checked the logs reluctantly. I'd missed several calls last night. Three from Abernathy, one from Steven Franke.

And now, a text from Abernathy.

Hanna? Are you okay?

I felt a stab of guilt. Abernathy hated phones, and here he was, calling and texting to check on me. Worried about me? *Or worried about what I knew?* Panic gripped my chest. Had I left the article?

I dug through my purse. Relief washed over me as I pulled the paper out and refolded it, tucking it safely away.

"Problems?"

"Nope, no problems," I answered, a little too brightly.

Another text. *Is thi sworking?*

I composed and recomposed a reply. *Hey there. Sorry for taking off last night. I think I ate something that didn't agree with me. Still feeling under the weather. Call if you need anything.*

His reply came a full minute later.

Okay. Feel butter.

Shit. Fell butter.

Better. Why does this ducking thing keep changing my swords?

I smiled in spite of myself.

Welcome to the world of autocowrecks, I typed.

No reply this time.

I thought of my empty desk, of Abernathy, of Steven Franke. The bitter taste of jealousy coated my throat. I didn't want life at the gallery to be happening without me. I didn't want to be in Morrison's car. I didn't want Penny to be dead.

The flash of blue and red bounced off the Crown Vic's gold hood as we pulled up behind a passel of cop cars clogging the entrance to the Clear Creek Greenway.

Yellow tape roped off a section of damp grass down by the creek's edge, where uniformed cops were milling around and chatting in scattered clumps.

Realization congealed in my stomach. "You brought me to a crime scene?" Morrison didn't answer. He maneuvered himself out of the car, came around to my side, and pulled the door open.

"Come on," he said. "Let's go."

I shook my head violently. "No. No way. Whatever is down there, I have no interest in seeing it."

"You need to see it."

"But I can't be here. I'm just a civilian."

"Unless you're my *expert witness*."

Fear crushed my chest like an aluminum can. Some part of me, however small, had to know. I wanted out of uncertainty's limbo. I needed something concrete.

I left my purse in the car and trailed after Morrison through the trees and down the small slope.

There, between the bodies clearing at Morrison's approach, I saw her.

A dead body. Mangled. Throatless.

Hers was not the first corpse I'd seen.

The car crash that had claimed my father in my eighth year had left him intact enough for an open casket.

My grandmother, my sweet Oma, who had survived eighty-four years on the planet only to be shot dead in a home invasion. Her good heart shredded by the bullet that tumbled through it sideways.

The death that had come for the woman down the hill hadn't been anything as swift as either scenario. Work had been required to relieve her of her throat. The kind of work that she would have seen with her open eyes before it was finished.

Morrison's breakfast lurched in my stomach. I sat down hard to keep it from climbing my throat.

Dead. Death. Dying.

A whole life running from these words.

They'd caught up with me at last.

"THE WOMAN YOUR BOSS LEFT THE GALLERY WITH LAST night."

Morrison's words were a haunting refrain.

Jealousy tore through me like a tidal wave, shocking me. A woman lay dead in my line of sight and jealousy was the chief emotion I felt?

Images assailed my mind like shrapnel. Abernathy and this dark-haired beauty. How long after I left had he bagged his prize?

How naïve of me to be surprised after all I'd learned of Abernathy's habits. Was discarding ruined women just another aspect of his carefully guarded M.O.?

"I want to go home," I informed Morrison.

"Can't," he said. "Not yet. I have some work to do here."

"Then you shouldn't have brought me here to play show and tell. Take me home. Now." I looked beyond him to the crime scene technicians, who had resumed their ministrations. Taking pictures, collecting samples.

Morrison turned his back to me and walked over to another officer, who cast a worried glance at me before waddling in my direction.

Without as much as a word to me, Morrison stalked back over to the crew hovering around the body like so many flies and resumed his work.

"Looks like I'll be taking you home," the officer said.

"Peachy. I'll grab my purse from Morrison's car."

The heady aroma of Morrison's breakfast still hung in the house when I arrived. I kicked off my shoes, crawled back into bed, and prayed that sleep would come before the tears.

I AWOKE TO A SOUND, SWEATING, DISORIENTED, UNSURE where my dreams ended and life began. A piteous animal wail followed by the ripping barks of a dogfight. I disentangled myself from my blankets and crept to the window. The darkness kept its secrets, its only movement the rustle of wind through dead trees.

I clicked on the lamp and bathed my small combined living and bedroom in the warm glow. The cats were curled into various spots on the deluxe scratching post Steven Franke had brought over.

My chest contracted. I missed him already. I should text him at least and let him know I was okay.

Was I okay?

The answer to that didn't matter. I didn't want him to worry.

I dug my phone out of my purse and saw I had more missed text messages. One from Steven, several from Abernathy.

I read Steven's first.

If you're receiving this text message, it's because you know me. Pat yourself on the back friend. You're a winner! Seriously though, are you okay?

I smiled, hearing his voice in my head, and clicked over to Abernathy's chain of texts.

Feeling any butter
Better.
What does this flushing green light mean?
Flashing. Cod damn it.
I give up. Hope you're feeling better.
Ha! First time!

Even now, Abernathy's technological ineptitude felt vastly endearing. I couldn't reconcile these parts of him. Helpless and charming, secretive and aggressive. He was all these things, yet try as I might, I couldn't make *murderer* stick. These texts. His kindness to Steven, Scott, and Mrs. Kass. His patience with me.

But there could be no denying that he cut a path through the world towing death in his wake. Two dead women in our town, one in Germany, others missing, all seen last with Abernathy. And that spoke nothing of strange habits and torn throats. What possible explanation could tie these facts up into a neat and acceptable truth?

I ignored this and other questions for the moment and composed a text thanking Steven for checking on me and letting him know I was okay.

Abernathy's messages would have to go unanswered. Everything I came up with seemed stiff and ridiculous. It was all wrong, and he'd know it in an instant. I powered the phone off, having had enough of both truth and lies today.

A brisk knock at the door sent me shooting out of my skin. I had come to recognize that particular pattern.

I opened the door but left the chain latched, feeling a little like Kirkpatrick as I spoke to him through the narrow gap.

"I don't like you very much," I said, by way of greeting.

"I suspected that might be the case, so I brought some friends." Morrison reached behind his back and produced a box of doughnuts.

"Bastard." He could have been holding a severed head in the other hand, and I probably would have let him in. I unlatched the chain and wandered over to the couch, leaving him to let himself in.

He set the doughnuts on the table and dropped his coat on the couch.

I tore the box in my haste and shoved a still-warm glazed doughnut into my mouth.

"This doesn't mean I forgive you," I mumbled around the melting mouthful.

"It doesn't mean I'm asking," he replied, selecting a raspberry-filled doughnut for himself. I tried not to notice as he addressed a blob of jelly with a precise, controlled flick of his tongue.

Dark shadows sculpted his jaw and lingered under his eyes. The slacks that had been neatly pressed this morning were now rumpled, his shirt stained with coffee and I didn't want to think what else.

"Her name was Amy Grayson," he said casually.

A tingle of recognition worked its way down my spine. *Amy Grayson from the Art and Frame shop.*

"I didn't ask." I leaned forward and snagged a maple-iced doughnut, brushing flakes of glaze from my lap with my free hand.

"She worked with your boss regularly, as it turns out."

The way he said "your" suggested pet ownership more than working relationship.

"Oh?"

"What do you mean 'Oh?'" He mimicked my tone with surprising accuracy. "You already knew that."

I said nothing.

"See that's the thing about being a detective. I find shit out. I talked to her office. They said she's been framing the gallery's works for about a year now. And that this time, she'd coordinated everything through you."

"I only talked to her on the phone. I had no idea what she looked like." I discarded the second half of my doughnut, my appetite suddenly gone.

"But I'll bet your boss did."

"If she's been framing art for him for a year, he ought to know what she looks like."

"Must be why he hunted her down last night." He let the word *hunted* hang in the air suggestively before continuing in his own time. "At the show, that is. That must have been after you took off."

I looked away.

"She was there for a long time, as I remember. Second to last person to leave. That is, if you count Abernathy holding the door open for her when they left together."

And didn't he know just what to say to wound.

"Third to last," I corrected. "As you were obviously still lurking around watching them."

Irritation creased his features. He switched tactics.

"Where was your boss today, anyway? I stopped by the gallery for one of our little chats, but surprise, surprise, he wasn't around."

"Beats the hell out of me." I shrugged. "I thought *you* were the detective here."

A disgusted sigh erupted from his throat.

"Are you ignorant or just stupid? How many more bodies do you need before you fucking get it?"

The dam broke, and I stormed over to the window. A flash of orange winked in the moonlight as something moved into the shadows.

Steam from my nostrils fogged the window, obscuring everything.

"Hanna—" Morrison began, softer now.

"What!" The volume of my own voice startled me. "What do you want to hear? You were right? Is that it? You were right, and Mark's a murderer, and my job is a sham to cover for him? The only thing I had going for me is a fucking sham and it's over?"

Over. That word again.

My throat shrank closed. I sat down hard and pressed the heels of my hands into my face until stars burst behind my eyelids. Could I hold my tear ducts closed by force? I'd never tried before. The first sob wrung my ribs. I swallowed animal sounds and fought the tears threatening to turn me inside out.

No. *No.* I focused all my thought on this word. Not in front of Morrison. Not in front of anyone. I wouldn't do this again. I couldn't. There was no surviving it.

Small hurt animal noises escaped through my clamped lips.

"My wife left me for a carnie."

Inside my head: the sound of a record screeching to a stop. I pulled my hands away from my face and found his eyes. He was staring at the floor.

"A fire swallower," he continued. "In the Haunted Circus. She met him at a bar."

"I'm...I'm sorry."

"They stripped the house. Took everything. The furniture, the cars. Even the dog. Been drinking every night since. Mornings too, sometimes."

"That's horrible," I said.

"I know." He paused and sighed heavily. "I really liked that dog." He looked me square in the eye and broke into a broad grin.

I felt my face split open and an absurd burp of laughter escaped, dragging up with it the buried sobs. Then I was shaking, laughing, and crying, unsure which emotion owned the tears streaming down my face.

Morrison placed a hand between my shoulder blades, unleashing a new torrent of tears by this simple gesture of physical kindness.

He curled me to his chest and banded his other arm around my back. He made no sound to quiet me, seeming content to let me soak his shirt with tears and heave gasping breaths in the circle of his arms.

When the tremors gentled to little sniffs, I pulled away and wiped my face on the sleeve of my t-shirt. "Sorry," I mumbled, "I don't—"

But the words died away against his lips as they crushed into mine.

CHAPTER 14

Someone else was eating my words. That was a welcome change. Shock faded to curiosity. So, this is what it felt like to be kissed by a man who knew the art.

He pulled my hair and smiled against my mouth as he slid his tongue across the seam of my lips. I captured it and sucked gently, drinking his moan.

Strong fingers found my thighs, and I was lifted until I came to rest straddling Morrison's lap. All reason and sadness were driven from me by the force of his insistent mouth against mine. Sudden aching hunger gnawed in the place it left behind. I wanted this fire to turn me to ash.

I kissed into his lips a wordless plea, knowing already it would be understood. I felt more than heard his answer: a moan deep enough to vibrate in my chest.

We sank down on the couch together and broke apart long enough to become only panting breaths and hungry hands. Grabbing at clothing. Yanking at zippers. Making projectiles of buttons.

My wrists were grasped and forced above my head, pinned to the couch as Morrison reclaimed my mouth in a hungry rush.

His entire naked body came down on me, reducing me to essential elements, drowning out every other stimulus until there was nothing but the place where our bodies met. This singular sensation ripped through my overwrought brain like a flash flood of hot summer rain.

There was no time for appreciation of his beautiful body. No time to determine which aspects echoed what I'd imaged. Any pause in the momentum might give us time to think, to reconsider.

He pushed inside me and stilled for the space of a heartbeat. "Oh God," he whispered against my neck.

"I know."

All questions between us were asked and answered in this simple four-word exchange.

How could two such completely fucked-up people find a moment of perfection like this? How long could the world and all its impossible choices be kept at bay by the meeting of two bodies in the dark?

For the space of this second, and the next, and the next. That was all.

He made only small movements at first, a careful foundation of kindling laid for the fire. Heat pooled and spread from the ache where he drove against me in a relentless, ceaseless pursuit toward madness. My legs fastened around his hips in an attempt to temper the sensation. It was met by arms shoved underneath me, lifting me with him as he came to his knees. His hands cupped my shoulders from behind to pull me further down onto him, deeper.

My cry of pleasure at this new sensation spurred him. The long muscles of his back built a miraculous arch over and over in time with his hips as he hastened the construction of unbearable pressure. He sent us over the couch's edge, and we rolled together to the floor in a tangle of sweat-slickened limbs.

And there on the wood floor, he fucked dirty.

Slow. Gritty. Leaving no place unreached as he shifted to explore every angle. Collecting gasps like a connoisseur and trading up to buy ever more precious sensations.

"Come for me," he breathed into my ear, coupling each word with a blow of crippling pleasure.

I bit into his shoulder to muffle the scream building in my throat and surrendered to the sensation of falling. My body folded in on itself, pulling the pleasure inward and condensing into one perfect rolling point I could no longer contain.

I cried out helplessly into his flesh as I contracted around him. The muscles of my stomach quivered and bunched in a dance older than time.

"Oh *fuck*," he panted. "Fuck. I can feel you." He rocked against me harder then, filling me with the full articulation of his barely restrained rage. I met him blow for blow, demanding of his body answers the world couldn't give me, ending my long isolation by the force of my own need.

In his eyes lived the understanding that I'd meant more than his body. More than the part of him that branded me inside out with cathartic fire.

And he complied.

The skin on my back burned as I was driven across the floor in time with punishing thrusts. Morrison was an anatomical wonder by lamplight. My mind's eye rendered each movement like a sketch in shadow. Proof that for a moment, for a season, I was wanted.

"Hanna! Christ!" His forearms collapsed on either side of my face, his hands buried in my hair as he murmured prayers against my forehead. I felt his every muscle tense as he came hot and hard, burying himself to the hilt. His face was a mask of desperation and ecstasy, the closest thing to redemption I'd known in ages. Our chests thrummed against each other in the lamplight.

We lay like that until our breathing slowed. When he stirred, I surprised both of us by speaking first.

"Don't," I said. "Not yet."

"Don't what?" he murmured against my shoulder.

"Don't get up."

I needed his weight, his warmth.

"No?"

"No."

"Okay."

"Thanks."

"Don't mention it," he sighed into my hair.

Our breathing settled into a regular offset rhythm like the lapping of waves on a shore. I let it lull me away, a little boat under the cover of heavy clouds, unreachable to the sun and safe from dangerous truths the light of day might bring.

THE STORMY SKY HUNG A LOW CURTAIN OF GRAY OVER the mountains. Rain deepened the colors of late winter to a palette of rust, gold, and mud. February was almost over, soon it would be March, and spring.

I backed away from the window and stretched.

"Ooh." I winced, unexpectedly sore in places that hadn't been sore since college.

Morrison, as it turned out, wasn't a one trick pony. More like a workhorse.

Sometime during the long night, he'd lifted me from the floor to the bed, but not to sleep.

He'd been absent when I awoke. Gone off to do cop things, I supposed.

A sly smile tugged my face into a sideways smirk.

I turned my attention to the box of doughnuts on

my coffee table. Dirty sex *and* he left the doughnuts. There was a lot to like about Morrison. I shifted to adjust my sore legs.

A whole lot.

On top of the doughnuts, I found a note. Next to them, I found a Taser and several shiny black cartridges.

I unfolded the note and deciphered the compact, scratchy script.

By now you're probably thinking, "This was a really, really bad idea." Well, you're right about that, but don't panic. I'm not boyfriend material, and I have no plans to complicate your life further. See ya around, - James (I figured after some of the things we did last night, we ought to be on a first name basis)

P.S. The Taser that's not on your coffee table isn't police issue and didn't come from me. You shouldn't Google Taser X26, learn how to use it, and put it in your purse. It would make me feel better. Hypothetically.

P.P.S. I've had a vasectomy and my ex-wife is the last woman I was with. I got tested after I found out about the carnie. You would have too, am I right?

P.P.P.S. I plan to fuck your brains out as often as you'll let me, just so we're clear.

Heat shot through my limbs like an electrical current.

He wanted me.

It only occurred to me to be offended several minutes later. Just where the hell did he get off assuming the doughnut box would be the first place I'd find a note?

I took a doughnut and sat back on the couch, bringing my pig slippers to rest on the coffee table's edge while I flipped open my laptop and did as I was bidden.

"Huh," I said to the cats, rewinding the video of a

man jerking and twisting on the sidewalk. "I didn't know a body could make those noises."

Amazing how much better I felt when I hadn't bathed in vodka the night before. Also, I didn't feel like I was trying to pass thoughts through cotton instead of brain matter.

Doughnut in hand, I could take on the world.

Three women, brutally murdered. Abernathy connecting them all. Abernathy, with his unlimited supply of money, priceless antiques, seriously old accounting documents, full moon episodes and furry shredded dry-cleaning. Occam's Razor said this dude was definitely a serial killer.

Then again, Occam's Razor didn't account for the existence of werewolves.

If I wanted answers about Abernathy, I'd damn well have to find them myself. Morrison, for all his efforts, had nothing concrete to offer me.

Well, at least not where Abernathy was concerned. And I sure as hell wasn't about to go all Diane Sawyer and sit a potential murderer down for a heartfelt chat.

Instead, I thought of the multitude of papers in Abernathy's office, the many cabinets, the crammed drawers, his careless hand with details.

My snooping efforts had been brought to a premature close last time. There had to be *something* in that office. Something to either condemn or exonerate him. I checked the time on my phone. 9:30 a.m. on a Saturday.

The gallery would be closed and locked. Whatever Abernathy did with his weekends, it generally took him elsewhere. I had a key. I could be in and out in the space of half an hour.

What was the worst that could happen?

Abernathy could eat you. Or leave you hideously maimed and throatless, the little voice in my head replied.

Right. But then at least I would know, one way or the other.

The little voice shrugged. *At least you wouldn't have to chew your doughnuts. You could shove them through a neck hole the size of a softball.*

Still. Death didn't seem as threatening as a repeat performance of the few months preceding my work at the gallery. The killing desperation of being trapped inside with no one and nothing. Being purposeless, jobless, lifeless, loveless. That, *that* was a fate worse than death.

I would confront the truth head on, even if it came at me on four paws.

Did werewolves even have four paws? Or was it a creepy man-wolf on two legs proposition?

You'll know soon enough.

God, I hoped I was wrong.

Wait. Had I just thought that?

Having had enough of my ceaseless inner wrangling, I showered, shaved, and put on my nicest bra and panties. On the off chance that I would be found in a bloody heap on Abernathy's floor, I would at least like to look decent on the coroner's table.

From the neck down, that was.

Considering this, I spent a little extra time on my hair and makeup. I'd been to enough funerals to know that the average mortician applied makeup with the precision of a dump truck. At least I could give them an idea what I was *supposed* to look like.

I took a cake pan from the cupboard, filled it with some extra cat food, and put out a large bowl of water. If I did end up as werewolf chow and it took a couple days for the cops to find my body, the cats would be all right.

On my way out, I shoved the Taser in my back pocket and pulled a bulky sweater over it. I wrapped a doughnut in a napkin and stuffed it in my purse, along with the Taser cartridges by way of a back-up plan.

I kissed each furry head goodbye.

Just in case.

BACK TO THE PLACE WHERE IT ALL BEGAN.

I parked a couple streets over from the gallery and walked around to the alley, not wanting to be spotted. I unlocked the door and slid in, clicking the deadbolt behind me.

What a strange place this was in the half-light of dying winter. Empty, but haunted by those who worked here even in their absence. Many of the pieces Abernathy and I had hung were now gone, taken away by those who had purchased them. Most evidence of the gallery show had been removed, save for a few crumpled cocktail napkins and programs. I picked them up and put them in the trashcan, tidying out of habit.

Climbing the stairs to the landing, I set my purse on my desk. Odd to be here when Abernathy was not.

Almost as odd as how much of my life he'd invaded in just a few short weeks. Not just his physical presence, but his entire being, his life. His body still filled the doorway to the office, all his words played on a continuous loop in my head. Every minute from the moment I'd met him to this very second in the empty building was consumed by some aspect of my relationship to him.

Here, in a space so completely his yet devoid of his presence, my world felt like a deflated balloon.

I backed into his office, closed the door behind me, and was rewarded with chaos of a magnitude I hadn't encountered since the day I started work here.

My carefully organized boxes had been torn open, their contents disgorged. The drawers hung dangerously askew. Cabinets flung their doors wide, revealing their scattered contents. I felt a little stab of sorrow. Gone for one day and his office had reverted to this?

The urge to begin shuffling papers back into neat piles was so dire that my palms began to sweat. But then, he'd know I'd been here. Of course, if he was a werewolf, he could probably know I'd been there just by scent.

A creak of the floorboards set my heart slamming into my ribs. I froze in place and stared at the closed door. When the knob began to turn, I ducked under Abernathy's desk and crouched in the space usually reserved for Abernathy's long legs. Thank God he was a big man with taste in quality furniture. Had he a cheap P-O-S from IKEA, my ankles would be spilling out from the desk like comical snakes from a can.

Then, I heard the endless slow squeak of the door opening its hinges. I made a mental note to pick up some WD-40 and bring it in on Monday.

That was, if Abernathy turned out not to be a ladyscarfing homicidal werewolf.

The blood rushed in my ears to the rhythm of my leaping rabbit heart as I held my breath.

"Mr. Abernathy? Is that you?" a familiar voice warbled.

All the air exited my lungs in a sudden rush. I unfolded myself from the little cubby and pushed up from behind the desk.

"Mrs. Kass!" I said. "I didn't think anyone was here."

"Sorry if I startled you. I came in to finish glazing a painting that Detective Morrison bought at the gallery show. I'll tell you one thing," she winked conspiratorially, "if I were forty years younger, I wouldn't kick him out of my bed for eating crackers."

If you were forty years younger, I thought, *you'd be about eighty.*

"I don't blame you." I laughed.

"He certainly is a nice young man, isn't he?"

"Yes." I was glad her impaired vision might take the edge off my predatory smile. "Very."

"I wonder what he could have done to upset Mr. Abernathy so," she added. "After that awful tirade last night, I thought he might have come back to clean up."

"He was upset at Morrison?" My heart relocated itself to my throat. Abernathy couldn't possibly know about my and Morrison's epic bone-fest.

Could he?

"My, yes. He certainly was in a mood. Overturning boxes, throwing things. My hearing's not so good," she said, tapping her giant hearing aid. "But even *I* heard him shouting *Morrison.* And some curse words, I think. It's been awhile since he had one of those fits of his."

"Fits?"

She chuckled and waved a hand. "You know how young men are when they're upset about something. Yelling, breaking things. More bark than bite really."

Her choice of words did little to ease my cartwheeling stomach.

She looked over her bony shoulder and turned back to me with a rueful smile. "Well, I won't bother you, dear. You go on with your organizing."

"Right." I laughed thinly, pretending to shuffle some papers.

When she was gone, I plopped down in Abernathy's chair and set my forehead on the desk.

He knew.

Somehow, he knew. Panic slid through my guts.

Focus. Get what you need and get out.

I took a deep breath and tried to channel inspiration. If I were Abernathy, where would I hide the key to life, the universe, and everything?

"Maybe under this phone I'm not supposed to touch," I reasoned aloud. I reached out and turned the ancient brass dial. The bookcase in the corner swung open neatly, revealing...another bookcase.

"You're shitting me. Really? A secret compartment?"

I gingerly stepped through piles of debris on the floor to survey the books lining the shelves. Some of them old and leather, some of them newer, bound in canvas. In stark contrast to the rest of Abernathy's office, these were pristinely organized and remarkably well kept. Not a speck of dust to be seen.

"Huh." I selected one of the tattiest books from the top shelf and opened it. A journal. The script was a looping scrawl I recognized. *Abernathy's*. Only it was dated Friday, November 9th, *1888*.

They found another one today in East End. Terrible business.

East End, I thought. *1888. Jack the Ripper.*

I returned the book and selected another, this one from the center of the shelves. I flipped to the center of the book and read an entry at random. February 15th, 1929.

Seven men gunned down last night. I'm beginning to think this Capone fellow might not be a reputable importer of liquor as he claims.

I slapped it shut and skipped further along the line. July 20th, 1969.

Americans put a man on the moon today. If by "on the moon" they mean, "in a small studio just outside of Hollywood, California." At least, this is what a gentleman named Neil informed me after his fifth boilermaker in a small pub about a fortnight ago.

The next book I grabbed fell open to Dec 8th, 1980.

Received a call from Yoko today. John has been shot. All

the good ones are taken too soon. I'll miss our late-night jam sessions.

Thunderstruck.

That seemed the only appropriate word. My brain slapped wetly against the conglomeration of facts opening before me. *Impossible.*

At last, I turned my attention to the book at the end of the last row. It didn't fit with the rest. It was much larger, newer, and bound in shiny leather.

I pulled it from the shelf and several yellowed newspaper clippings fluttered to the floor like dead moths. The pages were stiff with pictures, glued in and captioned. Names, dates, notes.

All women.

"Shit fire," I whispered. Helena's face smirked up at me from a wrinkled obituary taped onto the page.

I paged through several bank pages to the end of the book. There, on the second to last page.

My face.

Goosebumps worked their way up my neck over my scalp. Every hair on my body stood at attention, tingling. Flashes blinked like strobe lights at the edges of my vision.

Not just one photo, but many. More than had been dedicated to any other woman in the book. Candid shots of me in my cap and gown, receiving my Master's degree. Me at a bus stop. Me in the grocery store. Me walking to the Mustang from the old house where I lived.

The book slid from my hands and landed at my feet, sending a cloud of dust upward like a mini atomic bomb.

The floorboards creaked behind me.

"Mrs. Kass," I said, turning.

I was wrong.

CHAPTER 15

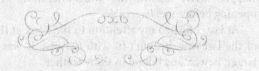

"*S*tay away from me."

"Hanna." Abernathy took a cautious step closer, hands extended. "You don't know what you're looking at."

I backed away, feeling my way through the piles with the soles of my shoes, unwilling to break eye contact.

"A murderous assface?" A hysterical laugh escaped my throat. "Because I'm pretty sure that's a scrapbook of dead women ending with me. Oh, and the diaries dating back a century or so ago. In your handwriting. But yes, fabulous. Glad to know I was mistaken."

He ventured another step. "I can explain."

"Splendid!" It was more a shriek than a word. "Let's have it."

He looked pained. "I can't explain *yet*."

"Figures."

"Hanna." Abernathy laid my name down like a stone, leveraging its solid sound to take another step in my direction.

"*Don't* come near me!" My knees threatened to give out. I felt blindly behind me for the desk's solid edge.

When my thigh collided with the corner, I scrambled backward, slipping on papers.

I slid behind the desk and yanked the Taser from my back pocket.

The second I broke eye contact with Abernathy, he was on me.

A terrified scream tore from my throat as his hand closed around my wrist and shook the Taser from my grip. It clattered to the floor and came to rest by my foot.

I made a lunge for it, but he pinned my hand to the floor.

"Stop." His growl vibrated in the wood beneath me. "Listen to me."

Give him what he wants. Don't argue. I tried to harness my hitching breath and pressed my lips closed. Warm tears leaked down my cheeks. Fear sent my heart leaping around my rib cage like a frightened animal.

Trapped. His hand was heavy as marble, his fingers digging like roots into the wooden planks.

"Hanna," he said slowly. "You are in danger."

"You don't say?"

His eyes darkened. "You have to come with me. Now."

"I *know.* Don't you get it? I know about all of them. Helena. Amy Grayson. *Penny.*"

"You don't know the first *fucking* thing about anything."

"Then *tell me* for God's sake!"

"You don't know what you're asking, Hanna."

A toxic brew of anger and frustration bubbled up from my guts. "I'm tired of not knowing."

Frustration rolled over Abernathy's face like a taut mask.

"Do you want to end up like them? Do you?"

The pressure of his grip tightened, crushing the

bones of my hand together. I wouldn't give him the satisfaction of flinching.

"Is that a threat?"

"I don't make threats."

"And this is supposed to convince me? I'm supposed to trust *you*?" I loaded the last word with as much disgust as it could carry.

Something flashed across his eyes. Hurt?

"Trust?" he asked. "Like you *trust* Morrison?" His dark eyes flicked over me as if I squatted there wearing not a stitch. "Was it the vodka talking? Or just one more example of that impeccable judgment of yours, Hanna?"

To hell with the Taser. I wanted to tear that insolent face apart with my bare hands. If I'd *had* a free hand, that is.

"Oh, and you're certainly one to talk," I bit back. "At least Morrison left my apartment with all his body parts still intact."

Dear God, what was I saying? What was I doing? He could destroy me quicker than I could snarf a Twinkie, and here I was standing before the bars, poking the bear with a stick.

His eyes went cold and distant. "You have no other choice," he said, quieter.

I exhaled deeply and looked down in desperation.

His grip loosened a fraction with my apparent acquiescence. I yanked my hand from his and grabbed the Taser.

He met my gaze with a mix of surprise and disbelief that promptly turned to glassy-eyed shock as I sent enough volts to barbecue an elephant arcing through his shoulder.

It was equal parts horrific and fascinating to watch every muscle in his body jerk to full tension. The collar of his shirt ripped open as the thick cords of his neck bunched wildly against the stubbled skin of his throat. His sleeves tore loose from his shirt as his arms snapped rigid and flailed at his sides. At the end of his long, powerful legs, his shoes danced a terrible jig, clubbing the wood floor. When a deep, agonized groan worked through his clenched teeth, it occurred to me I should probably stop.

Soon.

At last I released the trigger, and he shivered out straight like a dead fish.

I scrambled to my feet and kicked him as hard as I could in the ribs.

"How's that for a choice?"

I discharged the cartridge, dashed out to my desk, grabbed my purse, and flew down the stairs. I had every intention of being long gone by the time he woke up in a puddle of his own piss. At that point, I didn't give a rat's ass whether it was purple.

CHAPTER 16

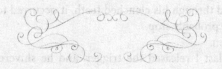

The way I figured it, I had about fifteen minutes' head start before Abernathy showed up on my doorstep very awake and very angry.

For the first time I could remember, I was glad to have brought so little of my previous life along to my divorcee's apartment. It made packing everything I owned so much simpler.

I stood in the tight wooden box of my closet, wrenching clothes from their hangers and disgorging them into my living room. There was no time for my customary pre-packing list, item sort, and check-off.

My largest suitcase slid down from the closet's top shelf, bringing with it an avalanche of items I'd neglected since moving day.

I tossed the open suitcase on the coffee table and began shoving armfuls of clothing in. Next came the books. Cookbooks from the 1950s, well-worn paperbacks, and my master's thesis, among other titles.

The kitchen presented more difficult decisions. My gadgets, my cookware, my beloved casserole dishes. I grabbed the smooth wooden rolling pin I'd inherited from my grandmother and held it for a moment while I considered. Its cool, heavy weight in my hand seemed to help me prioritize, as if I could draw from it the practical level-headedness of the women who'd used it before me. In the end, I took only the rolling pin, my German-forged steel meat cleaver, and a few other favorites I'd rather die than abandon. I returned to the living room with a black plastic lawn bag and began filling it with my shoes.

Wrestling the suitcase down the stairs made me wish I had left the bulk of my pretentious art historical tomes on the shelf gathering dust, as they were wont to do. After three trips up and down the stairs, I had the Mustang's trunk packed perilously full to bursting.

Enough procrastination.

I met my final task with a measure of dread.

"Oh, kitties," I chirped in what I hoped was my most motherly and soothing voice.

"Mommy has a very nice treat for you..." I lied.

Fat Gilbert had little chance of escape. I nabbed him football-style from the kitchen counter, shoved him in the carrier and zipped it shut. Stewie was not so easy, so I opted for psychological warfare instead. A piece of yarn dangled in front of his twitching whiskers proved the perfect foil. While he was distracted, I scooped him into the second carrier.

That left only Stella, who usually preferred to stay under my bed plotting the violent downfall of mankind. I elected to take the boys down first and deposit them in the Mustang's back seat, where I had stashed their food and litter box. I was long on cats and short on carriers, so hers would have to be a manual job.

Back in the apartment, I squatted down in front of the bed and ducked down to see her eyes shining in the dark space.

"Here, kitty, kitty."

She blinked at me as if to say, *"Has that ever worked?"*

Time to pull out the big guns.

I wiggled my fingers back and forth on the carpet. Usually this brought on a bloodlust in Stella matched only by berserkers of Norse legend.

But she wasn't tumbling for the cheap seats.

"Fine," I said. "Do you want to stay here and get eaten?"

She looked away, no longer willing to acknowledge my presence.

"Sonovabitch," I muttered, thinking of the Taser I'd tucked back into my pocket after zapping Abernathy. "If I Tase myself in the ass crawling under the bed to get you, I'm going to be very upset."

With some effort, I squeezed myself under the bed and dragged her out by her back paws—a hissing, scratching, squalling ball of fur and teeth.

I had to balance her on my hip as I pulled my front door shut and locked it behind me. It would have been worth a moment, bidding goodbye to all I knew, if Stella's claws hadn't been digging into my ribs.

"Ow, ow...OW!"

With one swift motion, I disengaged her claws, opened the driver's side door to the Mustang, and tossed her in. I squeezed myself in and quickly closed the door behind me.

"Everyone in?"

Gilbert wailed pitifully from the back seat.

"I know," I said. "This is less than ideal. But the alternatives are worse, believe me."

I started the engine and cranked the heat.

"Sorry guys, it'll warm up soon."

As I approached the freeway, it occurred to me I might need to decide in precisely which direction I would be fleeing for my life.

South.

In my mind's eye, I saw the little green house in

Abilene, Texas, shared by Mother and Oma, their pack of five dogs, and once upon a time, by me. It had been about ten years since I'd left for college the first time, but every time I'd visited since, I could step straight back through time and into my old room with its worn twin-size bed and faded floral curtains—ends gnawed lacey by my gay guinea pig, Benny. I had always thought it was his way of telling me he would have sprung for Ralph Lauren.

Under normal circumstances, nothing short of the zombie apocalypse could send me willingly in the direction of my mother. Considering I was in the employ of a potential murderer and werewolf whom I had recently incapacitated with about two gazillion volts of electricity, my mom's house didn't seem all that bad.

Even empty of my grandmother, the house still promised her echo.

I took the freeway ramp that would lead me on an undulating path through the mountains.

As we approached the last exit before civilization gave way to dodgy rest stops, Gilbert gave a low, worried whine from the back seat.

"I know. It's okay."

The only thing worse than putting a cat in a cat carrier was putting a cat in a cat carrier in a car. Especially if the cat happens to suffer from an anxiety disorder.

"Mrrroooow," he squalled again, more insistent.

"I'm sorry baby," I crooned. "It will be all ri—"

A powerful stench assaulted my unsuspecting nostrils. I sniffed, for God knows what reason, perhaps, wanting to authenticate my suspicions.

Yep.

"Gilbert!"

Heat from the engine block met Gilbert's deposit, multiplying its potency in the enclosed space.

"Mother of God!" I gagged, and my eyes started to water.

I cranked down the window and gulped in the jet of frigid air like the sweet nectar of life itself. If I could have managed it, I would have hung my entire head out of the window.

The car careened off the next exit and into a gas station parking lot, and I launched out of my seat even before the engine had settled.

Inside the convenience store, I passed by the alluring displays of Hostess Chocolate Frosted Gems in their sexy cellophane lingerie and instead grabbed baby wipes, paper towels, rubber gloves, and a dozen apple cinnamon air fresheners.

The clerk, a pimpled kid with muttonchops, raised an eyebrow at me as he considered my items.

"You don't want to know," I informed him, adding a handful of truffles to my purchase.

As I walked back toward my car, the gas station's bustling hum was shattered by an ear-piercing scream.

I jerked around to see where the sound originated and found a woman at the pump across from mine pointing to the parking lot across the street.

She'd captured the attention of a nearby gas station attendant and was shrilling in his ear. Several other people were now gathering around and following her line of sight.

"It was a *wolf*!" she insisted. "I saw it! It looked right at me! Then it ran into the bushes!"

She indicated the clump of hedges by the KFC across the street.

My first, and not necessarily most helpful, thought was something to the effect of: *Fried chiiiicken.*

My second thought: *Holy shit. A wolf!*

I scanned the bushes looking for eyes, teeth, a flash of fur. Nothing.

"Well, I don't see it now," one of the people said. "Besides, I don't think there are wolves in this part of the state. Coyotes maybe."

"It was a wolf," she repeated, shifting a fat baby to her opposite hip. "I'm not blind."

Just distracted, I hoped.

The woman beeped open her minivan's sliding door to reveal a set of four kids, all buckled in and watching a DVD. She deposited her fifth into his car seat and slid the door closed on her brood.

At this exact moment, I couldn't decide which would be worse to have in the back of my car: three cats or five kids.

I lingered for a moment, scanning the parking lot, looking for sleek gray movement. When nothing materialized, I let myself into the car, dealt with the mess, and settled Gilbert back into the carrier.

"We'll stop in Pueblo for gas," I informed the cats. "I'll let you out for some food and water then. Okay?"

I took their silence as complicit approval of my plan.

On the road before us, the slim, white windmill blades scissored a slow arch against the canyon's mouth. Eleven hours of road separated me from my family home. Daylight would be our companion for only five of those.

I hoped the Mustang's 195 horses were faster than a lone wolf's stride.

SUN DRAINED AWAY LIKE SAND THROUGH A SIEVE, leaving the red rock outcroppings to spill lengthening shadows across the desert floor. Soon it would descend fully, pulling all the light and heat with it to the other side of the world. I drank in the dying light casting an orange mantel over the dirt hills and scrub.

Every day required a dramatic close before it could be reborn anew the following morning. Shadows became deeper, colors became more intense—both in themselves and in relationship to one another. Now, against the backdrop of a fire-hued horizon, the day's blue sky gave way to shades of purple and gray. Too soon, the day would surrender to black. If only I could surrender to black and find the same peace.

I was a solitary agent now, at odds with Abernathy and unsure of Morrison. I'd been evicted from what was left of my life, and now there was only this road and the hope I could drive fast enough to leave the questions behind.

On the outskirts of Pueblo, hotels began to spring up on either side of the road. I looked longingly at the glowing signs knowing I couldn't afford to stop longer than it took to get gas.

At the opposite edge of town, I pulled into my favorite gas station. After cracking open a couple cans of cat food, I poured a little bottled water into their foldable travel bowls. I unzipped the carriers so the cats could eat and stretch their legs while I went inside to acquire the makings for a coffee and Red Bull special.

"I would just like to point out," I said, "that I have made a litter box available for your use. Should you feel the need to relieve yourself, please feel free to avail yourself of the facilities."

All three faces remained buried in their respective cans.

With the Mustang's tank filling, I walked into the mini-mart across the parking lot. My step was slower than it would normally be in the biting cold, owing to the need to look over both shoulders every few seconds.

Washed in the convenience store's eye-frying fluorescent lighting, I filled a cup with 70% French roast coffee and 30% half and half and shook in a flurry of dehydrated marshmallows for good measure.

For dinner I elected to snag a junky gas station hotdog loaded with ketchup, relish, mustard, and onions. I spied the nacho station nearby and added some nacho cheese and chili. Because it might be my last meal.

Tucking a bag of cotton candy under my arm on the way to the register, I took my place in line.

The doughy clerk looked at the items I schlepped onto the counter. "Now, honey, that hotdog don't come with chili and cheese," she explained, "I'ma have to charge you extra fer that."

"Fine," I said.

Her moon-shaped face relaxed a little. I didn't envy a job that required you to interface with people that were likely to haggle over paying for gas station chili and cheese.

Of course, she might not envy a job that required you to maintain a to-do list for a man that could relieve you of your throat if the mood took him.

With coffee, cotton candy, and hot dog balanced in my arms, I jogged back to the car. I set everything on the Mustang's roof and extracted and re-holstered the gas pump.

Gilbert was standing in the backseat with his paws on the window. His round, worried eyes looked at me through the glass.

I smiled and gave him a little finger wave.

He drew his ears back and hissed. I could hear his low, angry growl through the car door.

"What gives? You know I'll share the hot dog with you."

He hissed again took a swipe at the window with one paw.

Then I heard it.

Panting. Directly behind me. And a subtler sound too. Foot pads on pavement.

Prickling hairs rose up on the back of my neck.

Slowly, *slowly* I rotated my head to look over my shoulder, my body following by small increments.

The wolf stared at me from the little concrete island dividing the gas station from the road beyond. Its head was lowered, eyes fixed on me, velvety black nose twitching as it pulled scent from the open air. Its golden pelt was wet and matted with sweat.

Black lips tugged back to reveal teeth like little ivory daggers. Strings of crystalline saliva hung from its chin.

"Please, no," I whispered under my breath. Tears filmed my eyes, an unwelcome manifestation of fear.

I flattened my back against the Mustang, feeling the cold metal through my clothes.

Was anyone else seeing this? I didn't want to risk looking around to see if anyone had caught a case of the heroics and decided to come save my pathetic ass. Using the car's body as a guide, I scooted my butt along, inching around toward the driver's side.

I resisted the urge to say, "Nice doggy."

When I at last reached the front bumper, I made a run for it. I managed to get myself in the car in one piece, save for what I knew would become a giant bruise on my shin from swinging the car door closed before checking to make sure all my limbs were inside. Rookie mistake.

The wolf's claws scraped at the side of the car as it launched itself at the passenger's side window. I yelped and fumbled the key into the ignition.

We burned rubber out of the parking lot. Only

when I was half a mile down the road did I remember the hot dog, cotton candy, and coffee on the Mustang's roof. A fresh round of tears stung my eyes at the thought of my dinner lying in ruins on the concrete.

I sniffed.

"I will not cry over a hot dog."

But it wasn't just the hot dog. It had been the desire for something warm and familiar. A hot meal. Comfort food.

"Couldn't you let me have one lousy hot dog?" I asked the universe. "Isn't there even one aspect of my pathetic life you're not determined to destroy?"

Hunger had turned into a bittersweet ache in my stomach.

And then I remembered.

The doughnut! I'd packed a doughnut in my purse this morning. With jubilance in my heart, I wolfed—pun slightly intended—half of it in one bite.

Gilbert blinked at me from the passenger's seat.

Shit. I'd left so quickly I hadn't even had time to return the cats to their carriers.

"You already ate. This is all I have."

He continued to stare.

"Oh, fine." I tore off a chunk of the doughnut and set it down in front of him.

He snarfed it with gusto. If I could say one thing for Gilbert, it would be that he had decent taste. I had long suspected he'd survived on dumpster food before he found his way to my door. This was the only way I could account for his passionate adoration of nacho cheese, corn chips, and turkey bacon.

Thus satisfied, Gilbert curled himself into a contented crescent on the passenger's seat and tucked his paws neatly under his chin. If only I could be as regal directly after attacking a doughnut with my face.

I reached over and scratched behind his ear in the

place he liked best and was rewarded by his contented rumbling purr.

"Well, at least I still know how to do one thing right."

MORRISON CALLED EIGHT TIMES DURING THE LONG night. Each time, I stared at my phone and let it roll to voicemail. I wanted to call him back. I wanted his cocky, comfortable voice in my ear. Maybe I wouldn't feel as lonely here in the Land of Disenchantment. But if I did, he'd want to know where I was, and that was something I couldn't tell him.

I really did owe him one for the Taser. It had already saved my ass once today.

Speaking of ass, my left butt cheek had gone numb somewhere outside of Albuquerque. I had a knot the size of a grapefruit in my shoulder, and my eyes had taken on a perma-squint. My knuckles had gone white from gripping the steering wheel, and I wasn't certain I could unbend my fingers if I tried. The flash of headlights in the rearview mirror had burned a permanent rectangle into my retinas.

The road stretched out before me like an inscrutable black ribbon, and all I could do was follow the flashes of white reflective paint caught in my headlights' glare. In the dark, I could barely make out the menacing shapes of mesas pressing against the starless sky. In this place so far from the artificial light that kept us safe, objects lost all scale.

Then there was the howling.

At this distance from civilization, the radio only barfed out staticky bits of bible programs and songs I didn't recognize. Even the sound of snow turned to full blast couldn't block it out completely.

It could conceivably be coyotes, though they didn't typically wander this close to the road. I could be hearing things. I acknowledged that as a definite possibility.

The faces in the darkness were harder to explain away. Glowing animal retinas floated in my peripheral vision like burned-out after images from staring directly at the sun. When I tried to look at them directly, they disappeared.

The orange needle of the Mustang's gas gauge slouched a little below empty. If I didn't pull off soon, I would be trapped out here. Stranded on the side of the road with three cats and the contents of my life in my car trunk. I'd have to rely on some random motorist to take me into town to get gas, hopefully without violating me in some unthinkable way and dumping my body in the desert.

If we didn't get eaten by my boss first.

A green road sign materialized in the distance proclaiming that Texline—the subtle and clever name someone had come up with for the small and unremarkable town on the Texas/New Mexico border—was a mere eleven miles away.

At two o'clock in the morning, Texline was a ghost town, the main drag cast in the jaundiced glow from the sporadic streetlights on either side of the road. Sinister shadows and pockets of darkness lurked between run-down houses and empty lots.

"If you can just make it through this town," I told myself in a voice choked with fear, "you'll be in the home stretch."

Hot tears spilled down my cheeks as visions of a Texas sunrise broke over the surface of my tired brain. God, I hoped I lived long enough to see just one more. On the flat plains of my home state, the sky began at the curve of the earth, at the bottom of the road before you. The immensity of it brought to mind Dutch landscape painters from the low country, whose quaint bleaching fields and windmills were the merest green stripe under the drama of heavens and clouds. Van Gogh had inherited this tendency from his forbears with his visions of exploding stars and celestial vortices.

But this was not a night Van Gogh would have painted.

Under this starless blanket in a deserted town, I might as well have been the last person alive. A twenty-four-hour gas station was a little too much to hope for. I settled for one where the pumps were abundantly lit.

Gilbert yawned and stretched in the passenger's seat.

"Sorry," I said, "we're not quite to Grandma's yet."

Not wanting to spend any more time outside my car than I had to, I arranged my effects in advance. Debit card in my bra. Fresh cartridge loaded into the Taser. Taser tucked into the front pocket of my hoodie.

Thus prepared, I got out of the car and locked it before plugging the nozzle into the parched gas tank.

As soon as the sound of gas sluicing through the hose reached my ears, the urge to hit the little girl's room reached crisis point.

The convenience store was long closed, the windows dark and deserted. This left only one option.

Hopping over behind a scrubby bush at the parking lot's edge, I wiggled my pants and lucky giraffe undies down around my knees.

The wolf hit me low and hard from the side, knocking me ass over teakettle into the parking lot, my pants still down around my knees. Stunned, I rolled dumbly onto my rump and yanked my damp pants and underwear back up, crab walking backward on all fours.

I watched in morbid, disembodied fascination as the sleek, powerful body erupted toward me. Fear made the action blur, a replay in slow motion.

Pristine white fur, golden eyes, compact curving body. Definitely not the same wolf I'd seen twice today.

I was going to die.

The sudden knowledge hit me like a truck, my heart caught up in my throat as I thought about all the things I had never done. The cheeses I'd never eaten. The books I'd never read. The men I'd never stalked—Sir Patrick Stewart being the first on the list. The Williams - Sonoma copper cookware I'd never gone into debt for.

Eyes squeezed shut, bracing for the bite, I brought my arms and legs up in a protective fetal position out of instinct. When nothing began mauling my head, I peeked between my fingers.

Without warning, a blur of golden gray collided with the white wolf in mid-air, a stylistic symphony of destruction as both animals hung suspended, claws and teeth ripping and slashing at each other.

The gray wolf yelped in pain as it caught the worst of the mêlée, its soft underbelly revealing a deep purple-red split as it hit the parking lot pavement with a sickening thud. The white wolf flew to this new weakness in the space of a heartbeat.

I have never been a fighter. I have always been the first one to back down and always the one to walk the extra mile out of my way if the word "conflict" is even mentioned.

But I shocked myself as I leapt up to my feet and charged the white wolf from behind. Digging my fingers into its sumptuous fur, I howled a savage curse and shoved as hard as I could. Triumph surged into my heart as it yielded, stumbling off to the side.

The gray wolf looked up at me, its eyes hazed over

in pain. For a moment, I stood transfixed, watching its chest fail to rise, wanting to breathe for both of us.

A horrifying roar of red-hot murderous rage preceded the rising white wolf as it lurched at me like the Apocalypse on four paws.

A new screech of pain erupted from its blood-slicked maw as the gray wolf caught a delicate length of ankle and snapped pointed teeth shut over it. Bones splintering was a sound I'd never be able to erase from my auditory memory.

In an instant, the white wolf had doubled back over its haunches and caught a loop of viscera hanging from the gray wolf's wounded belly.

Terrible animal screams exploded as a chorus of steam on the air. White and gray, red and black tangled together in an unending fight to the death.

Desperately, I looked around for a way to help.

Spotting a good-sized rock behind the dumpster a few feet away, I sprinted over to grab it.

In this short time, the gray wolf had lost both blood and ground as the white wolf tore at the collapsing body with a potent, frenzied rage.

I prayed more than I aimed as I swung the rock back and hurled it.

Salvation came in the guise of a sickening yelp and a spurt of warm liquid against my cheek.

The white wolf tumbled to the earth and lie still.

"Holy shit!" I said to no one. "Did you see that?"

A weak whine at my feet broke my mini-celebration.

I squatted before the shuddering body and buried my fingers in the thick silver fur behind the ears. I stroked the sleek muzzle in the places not marred by deep gouges and scratches.

"Shhh."

It was beautifully made, this creature who'd fought

to protect me. The pads of its paws cracked and bleeding. Cockleburrs and thorns woven into the fur of its legs.

It had followed me all this way, running through God knows what until his paws bled.

Tears slid down my cheeks as I watched the life ebbing out onto the pavement.

"Aww. Look at the lovely couple. Aren't they sweet?" a silky female voice interrupted.

I glanced up to find a naked woman, covered in blood and gore and gashes. "I owe you for this," she said, rubbing gingerly at a large goose egg rising on her forehead.

If it hadn't been for the platinum bob, I might not have recognized her under all the meat confetti.

"Penny?"

CHAPTER 17

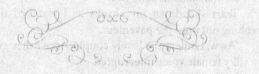

"That's right, love."

Words failed me. *Me*, Hannalore Harvey of the flowery master's thesis. The girl who produced thousands of words about the sun reflecting off a hatpin in a painting of Sarah Bernhardt.

"I must look a mess." Penny wiped her mouth with the back of her hand and licked the blood. "Not something I'd choose for myself," she said, stroking her tongue against the roof of her mouth like a sommelier. "But not bad, really."

I noted the gaping wound on her forearm where she'd been bitten. Her hair was streaked with grisly crimson highlights from wounds on her scalp and cheek.

"This isn't possible. I'm hallucinating. My love for mushroom risotto has finally caught up with me, and I'm hallucinating. I've heard of that happening. Retroactive tripping. Yes, I read that somewhere."

"Sounds plausible." Her breasts jiggled as she shrugged.

If this was a hallucination, it was a damned detailed one.

"But you're dead." I said this out loud as if doing so could make it real. "I saw the article. I saw the pictures."

She rolled her eyes. "How droll of you, Hanna. You think what you see is an accurate reflection of what's there? Think of all the things your senses have failed to tell you so far. Who do you think sent the article to you? Did you ask yourself that?"

In fact, I hadn't.

"I lay in that bloody ditch all night before they found me. Nearly froze my arse off in the process. I made a proper sight though. One of the bobbies was sick in a hedge."

"You weren't dead?" I asked stupidly.

"Not in the traditional sense."

I sat blinking like a dumb cow, trying to collect my thoughts.

"But why?" I asked, hating myself for sounding like every other victim chick in history.

"Simple transaction of business. I came to kill you; Abernathy killed me instead."

"Me? Why me?"

She laughed. The same tinkling sound that had so charmed me on our first meeting. "You mean he hasn't told you?"

"Told me what?" I asked.

Now she was really tickled. "If he hasn't told you yet, I certainly don't want to ruin the surprise."

"What surprise? So the noises I heard through the wall weren't you and Abernathy having wild gorilla sex?"

She made a disgusted face. "With my brother? Are you mental?"

"Wait, what?"

"Honestly, Hanna. Do try to keep up."

"But you said you were there to see him, not me."

"Well, you were in there together. I couldn't very

well ask to see you in private then, could I? Anyway, if Abernathy weren't thinking about shagging you constantly, we wouldn't be having this conversation."

"*Shagging* me?"

"Fucking you, jumping your bones—"

"Yeah, I got that part. Abernathy was thinking about that?" A little rush of pleasure darted to my heart.

Hello? Life being threatened! reminded the little voice in my head. I filed this information away for future consideration.

"As if you didn't know," Penny said. "Muddies his trace something awful though. Yours too. Pheromones can be a bloody nuisance during the full moon."

I felt like I had clam chowder in my head where the brains ought to be. Information kept dumping in, but understanding failed to materialize.

Penny read the confusion on my face.

"Up until about ten minutes ago, you weren't convinced that werewolves existed. About an hour ago, you thought that mess over there was *chasing* you. Pathetic."

That mess over there. The other wolf. I'd completely forgotten.

I looked past her to the crumpled figure on the concrete. It was no longer a wolf.

It was Steven Franke.

My heart. Oh, my heart. A void. A black hole. A blank space that all sunlight disappeared into. Not him. Not my friend.

My throat constricted with tears, and yet one word found its way out. Over and again. "No, no, no, no. No!"

I took off in his direction. Penny caught my arm and twisted it behind my back until I felt sure it would pop out of the socket. She tossed me forward with enough force to dent the Mustang's bumper where I slammed into it, chest first.

The impact knocked the wind out of me before the pain kicked in, rattling up my spine like a jackhammer. Copper on my tongue.

"Hanna, Hanna, Hanna. You really don't have any of this figured out?"

Presently, I couldn't figure out if my spleen was located in my ear. I shook my head in the negative.

She sighed, exasperated.

"Honestly, I thought you more resourceful than this. You really thought it was Abernathy? This whole time?"

I didn't respond. I didn't have to. She read my face like a dime store novel.

"And you're supposed to be the plucky heroine. How very ironic."

"It was you then," I whispered, fighting for breath. "The murders."

"I'm afraid it's not so simple as all that."

She padded over to me on bare feet and squatted in front of me. I had to look away.

Imagine if Goldfinger's schlong had been dangling in the breeze when he revealed his plans for world domination to James Bond. Rather put a different spin on things, didn't it?

"Look at me," she said.

"Could you not be so naked right now? I'm much too socially awkward to be a proper ingénue."

She pinched my chin between two powerful fingers and forced my face toward hers. The blood on her face was drying now, flaking off in little specks when she talked.

"You've a smart mouth on you, miss. I don't think I care for it. It would have been better for you if he'd only let me kill you in Germany. As it is, I have a little more time to be creative."

The thin thread binding me to what I thought I knew had finally snapped. I felt myself floating into new territory, a place where the rules no longer applied.

"Between you and me," I said, "I don't give a shit what you care for."

"Unwise." Her golden eyes took on a steely cast. "If I were you, I'd be groveling about now."

"You want me to beg for my life? Joke's on you then. I don't have dick to live for."

"Is that so?"

She took her time standing and making a leisurely stroll around to the Mustang's window. She pecked on the glass with her nail. "Here kitty, kitty," she purred. "Ooh, a nice fat one. I'm a little puckish, come to think if it." And with that, she punched her hand through the passenger's side window.

Pure, white-hot rage shot through my nervous system.

Oh, hell no, said the little voice in my head. *Please God, or Whoever, let it still be there.*

A sadistic surge of glee coursed through me as my hand found what it sought.

"Hey bitch."

Penny's head whipped toward me.

"Eat lightning."

I depressed the trigger and watched as the probes sank into her stomach, sending thousands of volts of electricity singing through her body.

She tipped backward to the concrete straight as a board. I took a measure of personal delight as her skull hit the road. Her naked flesh jerked and bounced. I sincerely hoped she got road rash on her perfect ass.

Whether I imagined or actually saw the smoke curling from her hair, I couldn't say, but only then did I release the trigger and shuck the cartridge.

I grabbed onto the Mustang and hauled myself to my feet. Gilbert had fled the passenger's seat and was huddled on the floorboards.

"Did that mean old lady scare you? Don't worry, Mommy will be right back."

I pulled a blanket out from the back seat and stumbled over to Steven.

His face was clammy between my hands. I dropped the blanket over him as much to warm him up as to prevent me from seeing his naked body. I'd had quite enough of that for one day.

I rubbed his skin through the blanket, willing him to breathe.

Let him heal like Penny. Let him live.

When he took a shuddering breath, relief sang through my soul.

"Come on," I said. "We have to get you to a hospital."

"No," he half whispered, half gurgled. "No hospital."

Based on the sounds he made, I suspected part of his voice box might be missing.

"Steven, you're hurt. Badly." Like, I could see what you had for dinner on account of the intestines hanging out of your body badly.

"Take my pulse."

Given the purple-red hamburger at his neck, I reached for his mangled arm instead. "I'm pretty sure the bones aren't supposed to stick out like that," I said, hoping to lighten the mood.

I rested two fingers on his slick wrist. No delicate throb of life rose beneath my fingers.

"You're dead!"

"Neat trick, huh?" He coughed. A wet, terrible sound.

"I can see where this would make an E.R. visit a little awkward."

"Digging your way out of a coffin and six feet of dirt

can be a real drag. Not to mention hospital morgues. Autopsies blow. And you'll freeze your ass off on those metal slabs."

"Okay, no hospital then. Where should I take you?"

"Back," he said. "To Abernathy."

My intestines relocated themselves several inches south. I had sort of planned on never seeing him again. There was nothing for it though. I'd drive to the devil's doorstep and dick-punch 'Ole Scratch himself if Steven Franke asked me to.

"I'm sorry," I said. "There's no dignified way to do this." Catching him under the armpits, I lifted his torso while trying to keep the blanket wrapped around him.

Together, we stumble-dragged his lanky body to the Mustang, where I rested him against a gas pump while I opened the passenger side door and brushed broken glass out of the seat. Leaning the seat back as far as it would go, I eased him in and tucked the blanket around him.

Penny began to twitch.

"Time to blow this Popsicle stand."

I returned the gas nozzle to the pump, slid behind the steering wheel, cranked the ignition, and backed the car over Penny a couple times for good measure.

"Oops," I said.

Steven's face shifted into a pained smile as we both felt her catch on the Mustang's undercarriage.

"Imma shut down now, doll. Healing coma. Makes the magic happen faster."

"Sure." I looked over at him, my heart full with hope. "Whatever you gotta do."

"Sorry about the hotdog," he mumbled, his eyelids falling closed.

"Yeah! What was with growling and baring your teeth at me and all that business?"

"Starving," he sighed. "You try running two hundred miles on an empty stomach."

I LISTENED TO THE WHISTLING SOUNDS EMITTING FROM Steven's throat for the better part of eight hours. In a hideous way, it assured me he was still alive. Parts of his trachea were still exposed, though the skin had crept farther over the wound every time I dared look over at him.

Presently, he sounded a little like a teakettle. So much for the nightly herbal chai ritual I'd hoped to institute at some point.

As the shape of mountains became more familiar, my hands began to sweat. We'd be home soon. I'd have to talk to Abernathy.

Maybe he'd be so distracted by Steven that he'd forget all about the whole Tasing thing.

As I often did in the car or shower, I mentally rehearsed what I could say to approximate a responsible adult human.

"Mark! It's Steven! He's been hurt!"

Nah. Too Lassie.

"Mark! Thank goodness you're here! Steven's been hurt!"

Definitely too Lois Lane.

"Mark! Steven's been hurt! And you're not going to believe this! It was Penny all along!" Scooby Doo much?

"There is no way to have this conversation," I said to Gilbert, who had curled up on Steven's lap. "It's not like I Tased him for fun." Gilbert rotated a single ear in my direction—the cat equivalent of a pity date.

"Anyone would have done the same thing in my situation."

Gilbert opened one eye and blinked it shut again. I

took this as an indication he found my argument spotty at best.

"Seriously. I thought he was going to eat me. What was I supposed to do? *I* don't have big books full of newspaper clippings of murdered women. No one *else* I know has books full of clippings of murdered women. I mean, he looks guilty as hell. Amiright? I'm sorry, but I know that handwriting, and those diaries are his. They have to be. Jack the Ripper? Al Capone? John Lennon? I mean really. How old is this guy anyway? He can't be human. Did you see the way he shoved Dave up the wall? It was poetic as fuck. And the appetizers! He picked the prosciutto off and threw the rest away. I saw him. Those smoked Gouda beggars' purses were to die for. Sure, Gouda can be a little overpowering sometimes, but the way they married it with the apricot chutney was spot on. And the Stilton crostini, don't even get me started on those. God, I love cheese."

I looked over at Gilbert, who was sound asleep with his head resting against Steven's stomach.

"Right. If he'd just told me what was going on from the beginning, we might have avoided this whole mess."

If only Hallmark made a "Sorry I Tased You" card. I could write a nice note in it, slide it under his door, hide in my closet, and wait for this whole thing to blow over.

Sure. And you could just hang around waiting for Penny to come turn your skin into a nice pair of stilettos.

"And that's another thing—holy shit, assclown, get off my tail would ya?"

I squinted into my rearview mirror at the tank that had crept up to my back bumper. Light from the morning sun reflected off the shining chrome grille, blinding me temporarily.

Ahooga! screamed the car's horn.

My sphincter tightened. I knew that sound. Last

time I'd heard it, Abernathy had folded up the Roll's hood like a tin foil taco.

I did a double take as a last resort. My mind could be playing tricks on me. I hadn't slept in twenty-four hours. And I'd witnessed a werewolf fight. I could be losing it. *Please let me be losing it.*

No such luck.

The Wraith's engine roared as it pulled up along beside me in the opposite lane.

I stared straight ahead. Maybe I could pretend I didn't see him. Maybe he'd just go away.

Ahooga!

Definitely not going away. When I glanced over at the Wraith, it wasn't Abernathy, but Rob Vincent I saw. He gave me an awkward smile from the passenger's seat and motioned for me to pull over.

In the end, it was the Mack truck in Abernathy's lane that made my decision. I wasn't entirely sure Abernathy would blink first.

The Mustang fishtailed on the gravel as I rocketed off to the side of the road. The rumble strips awoke Steven, who yawned and cracked his neck. The gaping wound in his throat was mostly closed, save for a raw-looking abrasion on his protruding Adam's apple. It might be mistaken for a really unfortunate shaving accident now.

The Wraith pulled in behind me, and Abernathy and Rob Vincent both got out. I fought the urge to hunt up my license and registration from the glove compartment beyond Steven's knobby knees.

"Just act natural," I instructed the cats.

Abernathy came around to the driver's side and yanked on the door handle. When he found it locked, he leaned close enough to fog the window.

"Unlock. The. Door." he mouthed.

I cupped my hand to my ear and pretended not to understand him.

Steven reached across me and popped the lock.

I turned to him, on the point of asking "whose side are you on, anyway?" when I realized how utterly stupid a question it was.

On the side of the guy that could break me in half and use me for a toothpick. Duh.

Abernathy wrenched the car door open and staggered backward.

"Pwah!" he grimaced, covering his mouth and nose and stifling a gag.

Until this moment, I hadn't considered what the inside of the Mustang must smell like. My nose had gone on strike about seven hours ago.

I didn't even *want* to think about how I looked. Without the aid of a mirror, I had brushed dried blood from my face and absently picked at the mats of gore in my hair while I drove. My shoes were beyond help. There wasn't enough hand sanitizer in the free world to handle this mess, much less the half-empty tube in my purse.

Abernathy looked like hammered shit, I was both delighted and horrified to note. He had the makings of a lumberjack beard sprouting over his jawline, his usually golden skin sallow and covered with scratches and wounds. Disheveled hair stuck up in strange cowlicks all over his head. Like he'd stuck his finger into an electrical socket.

Or like someone had Tased him.

Oops.

Like me, he wore the same clothes he'd had on yesterday, torn shirtsleeves and all. He glanced at the Taser still resting in my cup holder and narrowed his eyes.

"Get out of the car," he said.

"I'm okay." I pretended to fiddle with the heat. "But thanks."

"It wasn't a request."

"Oh?"

"Get out of the car, or I'll *pull* you out of the car."

I considered my arm, the one nearest to him, the one Penny had nearly dislodged from its socket earlier that morning. It still ached.

"I would...but my cats—"

He moved faster than I could see. I felt the rush of cold air and the blur of violent movement. Then blood rushing to my head as I dangled over his shoulder like a sack of dirty laundry.

"Hey!" I said. "Put me down!" We both knew it wasn't going to happen, but I felt compelled by all members of the female sex to make the request in any case.

He ignored me, and spoke to Rob instead, tossing him the Mustang's keys.

"You want to follow me?"

"Sure thing," Rob said.

As he turned to walk back to the Rolls, Rob gave me a wave and a nod.

"The Mustang sticks a little in third," I warned him behind Abernathy's back.

"Got it."

"Oh. Sorry about the smell. Gilbert's mostly emptied out now I think."

Abernathy opened the door and flung me into the back seat. Under different circumstances, this might not be such a bad gig.

"What? I've been fired from sitting in the front?"

The engine turned over with a throaty growl. Abernathy sent a spray of gravel flying as we sped off.

I looked out the small back window and saw Rob pull the Mustang out after us. Gilbert's perpetually worried face popped into view over the dashboard. Stewie and Stella were probably attacking Rob's ankles about now. I hoped they would be okay. I was almost positive Rob wouldn't eat them.

Propping my elbows up on the back of the front bench seat, I accidentally caught a glance of myself in the rearview mirror and scooted a foot to the left.

"How did you find us?" I asked.

The muscles in Abernathy's jaw worked beneath his dark scruff.

"Does the Wraith get decent gas mileage?"

His face was expressionless. Solid as the surface of a frozen lake.

"'Cause the Mustang is terrible."

His right eyelid twitched. *Now* I was getting somewhere.

"Are you all werewolves, then? You, Steven, Rob, Kirkpatrick?"

Abernathy's lips flattened into a stubborn line.

"Silent treatment, huh? Normally that works great because I'm super-sensitive to rejection, but I haven't slept in forever and I'm feeling pretty punchy. I'll probably keep talking until you say something, just so you know."

He stared ahead with laser-like focus.

To hell with it. I leaned forward to climb into the front seat and wriggled my body over the back of the bench. My knee caught Abernathy's elbow, and when the car lurched to the left, I kicked him in the back of the head getting the last of my leg over.

"Jesus Christ, Hanna!" he growled, righting the car back into the proper lane.

At least he was talking to me.

"Sorry. If you hadn't shoved me in the backseat..."

"You *Tased* me! Do you have any idea how painful that is?"

"Actually," I began, fully prepared to launch into all I knew about the effects of Tasers having researched the topic before I left. But catching the shape of his hair in my peripheral vision snapped my mouth shut.

"No," I said, picking at a bloodstain on my jeans. Beyond the windows, the first fingers of gray dawn crept over the distant mesas.

"*No.*"

"In my defense, I thought you were going to eat me. I had just discovered diaries from a couple hundred years ago *and* a book with dead women and my picture in it, which, by the way, you *still* haven't explained to me, and then you get there and you're being all creepy and obscure—"

"If I had wanted to *eat* you, Hanna, you wouldn't have had a snowball's chance in hell of stopping me."

The way he said "eat" had me wondering how he meant it.

"Nice reassurance, boss. You been reading Hitler's *How to Skin Friends and Influence People*?"

"Can't you just accept that there are things you're better off not knowing?"

"You *do* know who you're talking to, right? And since when was lack of information considered a good strategic position? That's a war thing, isn't it?"

"Assuming you have the *correct* information and not just a loose collection of assumptions. A loose collection of assumptions puts you precisely where we are now. The intersection of fucking nowhere and fresh hell."

Perhaps I had acted a *tad* rashly. I considered the absurdity of all that had occurred in the last twenty-four hours as a result. He'd left me with too many questions. Questions I still didn't have answers to. I regretted that I'd left my composition book in the Mustang. I could be writing them all down.

"Did you know about Penny?" I asked.

"I was aware of her, yes."

"Aware of her? Apparently you two aren't tight then." I felt at a distinct disadvantage, having no siblings of my own to form a basis of comparison.

"Tight?"

"Tight. As in tight-knit family."

Abernathy looked at me like I had a birch tree growing out of my head. For all I knew, I just might.

"Penny, your *sister* Penny."

"Penny's not my sister. What the hell gave you that idea?"

"She did. When she was all naked and covered in blood and getting her bragging-villain strut on, I asked about you two having gorilla sex in Germany and she said 'With my brother? Are you mental?'"

"She's more unhinged than I thought."

"You think?"

He stared past the horizon, his thoughts having moved on to country whose terrain he wouldn't share.

"Do you have siblings? Real ones?"

"A sister."

I tried to imagine what she might look like. Penny had been difficult to accept as a relation to Abernathy, with her petite frame and light coloring. No, Abernathy's sister would be dark. Taller than average perhaps.

A wild idea bounced through my tired brain.

"Oh my God. The pictures! Sending Steven Franke after me. Oh my God. It all makes sense!"

Abernathy said nothing.

"I'm your sister, aren't I?"

He looked at me, his face a mixed mask of regret and sorrow.

I felt the blood drain from my head as my vision

shrank to a single point. Abernathy's wide shoulders shook inside his shredded shirt. Was he crying?

"Oh my God." I leaned forward to let my elbows rest on my knees.

Then his face broke. He threw his head back and howled. His booming laughter rippled through his throat, filled the entire car.

I'd been had.

"You son of a bitch." I punched his massive arm as hard as I could. Pain rang through my scraped knuckles. "You jerk!"

"Sorry. You walked right into that one."

"You don't *sound* sorry." I crossed my arms and turned my face to the window. I felt my nose rise toward the Wraith's roof.

"Oh, come on. You know you deserved that."

Maybe. Probably.

"Hanna, you are *not* my sister. You couldn't be further from her. She's batshit crazy. Not to mention about four hundred years old and kind of a bitch."

My antennae perked up. *So how old would this make Abernathy?* I turned further away, not quite willing to give it up yet.

"I would have had *you* up against the gallery wall instead of your piss-ant ex-husband, if he hadn't interrupted. Do you honestly think I'd have done that to my sister? Even wer—"

But he caught himself and stopped.

Meanwhile, my heart was climbing my ribs like a jungle gym.

I would have had you up against that gallery wall. He'd said this. Out loud. With his mouth.

"That wasn't nice," I said.

"Really? You seemed to be enjoying it at the time."

I *really* hated it when he was right, and he knew it. "You know what I meant."

"Tasing me wasn't nice either."

"Fair enough."

The hurricane of questions swirling around my brain began to die down to a whisper. Whether they were gone, or I was just in the storm's quiet eye, I couldn't say.

I glanced in the side mirror and saw the Mustang faithfully following after us like a happy caboose. Steven and Rob were talking. I slid down in my seat and smiled, glad for the simple knowledge that Steven was still here. The world would have lost something in him. *I* would have lost something.

The Wraith's rumbling lullaby gentled away the last of my conscious thoughts. At last, I gave in to sleep.

CHAPTER 18

*M*y ear hurt.

Consciousness returned to me in degrees. I felt like I'd been sleeping on a rock.

"Hanna," the voice said, "we're here."

I blinked my eyes against the daylight and peeled my wet cheek away from my rocky pillow, otherwise known as *Abernathy's thigh*.

He had a dark pool on his pants where I'd drooled on him.

Again.

I sat up straight and glanced around. We were still in the Wraith but parked in front of the gallery.

"I would apologize, but I'm too delirious to be mortified at present."

"Hey, don't sweat it." Abernathy tugged the knee of his slacks. "These will match my suit jacket now."

"I think I liked you better as the silent stoic type," I said, climbing out of the car and into a full-body stretch.

Everything hurt.

Behind me, Rob Vincent helped Steven out of the Mustang.

"Wouldn't he be more comfortable at home? Actually, wouldn't we all be more comfortable at home?" I asked, thoughts of a hot shower and my warm bed unfurling like a fairy tale tapestry.

Abernathy shook his head. "Not safe."

"And this place is?"

"The Crossing has certain," he paused, "advantages."

"Ohh right, like a magic force field or something."

Hell, I didn't know how this shit worked. I'd only found out that werewolves existed earlier that morning. For all I knew, the whole wheelbarrow of happy horseshit could be true. Werewolves, vampires, nymphs, satyrs, Nickelback fans...

"No. Like a state-of-the-art security system from Bosch."

"Wait. You didn't even have a cell phone or a computer when I met you, but you have this place wired for security? Since when?"

"Since forever."

"You don't even lock your office door."

Abernathy shrugged. "There's nothing in my office I care about."

"But I got in here yesterday morning with just a key."

"Steven was already here."

"Wait, what?" The more I learned, the less sense everything seemed to make.

"We'll talk inside."

Rob flipped open a brick to the side of the door, punched in a code, and tossed the Mustang's keys to me as he helped Steven limp in.

I glanced over to the Mustang and saw Gilbert sniffing at a side window.

"The cats," I said. "We can't leave the cats in the car."

"We can't?" Abernathy asked.

I gave him a dirty look.

"Either they come in, or I go home."

He considered this for a moment. "I'm going to regret this."

"Here. You take Gilbert and Stella, and I'll get Stewie and the food."

Gilbert hissed and growled, his paws flailing in the air as Abernathy grabbed him by the scruff of the neck and held him out at arm's length.

"Hey! He's not a damn kitten. You can't hold him like that."

"Most Wagstaff cranes couldn't hold him like this," Abernathy grunted. "Do you want them brought in or not?"

"He's on Iam's Lean! He's diab—"

"Just give me the other fucking cat!" His arm swung wildly as Gilbert hissed and rolled, clawing at the air.

I pulled Stella out of the back seat, and Abernathy snagged her scruff, holding her at the full length of his opposite arm.

Balancing the bag of cat food on one hip and Stewie on the other, I followed Abernathy into the gallery. We ran into Rob Vincent at the door.

"I've got Steven all settled in my studio," he reported. "Why don't we put them in Steven's space?"

Stewie didn't seem to have any definitive opinions on the subject. "Works for me," I said.

Rob opened Steven's door, and Abernathy tossed Gilbert and Stella in.

I set Stewie down and shook a little cat food onto a paper plate on the floor. Rob arrived with the litter box. "Figured they might need this," he said.

We closed the door behind us to keep them contained.

"Hey!" Steven bounced out into the hallway.

I looked over just as he whipped open the blanket. "Intestines back in place and covered by—" he patted his belly "—these amazing abs!"

"That's great." I directed my gaze to the gallery's ceiling of exposed vents and pipes.

"Oh, sorry." Steven wrapped the blanket around his hips like a bath towel. "Kind of forget I'm naked sometimes. You know?"

"I can't say I do, actually." For me, being naked was akin to a Master's thesis defense: lots of preparation before, expectations of heavy criticism during, and anxiety about my performance afterward. My wild night with Morrison notwithstanding.

Rob helped Steven back into his studio and went in after him. I trailed Abernathy upstairs, pausing at the landing to raid my desk for the essentials: bleach wipes, hand sanitizer, and a Milky Way bar. I brought my collection into Abernathy's office where I plopped down on the couch and took a bleach wipe to my face.

Perhaps not the best idea, but their clean, chemical smell did wonders to refresh my soul. Wipe after wipe came away smeared with rusty brown smudges of dried blood and the remnants of yesterday's makeup.

Abernathy sat down in his chair and propped his feet up on his desk.

"What now?" I asked.

"Now, you lie down on the couch and get some sleep."

"I'm not tired."

"If *I'm* tired, then I know you have to be."

"That reminds me," I said stifling a yawn. "Where do you sleep?"

I had begun to suspect that, like an elementary school teacher, Abernathy might just tuck himself into an office cupboard at night.

"In my bed," he answered.

How could three simple words carry such heavy implications?

"Yes, and your bed is where?"

"In my bedroom."

"Where the hell do you live?"

"In my home."

I flopped back on the leather couch. "Do you have any idea how irritating you are?"

"I might." He cast a meaningful look to the spot next to his desk where I had Tased him.

"Still hung up on that whole Tasing thing, huh?"

God but this couch was comfortable. I rolled onto my side and rested my head against the crook of my elbow. I bit into my Milky Way bar and chewed slowly.

"When do I get to know why Penny wanted to kill me?"

"After you sleep."

"I told you, I'm nottired. I'm tootired tobe tired." I hoped my words were making more sense to Abernathy than they were to me.

"Right," he said.

"What about the murders? D'you thinkit wasPenny?" Why were my words sticking together? Was it the caramel?

I tried to swallow a yawn but ended up snorting instead. So many questions.

"Thanksfer not eating me."

Abernathy might have said "the day is young," but I can't be sure.

I slept.

RIDING THE WAVE, PROLONGING THE MOMENT BETWEEN sleeping and waking, I could feel peace. Knowledge distant enough not to bother, and dreams close enough to keep the pleasant heaviness in my limbs.

It was the smell that forced me out of my happy place.

At once recognizable and unwelcome. Dark, musty, medicinal...chocolatey.

The chocolatey part was me, as it turned out. I'd fallen asleep with the Milky Way in my hand. I could feel it in my fingers as I rolled onto my back on Abernathy's leather couch.

"You're awake," said the voice, familiar and unfamiliar. "Good."

I stretched and blinked the sleep funk out of my eyes until the face swam into focus.

"Hi, Mrs. Kass. Where is everybody?"

My legs were tangled up in something. I pushed on to my elbows and glanced down.

Abernathy's pants. He'd covered me with his dry cleaning. My heart fluttered a little at his sweet and simple—if totally odd—gesture.

"Downstairs I expect."

"Is Steven doing okay?"

"How would I know, Hanna?" She ran a bony, gnarled hand over my hair. "Such a pretty girl."

A cold, creeping dread settled into my chest as the realization hit me. Mrs. Kass wasn't wearing her glasses. Mrs. Kass could see me.

I knew that older people suffering from dementia or Alzheimer's would have occasional moments of lucidity, but I didn't think the episodes included the patient's suddenly having 20/20 vision and perfect hearing.

"Are you okay Mrs. Kass?" I asked, pushing myself into a sitting position.

Her dry, cracked lips drew back into an ugly rictus smile. Red, swollen gums peeked through where her dentures should be.

"I think I should check on my cats," I said, rising from the couch.

She planted a hand on my sternum and shoved me back into the couch with surprising force.

"Oh no dear, you're not going anywhere." The frightening smile deepened, pushing the papery skin up her cheeks in hundreds of impossible folds.

"Mrs. Kass, what are you doing?"

"I wasn't sure it was you." Her hand crawled along the couch's arm as she leaned toward me. She sniffed the air by my face and licked her lips. "Not at first."

"What was me? What are you talking about?" I glanced at the door to the office. Mrs. Kass had locked it. *Where was Abernathy?*

"He's had so many women, you see. So many. It could have been any of them."

Her normally wobbly voice was solid and clear. Perfectly, terribly calm.

"I don't understand." *Keep her talking, Hanna.*

"But when he hired you, I thought, 'It must be her. It has to be.' But I still couldn't be sure, could I?"

"Couldn't be sure I was *what?*"

"Don't pretend you don't know!" Sudden anger brought a pink flush to her scalp. "It won't save your precious *skin.*" Flecks of spittle flew out and landed on my cheeks.

"And that walking accident of nature, Steven Franke. Always following, always interrupting. When all I wanted is some *time* with you."

Her breath singed my nose hairs with the scent of decay. She trailed her knuckles down the front of my neck and across the curve of my collarbone.

"I'm going to enjoy eating your heart. So tender."

And exactly how did she know I had a tender heart? Okay, so I once rescued a burnt corn flake from my cereal bowl because I felt sorry for him. I named him Cornelius and kept him in my jewelry box. But *she* didn't know that.

Or did she?

Her dowager's hump made a sickening cracking noise as her spine folded forward on itself. The middle of her face began to swell outward, shaping into a short, brutal muzzle. The gnarled hand at my throat began to contract, and claws dug into my windpipe. Fur sprouted in patches over her liver-spotted skin. Rotten yellow fangs pushed through her slick red gums.

She was neither wolf nor woman. She was a monster in a housedress. Her coated purple tongue snaked out and licked my cheek. A scream pealed out of my throat and sent her staggering backward.

Someone had forgotten to take out her hearing aids. It must have been especially unpleasant since she didn't really need them in the first place.

Just as I launched myself toward the door, it exploded into the room.

Between the splinters and flying debris, I caught an ephemeral glimpse of the last of Abernathy's features before he had completely transformed.

He was a wolf.

His body was a ballad to animal grace: perfection in predatory design. A thick pelt the color of dark chocolate, eyes the color of milk chocolate (hey, I'm working on a theme here), a muscled flank, long powerful legs, rows of white teeth like daggers.

Also, he was huge. Like, a Bull Mastiff on steroids huge.

I kind of wanted to pet him.

He was on Mrs. Kass—or what used to be Mrs. Kass —in a fraction of a second.

I fumbled the lock open and ran to my desk, knocking my pencil cup over as I looked for my sterling silver flying pig letter opener. I had no idea if the legends about werewolves and silver were true, but I figured a little insurance couldn't hurt.

I found it in my top drawer and tucked it into the band between the cups of my bra for easy access. One of the wings dug into my sternum, half annoying, and half reassuring.

Steven and Rob. I had to get to them.

I flew to the stairs and froze halfway down as a deep, vibrating boom rumbled through the gallery. Plaster dust rained from the ceiling, and a deep crack opened in the exposed brick wall facing the street.

"What the he—"

This time, the wall gave way, collapsing into the gallery like a tapestry of falling brick. The dust cleared, revealing the grill of a Mack truck.

So much for Abernathy's state-of-the-art security.

Whoever was driving the truck, I took a chance that it would take them a moment to get out and over the debris.

I tripped down the last few stairs and scrambled over the bricks toward the artists' studios. Rob and Steven were already way ahead of me, sprinting into the gallery. By the time I turned to watch, I saw only retreating hind legs and tails.

A flash of orange.

Rob Vincent, when he was on all fours, had a distinctive copper sheen. Had they all been watching over me? All this time?

In the settling dust, Steven and Rob squared off with wolves I'd never seen.

They moved like separate pieces of a single machine. The slightest twitch in one haunch was enough to send ripples of coordinated movement through the rest of the pack. These were not decisions, but instincts. Actions performed without thinking.

Meanwhile, thinking was all I could do.

Three on two seemed like unfair odds, with Abernathy otherwise engaged.

Creeping down the hall, I paused by Steven's studio, where a sliver of yellow light leaked from under the door. Rob had turned on a lamp for the cats.

I inched the door open and saw Stella, Stewie, and Gilbert curled up on his desk, in his armchair, on his worn ottoman.

"No worries," I assured them. "Just an apocalyptic werewolf battle going on out here."

Stella rested her chin back on her paws, untroubled.

I tiptoed out to the silent oddities shop and slipped through the front door.

The cold half-light caught between the end of one day and the beginning of another smudged greasy shadows in the deserted street. The world had entered into the tense, paranoid silence of a Surrealist painting. What happened now beyond the breached gallery wall could be felt by the terrifying absence it created. No sirens wailed in the distance, promising to bring trouble, or help. No gawkers or bystanders to offer confirmation or compare accounts.

I couldn't decide which was worse: if nothing was real, or if everything was.

I moved toward the Mustang in the weightlessness of dreams. The Taser was still in the cup holder where I'd left it. I grabbed the reassuringly heavy object, loaded my last cartridge, and tucked it back into the front pocket of my hoodie.

Mission: Impossible theme music played on a loop in my head as I snuck into the building and slid along the wall, careful to keep in the shadows.

Back inside the gallery, Rob tangled with a rangy black wolf on the scattered pile of bricks. They tore at each other with teeth glinting under the gallery's track lighting and collided into the side of the truck, yelping, biting, rolling, righting themselves for a new onslaught. Rob fought to get toward Steven, who had been backed into a corner by the other two wolves.

Hunkered down, hackles raised, Steven growled as they advanced. The smaller, mud-brown wolf inched closer by slow degrees, savoring the kill while the blue-gray wolf tensed and made strange coughing sounds.

I stuck two fingers in my mouth to whistle and blew a gob of spit down my wrist.

So, I wasn't so good with the wolf-whistling. It had always worked in the movies.

Time for plan B.

"Here boy!"

All five wolves froze mid-fight and turned toward me.

Shit. I hadn't counted on that.

Before they could leap on me in a frenzy of claws and teeth, I aimed my Taser and took out the blue-gray wolf closest to Steven. He was the bigger wolf, after all.

He yelped and went down in a twitching pile of fur.

Steven winked at me and seized upon this opportunity to launch himself on the mud-brown wolf. They went at each other on hind legs, clawing and snarling as they crashed into the white gallery walls and sent paintings hurtling toward the ground.

The blue-gray wolf was no longer a wolf, but Basil Hackett, the ancient auctioneer Penny had pointed out at Bonham's in Germany. The one who'd called me the "ginger miss."

Been around since 1793 indeed. Take *that*, werewolf jerk.

Now for the mud-colored wolf.

I bent down to grab a nearby brick to lob at its head, hoping for a repeat of my performance with Penny at the gas station.

The universe had other plans.

A forceful kick to my ass sent me sprawling face-first into the gallery.

My teeth punctured my lower lip on impact but felt no pain, only warmth spreading down my chin.

Penny was dressed now. That was an improvement at least. Her scars were healing nicely, I was discouraged to note, though one of her arms was bent at a completely unnatural angle to her body. I secretly hoped this was a remnant of her run-in with the Mustang.

"Someone really ought to take that toy away from you," she said, glancing at the Taser.

"Glad to see they got most of you off the concrete," I said. "Did you have to use a spatula?"

She narrowed her eyes at me. "You'd better—"

Rob and the black wolf rolled between us, growling and snarling, drowning Penny out.

I cupped my hand to my ear and shook my head.

"You'd better—" she began again, as Steven and the brown wolf came tearing across the gallery.

"Come on, you grotty wankers! Take it somewhere else!"

The black and brown wolves took off down the hall toward the oddities shop with Steven and Rob on their asses like a pair of cheap leather pants.

"Right," she said. "What was I saying?"

"I believe you were about to threaten me."

"Yes, that's right. Oh, sod it all."

She leapt at me without warning, her bones cracking and shifting as she transformed in mid-air.

Her paws hit my shoulders, driving me back into the bricks. She caught hold of the sleeve of my hoodie and shook it like a rat. I swung my leg around and kicked her ribs, but to little effect. If only I had opted for boots rather than Chuck Taylors when I'd picked my "fleeing for my life" outfit the day before.

As I struggled to put elbows and knees between her maw and my neck, her powerful jaws snapped and clicked toward my face.

The pain of my skin tearing between her teeth was unbearable, but brief. Better an elbow than a jugular.

A chocolate-brown blur streaked over my head, and Penny was gone before I could even scream.

Now I understood exactly what I'd heard that night in Germany. The growls, the screams, the banging walls and breaking glass.

This was the sound of Abernathy saving my life.

He and Penny wasted no time with the customary dance. Their assault was primal, brutal, and perfectly efficient. To watch them was to understand the terrible consequences of duality unraveled: light and dark, male and female, life and death. The elemental forces of nature at each other's throats.

Penny aimed low, using her smaller size to attack Abernathy's vulnerable underbelly. She caught his pelt and ripped at the skin at his flank, exposing silvery connective tissue and torn flesh.

Abernathy came over top, catching her by the scruff of her neck and throwing her over on her back. He lunged at the underside of her throat, his powerful jaws closing on her windpipe.

Her yelp turned into a wet gurgle.

A terrible animal scream of pain jerked Abernathy's attention from Penny's open throat.

We both knew the source.

Steven Franke.

Abernathy flew down the hall toward the sound. Within seconds, I heard crashing shelves and foreign yelps. Abernathy exacting his revenge on whoever, and whatever, hurt Steven, no doubt.

Rob's copper body came flashing past me. The black wolf, close on his tail, sprang onto Rob's back, forcing him onto the ground. Penny, as if revived by these new yelps of pain, scrambled to her feet and leapt at Rob from the other side.

"No!" I screamed. "Get away from him!"

I picked up bricks and started heaving them at Penny, and at the black wolf.

"Leave!" *Brick.* "Him!" *Brick.* "Alone!" But before I could hurl another, a gnarled, bloody hand-claw caught my wrist and forced it up behind my back.

The Mrs. Kass-wolf-thing wrapped her other claw around my neck. "Don't move," she growled, "or I'll open your pretty throat." The mineral-rich scent of blood now accented the heavy aroma of death on her hot breath.

I watched, helpless and hurting, as the black wolf crushed its jaws around Rob Vincent's neck while Penny buried her muzzle in his chest.

"Rob!" I shrieked, squirming against Mrs. Kass.

Penny had broken through the muscle wall and held between her jaws Rob Vincent's good, kind heart. She tossed it up in the air and snapped it down like a fox would a muskrat.

Sobs caught in my throat, squeezed beneath Mrs. Kass's grip.

"That, Hanna," Mrs. Kass said, her sticky lips brushing my ear, "is how you kill a werewolf."

CHAPTER 19

CHAPTER 19

*R*elieved of his heart, Rob Vincent's naked body lay lifeless on the floor in a widening pool of his own blood, staring endlessly at something his waking eyes would never see.

He was human again. At least, he was as human as he'd ever been. His chest and throat were torn open, and his body was a purple-red carpet of wounds. There would be no healing coma for him.

Penny and the black wolf backed away from Rob's body, each taking their own time to transform. Penny was naked again, as was her companion. I recognized him as another Bonham's agent I'd met at the auction.

Just how many werewolves are there in the art world?

"Ugh." Penny grimaced. "Tree hugger. They're always so bland." She wiped her bloody mouth on her naked shoulder.

Abernathy bounded into the room with Steven on his heels.

"Stop!" Mrs. Kass ordered.

His animal gaze flicked over the room, taking it all in. Penny and her goon, Rob Vincent, Mrs. Kass, and me.

"Sit."

When Abernathy hesitated, Mrs. Kass wrenched my arm higher to renew the pain.

He brought his haunches to rest on the floor. His body remained on high alert even in this resting position. Ears cocked, muscles tensed, ready to spring.

Behind him, Steven had begun to lose his grip on his wolf form. His face was nearly human now, save for wolf ears and a shiny black nose. The rest of his body was lengthening, the fur retracting into his white skin. He still had a tail.

"Good boy." Mrs. Kass had recovered some of her former syrupy sweetness.

"What is it you want?" Abernathy asked.

I stifled a giggle that I hoped sounded like dismay. Abernathy was a wolf. A *talking* wolf.

"What do I want? *What do I want?* Not much." Mrs. Kass's fingers trailed down my neck, pressing briefly against my throbbing jugular vein. "Just your heart, Abernathy."

"Mother!" Penny hissed from across the gallery. "What are you doing? Kill her!"

"Mother?" Abernathy's head cocked to one side in the universal gesture of canine bewilderment.

"Yes," Mrs. Kass said. "*Mother.*"

"Why *my* heart?" Abernathy asked.

"Look at me! Look at what I am!" The force of Mrs. Kass's words rattled through my ribs. "You would have done the same to all those women, if I hadn't killed them! Just like your father!"

"What about my father?" Abernathy's features sharpened with a predatory keenness.

"Your father made her!" Mrs. Kass shouted, looking toward Penny. "And carrying her, made me! A half wolf with a half-life! Living through centuries only to see my body decay bit by bit as everyone I loved died. He abandoned us. Threw us aside like garbage for you, his precious son."

So, Penny *was* Abernathy's sister. His half-sister born of a half-wolf mother. We all soaked in this knowledge. Mrs. Kass, the murders, her identity.

"Joseph Abernathy was a bastard." Abernathy's sleek head canted downward. "But I am not my father."

"No. You're worse! All the women you've paraded through here. The women you *ruined*. I gave them mercy. I *saved* them."

"Rosemary." Abernathy's voice held a gentleness I had never before heard. "That's not how it works. What my father did—"

Mrs. Kass shoved my arm up my back until the re-sounding pop echoed through the gallery. Hot, searing pain burned through my shoulder and shot through the nerves into my fingers. Agony erupted from me in one, long howl.

"Her, or your heart! Your life, or your precious *heir*."

Heir? This one word penetrated the red-rimmed haze of pain. Heir to *what*?

Across a distance now populated with impossible knowledge and the destruction it wrought, Abernathy's eyes found mine. In them, I read a volume of suffering. Of conflict. Of scenarios hoped for and lost. The tying of all ends.

"Make one move, *sweinhund*," Mrs. Kass growled, "and I will *end* her. You know I can."

To my horror, Abernathy lowered himself to the ground.

In a calculated surrender, he relinquished control of one muscle at a time, never taking his eyes off Mrs. Kass. At last, he stretched out his long limbs, rolled to his side, and exposed his heart.

Panic took me. "Mark, no! You can't—"

Mrs. Kass tightened her grip on my throat until her claws pierced my skin and drops of warm blood rolled down my neck. She sniffed the air, sensing this new scent.

Her long purple tongue traced the length of my throat. "Someone has a sweet tooth."

"Don't judge," I choked.

"Penelope! Take him now!"

Penny failed to launch into action. "If we don't kill Hanna, she won't complete your transformation. Everything we've worked for will be lost."

"He has to pay," Mrs. Kass said, ignoring Penny. "Sins of the father. Take hi—"

The muzzle signature slammed the air a split second before the hot wall of chunks and blood covered my back and head. A curtain of red mist exploded in my peripheral vision as fragments of skull and skin rained to the gallery floor.

Mrs. Kass's claws dropped away from my arm and throat as what was left of her body tipped backward and hit the bricks.

Kirkpatrick shucked his shotgun, sending shell casings tinkling to the floor. He stood at the end of the hall to the artist's studios like a miniature Rambo clad in fishing gear. We all gaped at him.

"How am I supposed to work with all this racket going on out here?"

Penny's howl of rage broke the stunned silence. Sprinting toward Kirkpatrick, she changed in midair, colliding with his chest. The shotgun flew from his hands—*shame about those stubby fingers*—clattering across the floor.

I reached into my shirt and palmed the silver letter opener, a comforting body-temperature weight in my hand. "Okay, Clancy," I whispered. "Let's do this."

When Penny loosened her hold on Kirkpatrick to get better purchase, I lunged, burying the letter opener as far as it would go in between her ribs. Her howl of pain shattered the gallery's remaining windows.

Smoke curled from the wound and dissipated into whisps on the gallery air. "Holy shit," I marveled. "It really works!"

Penny collapsed onto her side, writhing paws lengthening into fingers and fur giving way to flesh. Then, at last, she was still.

"I could have fought her off." Having regained both his footing and his reprehensible personality, Kirkpatrick brushed broken glass from his fisherman's vest.

"I'm sure you could have." Not the response I wanted to give him, but I figured saving me from being gnawed to death by a hideous half were-lady had to buy him something.

A pained groan wrested my gaze from the ruin at my feet.

Abernathy lay panting on the gallery floor, arms outstretched and bleeding from too many places to count. I knelt beside him and placed a hand on his massive shoulder.

His massive *naked* shoulder.

I restricted my eyes to chest level, telling myself there was plenty to see there, in any case.

"Ow." He winced, trying to sit up.

"Let me help you."

The arm Mrs. Kass had cranked behind my back hung numb and tingling at my side. I scooted my good arm under Abernathy's shoulder and tried to coax him upright, but only managed to pull myself on top of him.

On top of *naked* Abernathy.

I quickly scooted away. "Sorry, boss. There's no way in hell I can lift you."

He only grinned. "I know."

"Hey look!" I said, desperately trying to keep my eyes from wandering south. "Mrs. Kass!"

The remnants of her head were beginning to smoke and sizzle.

"Silver filings in the shells," Kirkpatrick said. "Makes healing damn near impossible."

"Speaking of impossible," I said, taking in the gallery with growing horror.

Four dead bodies—one of them missing its head— collapsed walls covered with blood and gore, splintered furniture, broken pictures, and a diesel truck parked in the middle of the gallery floor.

I didn't even want to think about what the oddities shop must look like.

"How in the hell are we going to explain all this?"

"I'll take care of it." Abernathy stood behind me, his face showing no measure of the shock I felt.

"What do you mean *take care of it*? There are dead bodies."

"I have people."

I thought back to Abernathy's pristine hotel room the morning after his epic werewolf brawl with Penny.

"Ahh. *Those* kind of people."

He smiled. "You can't live as long as I have without being able to clear away a few messes."

"And just how long would that be?"

"Tomorrow," he said. "Go home and get some rest. It would be better if you're not around for this."

"Why?" Not that I wanted to argue too insistently. I had about half of a quasi-werewolf head congealing in my hair.

"Because when Detective Morrison questions you, you won't have to lie." I detected a lingering note of irritation in Abernathy's voice when he spoke the name Morrison.

Detective Morrison. Shit. What in the hell was I going to tell him?

"Go home."

"Whatever you say, boss." I picked my way through the rubble and went upstairs to Abernathy's office to gather my purse and coat. Unable to accomplish the basic maneuver of getting my useless arm in the sleeve, I used my one working hand to drape it over my shoulders.

When I turned to leave, I found Abernathy leaning in the doorway, much the same way I had encountered him on our first meeting. Shirtless and stubbled, smudged with dark shadows like a charcoal drawing, he looked like an ad Satan's Director of PR might produce.

"What is it?" I said.

"Turn around."

"Excuse me?"

"Turn *around*."

"Why?"

Then Abernathy was gone, and the world became a streak of colors on the air as I spun to face the desk. Hands were on my sternum, at my hip. Lips were on my ear. Abernathy behind me, holding me fast.

"When are you going to learn to do what I say?"

"When what you say makes fucking sense." I squirmed against the arms crushing me to his body. His warm chest pressed against my back like a stone wall holding the sun's last warmth at dusk. How I wanted to lean against him to rest, to let someone or something else hold me up for a while.

He pulled the purse from my hand and dropped it on his desk.

"Hold still." His hands slid over my shoulders, finding the edge of my coat and peeling it from me. It fell to the floor between us with a sigh. Specters of fire danced across my neck where he'd touched. My wrist was lost in the grip of his hand, solid as an iron cuff.

"Don't." I winced. "Mrs. Kass—"

"Shh." The fingers spread against my stomach flexed. Lips found the tender spot where neck met shoulder and brushed a kiss there.

A sharp intake of breath was enough to send a new jolt of pain through my shoulder. Mark slid my wrist up my body and lifted it as he stroked the hollow behind my ear with his tongue.

Breath sawed out of my lungs. "Mark, what are you doing?"

"Distracting you." The words tickled the cool spot his mouth had left.

"From wha—"

Pop.

Electricity sizzled from my shoulder to my palm. Warmth bloomed, and feeling began to collect in my fingers. I gave them a wiggle. "Hey! You fixed it!"

"You're welcome. We're lucky she didn't break it. I can fix dislocated shoulders all day long. Broken bones require more," he paused, searching for a word, "*invasive* solutions."

"Good to know." I thought about how much distraction that might require and briefly considered throwing myself down the stairs.

Steven helped me get the cats packed back into the car and set down a garbage bag in the driver's seat.

"You know," he said. "To keep bits o' Kass from getting on your leather."

"Thanks, Steven. That's very thoughtful."

His chest puffed with pride, and he flexed his pecs. "I try."

I SAT IN THE SHOWER FOR ABOUT A YEAR. AFTER ABOUT twenty washes, my hair was free of chunks, and the water coursing down me ran clear.

Eyeing the drain, I made a mental note to pour down a bleach and Drano cocktail. If anyone ever had cause to go swabbing for DNA in this tub, it might not completely erase the evidence, but it might destroy enough to make an investigation tedious.

I slid into a t-shirt and panties and went to bed with my hair still wet. The cats piled on my feet like a heated blanket.

My last thought, before sleep took me, was that Abernathy has still managed not to answer a single question I'd asked him.

Damn, he was good.

CHAPTER 20

When I arrived at the gallery the following day, I found the street blocked off with cop cruisers and flashing lights. Parking around the corner, I hoofed it down the sidewalk to yet another yellow crime scene tape barricade. Onlookers coagulated in clumps around the periphery, stretching their necks in search of carnage. I'd seen enough to satisfy them all, and would gladly sign over the memories, free of charge.

Ducking under the barrier, I drew the notice of an officer who looked more like a bouncer than a cop. Big, but young.

"Sorry, miss. Gallery's closed."

"But I work here," I said, hoping my face bore a convincing likeness of shock and concern. "What's going on?"

"I'm afraid I can't discuss the details." He glanced over his shoulder, silently willing reinforcements to float in his direction.

"And I'm afraid I'm late for work. If you'll excuse me—"

He held out an arm and herded me back toward the tape.

"What's the problem?" The voice belonged to an officer I recognized. The same one who'd been saddled with the unenviable task of shuttling me home from Amy Grayson's crime scene.

"Officer Birch. I'm Hanna Harvey. You remember me?"

Recognition kneaded his doughy features into a smile. "Oh hey! It's you!"

"Yup. I just need to get into the gallery. My boss's car is over there, so I know he's here and—"

"Of course!" Birch elbowed his fellow officer. "This is *Hanna Harvey*. Morrison told us about her, remember?"

A hot flush of anger and embarrassment shot through my cheeks. *Morrison wouldn't have—*

"Oh! *That* Hanna Harvey. Sorry, miss. If I had known—"

"Now wait just a minute," I protested. "That was a one-time thing. Well, a one-night thing. I'm not the kind of girl who—"

"Miss Harvey," Birch said. "You don't have to—"

"Yes, I do," I insisted. "I don't sleep around, okay? It's just, I've been through this divorce, and it had been three months, and I was scared, and he smelled really good and there I was all alone and vulnerable and he shows up with these doughnuts—"

I could have warmed my hands by the bright red ears of Officer Bouncer.

"Sorry," Birch said, his cheeks pink as the frosting on sugar cookie. "I should have been more clear. Detective Morrison gave us orders to send you straight into the gallery when you arrived. That's all I meant when I said he—"

"Okay then! I'll just be going. Lovely to see you again, Officer Birch. And you, uh, whatever your name is. Pleasure." I slid around them and let the crush of bodies absorb the shame trailing in my wake.

The wall facing the street had been completely repaired, and there was no sign of the truck that had broken through it. The gallery's interior walls were back in place, and the debris had been completely cleaned. Even the paintings had migrated to their requisite spots.

Thankfully, no bodies remained in the gallery. Only black bags in the places where Rob Vincent and Mrs. Kass had fallen. I tried not to look at either. Kind Rob and his Buddy Holly glasses who'd been watching over me. Rob who had driven my shitty car full of cats back to Utah without eating a single one. I had dreamed of distant howls filling the night with a song of mourning. Sadness gripped my heart with an iron fist as I silently added my own voice to the chorus of lamentation.

What Abernathy's *people* had done with Penny and the brown wolf's bodies, I had no idea, and that was just fine by me.

Kirkpatrick, the hero who had shot Mrs. Kass when he'd discovered her disemboweling Rob Vincent (*cough cough*), stood nearby giving a statement to a couple uniformed officers.

I found Morrison in Abernathy's office when I slogged up the stairs. Both men looked up when I limped in. Morrison smirked. Abernathy grimaced. I think it would be safe to say that each was making assumptions slightly to the left of accurate.

"Hanna," Abernathy said. "We were just talking about you."

"That can't be good."

"Have a seat," Morrison invited, indicating the chair next to him.

I opted to plop down on the couch instead, the chair

feeling entirely too close to that much alpha this early in the morning.

"Don't mind me," I insisted.

Morrison cleared his throat and turned back to Abernathy.

"As I was saying, when I picked up the painting from Mrs. Kass on Saturday afternoon, she made a comment about Hanna."

"You don't say." I shifted on the couch, gently maneuvering my arm to rest on one of the many throw pillows I'd introduced to Abernathy's office.

Morrison nodded. "Said she was afraid that Hanna was going to end up just like *them*. Seems your dating habits really pissed her off. I did a little digging, and it looks like our Mrs. Kass had a string of unsuccessful marriages. Something must have snapped."

Yeah. Like her spine. But mostly when she was transforming...

"Anyway," he continued, "I tried to call Hanna last night to let her know about Mrs. Kass, but she was *unavailable*."

Right. Unavailable being chased across the country with a psychotic werewolf on my heels. Details.

"Yes," Abernathy said. "I'm afraid Hanna and I were engaged in other *pursuits*."

Morrison sat up straighter in his chair. "Is that right?" I felt his energy turn to me, though his eyes remained fixed firmly on Abernathy.

"Yes. It was an overnight trip. We barely got a wink of sleep. Isn't that right, Hanna?" He let the suggestion linger in the air.

Not exactly how I would have described our awkward car ride back, but then, I wasn't in the business of measuring dicks. Though technically I could, as I'd seen them both naked in the last forty-eight hours.

Again. Details.

279

"Did Mrs. Kass say anything else?" I asked, hoping to steer this conversation back to safer ground.

"She mentioned details about Helena's murder that we hadn't released to the public."

"Yikes," I said.

A predatory grin spread across Morrison's face as he relived the memory. "Exactly. Since I happened to be right there in her studio picking up the painting, I offered to take her trash out for her. And wouldn't you know it? She let me."

Any self-respecting watcher of crime shows knew that once the bag hit the street, it was fair game.

"Not only was Mrs. Kass's DNA a perfect match to the DNA found at the crime scene, but we also identified animal fur in her trash. Fur that matched the canine DNA found at both crime scenes."

My stomach did a little flip-flop as I recalled Mrs. Kass's twisted body pressing into my back. The end Helena and Amy Grayson had met was not a pleasant one.

"And there you have it." Morrison closed the pad he had spread on Abernathy's desk and tucked it under his arm.

Rather Perry Mason of him, I thought.

"Would it be safe to assume," Abernathy pressed, "that I am no longer a suspect?"

"That would be a safe assumption." Morrison cleared his throat, tugged at his pants leg. "And, you know."

Abernathy jerked his chin in non-acknowledgement of Morrison's non-apology. "Just doing your job."

"Speaking of my job..." Morrison rose, grabbing his coat, "I better get back to it." He looked at me and winked with his back to Abernathy. "I'll be in touch." Though I wouldn't mind another *visit* from Detective James Morrison, it would be at least a few weeks before

I gave him an all-access pass to Adventure Island. One look at my body, and the story Abernathy's *people* had woven would be blown all to hell.

I waited for the heat to disperse from my cheeks before I closed the door after him and seated myself in one of the chairs facing Abernathy's desk.

"That's it then?"

"For the moment," Abernathy said.

"And you don't think this will come back on you?" I asked.

"It hasn't yet."

"And exactly how many times have you done something like this?"

"A few," he answered.

"Like, a few hundred?"

"Now that would be telling, wouldn't it?" Abernathy leaned back in his chair and propped his feet on his desk.

"I really wish you'd stop doing that. You get *schmutz* all over your papers."

He righted himself and put his feet under his desk like a chastised schoolboy. "Better?"

"Better," I said. "Speaking of telling, if I recall, someone promised me answers after I got some rest, and I've slept *twice* since then."

Abernathy folded his arms across his chest. "A deal is a deal. But I'll warn you in advance, there are some questions I still can't answer."

"What? No! That's not how it works. This is the part where you reveal everything to me that I've wondered about all this time. You know, big dramatic conclusion, ah-ha moments..."

"Sorry to disappoint," he said. "Orders."

"Orders from whom?"

"Can't answer that."

"This is stupid," I said, folding my arms across my

chest like the brat I was. Well, *am*. "I don't want to do it like this."

"No questions, then?" He grinned at me. Big stupid sexy werewolf and his stupid sexy werewolf grin.

"Fine." I opened my purse and pulled out the list of questions I'd written down last night.

"You made a list?"

"Of course, I made a list. Don't knock it till you've tried it."

"Don't have to. I have you, remember?" The smirk lifting one corner of his mouth would have driven lesser women to madness. Or at least, less determined women.

My heart thumped. He was *not* going to distract me, dammit.

"First question. Mrs. Kass referred to me as an *heir*. What did she mean?"

"Straight for the heart," he said.

"I learned from the best."

Abernathy took a deep breath and let it out slowly. "How much do you know about blood?"

"That it really enhances the richness of broths, soups, and stews. In fact, in Norway, they make it in—"

"Jesus Christ, Hanna." Abernathy interrupted. "Are you ever not thinking about food?"

While I thought about this, a frosted pink doughnut floated through my head like a mental screensaver. "I'd prefer not to answer that."

"Doughnuts?"

"How did you—"

"Never mind. About the blood. There's something in yours. It's rare. Pure."

I snorted. "Butterfat?"

"A gene. Passed to you from your mother, and her mother before her. It's *there*." His eyes went liquid as they passed over me, his cognac-colored gaze soaking into my skin like the summer sun. "*Inside* you."

Swallowing was a Herculean effort. "What? What's inside me?"

"Everything."

Had there been a chaise lounge nearby, I might have stood for the sole purpose of swooning into it. "Wait a minute," I said. "You're being all sexy and vague to avoid answering my questions, aren't you?"

His Adam's apple bobbed beneath its cloak of stubble.

"Uh-huh." I smoothed my list and leaned forward in my chair. "Spit it out, sir."

"You're from a pure bloodline, Hanna. That makes you an heir."

"An heir to what?"

"Can't answer that, next question."

"You *would* say that."

"Next question," he repeated.

"Penny kept referring to a 'she' when she talked about killing me. Who is the 'she'?"

"'She' would be my sister. The one I mentioned on the way back from New Mexico."

"What makes you think your sister is involved?"

Abernathy opened his top desk drawer and pulled out a silvered daguerreotype. He handed it to me across the desk. "Look familiar?"

Chills galloped across my skin. Dark hair, wide set eyes, olive skin. All the ghosts of her face stored in my brain pulsed into one common electrical current anchored by this new image. "It's her," I gasped. "I've been seeing her everywhere. I ran into her at the deli on my first day. She was in Germany. She was at the gallery show."

"She's been following you. At least, that's what my father told me when I went to see him in Germany.

283

After he had been attacked. He knew I had been protecting you."

"Wait, your father? That's why we went to Germany? How did your father know about me?" *Joseph*, the German man who'd called for Abernathy. "Joseph Abernathy was a bastard," Mark had said.

"Can't answer that," he replied.

"What about the auction? And the moonstone pendant."

"I had to stash you somewhere. I couldn't very well take you to meet him. I have lots of friends at Bonham's. They said they'd keep an eye on you."

So, he *had* been dropping me off at the babysitter.

"Except for that whole part when your psychotic sister showed up."

"I hadn't planned on that."

"You said you went to meet Joseph to get a spoon. Was that a load of malarkey as well?"

"No, that part was actually true. My father called because my sister came to confront him. That's when she mentioned you. He wouldn't give her what she wanted, so she stabbed him through the heart with a silver spoon. He couldn't heal from it. He was dying."

"I'm so sorry."

"Don't be," Abernathy said. "Next question."

His matter-of-fact tone invited no further discussion on the point.

"Didn't your father tell you about Mrs. Kass? And Penny?"

"I doubt he knew himself. He got around. He wasn't careful."

"You're saying you could have more brothers and sisters out there?"

"I run across them now and then. It usually doesn't end well."

I thought of what the gallery had looked like when

I'd left last night. 'Doesn't end well' seemed a ridiculous understatement.

"But why would your sister want Mrs. Kass to kill *me*?"

"There aren't many pure bloodlines left in the world. What you carry in yours is rare and powerful. That kind of power makes some people nervous. My sister is one of them. I expect she knew Mrs. Kass had a grudge and convinced her it would be to her advantage to take you out."

"When you said you were *protecting* me…"

"Keeping things from killing you," he explained helpfully.

"This job, your hiring me, all of this was so you can keep an eye on me?" No wonder he'd been so cranky when I kept trying to organize him.

He was smirking again, damn him.

"What about Steven? Did you ask him to follow me?"

"We took shifts after hours. Sometimes me, sometimes Steven, sometimes Rob."

"Was Steven following me yesterday when I came to the gallery?"

"Indeed," Abernathy said. "And he gave me a heads-up when you got here."

Sonovabitch.

"Did he happen to give you a heads up when I came into clean your office while you were still in Germany?"

"I'm afraid so."

I blew hot air out of my nostrils. "And here I was thinking I was being all stealthy."

Abernathy snorted.

"What? I could be stealthy."

"Like a musk ox," he said.

To prevent myself leaping cross the desk to throat-punch him, I turned my attention back to my list.

"And the box I found in your cupboard? Was it Steven who took it?"

"I asked him to," Abernathy confirmed. "I'd forgotten to get rid of it before I left."

"The papers in it, what were they?"

"Next question."

"How did I know you were going to say that?" I read down through my list and checked off the ones he'd answered directly and indirectly.

"Mrs. Kass. You had no idea she was the one committing the murders?"

"I knew something was up with her when Steven said he thought she was following you too, but I wasn't sure what. As to the murders, I knew someone was out to get me, but hell, who isn't? It wasn't the first time; it won't be the last. I've been around long enough to make a few enemies."

"How long, exactly?"

"Four hundred and thirty-one years."

I accidentally inhaled my gum and spent a moment hacking it back out of my lungs.

"You asked."

"Well," I coughed, "you look great."

"You should see me naked."

"Like last night?" Had he forgotten so quickly? I sure as hell hadn't. Naked Abernathy was the chief reason I'd woken up sweating in the middle of the night and poured my sexual frustration into a list.

"Post-wolf naked doesn't count."

"And why not?"

"Because there's naked, and there's *naked*."

"What's the difference?"

He discarded his careful control like a mask. Behind it, I found undisguised need. "Want to find out?"

And here, his totem animal—wolf—met my totem

animal—chicken. "You're trying to distract me again. It won't work."

"Tell that to your pencil." That damnable smirk again.

A distinctive yet familiar flavor registered on my tongue. Shit. I had a pencil in my mouth. When had that gotten there? Teeth indentation marred the paint. The metal ferrule had been crushed like a soda can.

I cleared my throat, as much checking for eraser shrapnel as to create a break in the conversation. "As I was saying, how long have you been protecting me?"

"Can't tell you that."

"Where did you get those pictures of me?"

"Can't tell you that either."

"Why not?"

"Because the person who asked me to protect you would rip my spleen out and make it into a doily."

"But I still don't understand. Why would you need to protect me in the first place? Why on earth would your sister consider me a threat? What does it matter what bloodline I'm from? She's a *werewolf*."

A small smile played across Abernathy's lips as he leaned forward and looked me directly in the eye.

"So are you."

Bestselling author Cynthia St. Aubin wrote her first play at age eight and made her brothers perform it for the admission price of gum wrappers. A steal, considering she provided the wrappers in advance. Though her early work debuted to mixed reviews, she never quite gave up on the writing thing, even while earning a mostly useless master's degree in art history and taking her turn as a cube monkey in the corporate warren.

Because the voices in her head kept talking to her, and they discourage drinking at work, she started publishing books instead. When she's not standing in front of the fridge eating cheese, she's hard at work figuring out which mythological, art historical, or paranormal friends to play with next. She lives in Texas with a handsome musician and one surly cat.

I love stalkers! You can find me here:
Like me: https://www.facebook.com/cynthia. saintaubin
Visit me: http://www.cynthiastaubin.com/
Email me: cynthiastaubin@gmail.com
Join my Minions: https://www.facebook.com/ groups/Cynthiastaubins/

Subliminally message me: *You were thinking of cheese just now, right?*

And here:

ALSO BY CYNTHIA ST. AUBIN

CPSIA information can be obtained
at www.ICGtesting.com
Printed in the USA
BVHW081436070121
597265BV00009B/574

9 781648 390050